PUFFIN BOOKS

THE SUDHA MURTY CHILDREN'S TREASURY

Sudha Murty was born in 1950 in Shiggaon in north Karnataka. She did her MTech in computer science, and is now the chairperson of the Infosys Foundation. A prolific writer in English and Kannada, she has written novels, technical books, travelogues, collections of short stories and non-fictional pieces, and four books for children. Her books have been translated into all the major Indian languages. Sudha Murty was the recipient of the R.K. Narayan Award for Literature and the Padma Shri in 2006, and the Attimabbe Award from the government of Karnataka for excellence in Kannada literature in 2011.

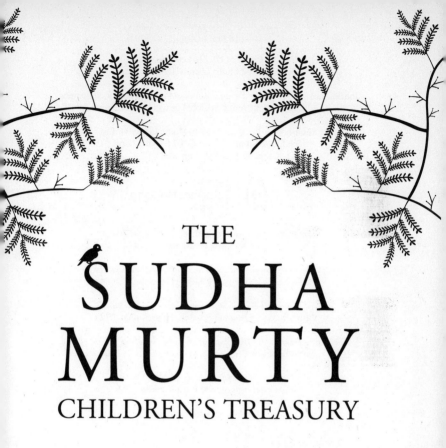

THE
SUDHA
MURTY
CHILDREN'S TREASURY

Illustrations by Priya Kuriyan

PUFFIN BOOKS

An imprint of Penguin Random House

PUFFIN BOOKS

USA | Canada | UK | Ireland | Australia
New Zealand | India | South Africa | China

Puffin Books is part of the Penguin Random House group of companies
whose addresses can be found at global.penguinrandomhouse.com

Published by Penguin Random House India Pvt. Ltd
7th Floor, Infinity Tower C, DLF Cyber City,
Gurgaon 122 002, Haryana, India

This omnibus edition published in Puffin Books by
Penguin Random House India 2019

How I Taught My Grandmother to Read and Other Stories was first published in
Puffin Books by Penguin Random House India 2004

Grandma's Bag of Stories was first published in
Puffin Books by Penguin Random House India 2012

The Magic Drum and Other Favourite Stories was first published in
Puffin Books by Penguin Random House India 2006

Text copyright © Sudha Murty 2004, 2006, 2012
Illustration copyright © Priya Kuriyan 2015

The views and opinions expressed in this book are the author's own and the
facts are as reported by him/her which have been verified to the extent possible,
and the publishers are not in any way liable for the same.

ISBN 9780143450146

Typeset in Sabon by Manipal Technologies Limited, Manipal
Printed at Replika Press Pvt. Ltd, India

www.penguin.co.in

*To all the children who read,
may you continue reading and
ignite the spark of creativity*

Contents

Book I: How I Taught My Grandmother to Read and Other Stories

1. How I Taught My Grandmother to Read 3
2. Books for 'At Least One Library' 11
3. Salaam Abdul Kalam 17
4. Hassan's Attendance Problem 28
5. The Red Rice Granary 37
6. The Real Jewels 44
7. A History Lesson on Teachers' Day 52
8. 'Appro J.R.D.' 58

Contents

9. Heart of Gold   71

10. A Wedding in Russia   77

11. 'Amma, What Is Your Duty?'   84

12. The Story of Two Doctors   92

13. A Journey Through the Desert   98

14. Dead Man's Riddle   110

15. 'I Will Do It'   116

16. The Rainy Day   122

17. Doing What You Like Is Freedom   129

18. Gowramma's Letter   139

19. Who Is Great?   148

20. Balu's Story   156

21. 'A' for Honesty   164

22. A Lesson in Ingratitude   170

23. My Biggest Mistake   179

24. The Secret   185

Book II: Grandma's Bag of Stories

25. The Beginning of the Stories   195

26. 'Doctor, Doctor'   198

Contents

27. Kavery and the Thief   210

28. Who Was the Happiest of Them All?   221

29. The Enchanted Scorpions   231

30. The Horse Trap   240

31. A Treasure for Ramu   250

32. The Donkey and the Stick   257

33. 'What's in It for Me?'   263

34. The Princess's New Clothes   272

35. The Story of Paan   280

36. Payasam for a Bear   288

37. Fire on the Beard   298

38. The Way You Look at It   306

39. Roopa's Great Escape   313

40. Five Spoons of Salt   326

41. How the Seasons Got Their Share   337

42. The Island of Statues   344

43. The Kingdom of Fools   352

44. The Story of Silk   360

45. When Yama Called   367

46. The Unending Story   374

Contents

Book III: The Magic Drum and Other Favourite Stories

47. The Supermen   387
48. A Fair Deal   393
49. The Seed of Truth   398
50. Haripant the Wise   402
51. The Last Laddoo   408
52. The Tastiest of All   413
53. The Cunning Fruit   418
54. Nine Questions for a Princess   423
55. Dead Man's Painting   427
56. The White Crow   434
57. The Horse in the Burrow   439
58. The Very Expensive Coconut   443
59. The Wise King   448
60. A Bottle of Dew   453
61. Two Thieves   458
62. The Best Friend   465
63. Good Luck, Gopal   470
64. Nakul's First Lesson   476
65. Golden Silence   481

66. Emperor of Alakavati   486
67. The Case of the Missing Necklace   496
68. A Question of Maths   502
69. The Clever Brothers   506
70. The Lucky Purse   510
71. Two Unforgettable Lessons   517
72. United We Stand   524
73. Where Did It Go?   529
74. The Princess Who Was a Bird   534
75. The Price Is Right   540
76. A Lesson for the Uncles   544
77. A Bag of Words   550
78. Magic in the Air   556
79. The Selfish Groom   562
80. The Tired Horse   567
81. A Minister's Test   570
82. A Cure for Laziness   575
83. The Magic Drum   581

BOOK I

How I Taught My Grandmother to Read and Other Stories

How I Taught My Grandmother to Read

When I was a girl of about twelve, I used to stay in a village in north Karnataka with my grandparents. Those days, the transport system was not very good, so we used to get the morning paper only in the afternoon. The weekly magazine used to come one day late. All of us would wait eagerly for the bus, which used to come with the papers, weekly magazines and the post.

At that time, Triveni was a very popular writer in the Kannada language. She was a wonderful writer. Her style was easy to read and very convincing. Her stories usually dealt with complex psychological

3

problems in the lives of ordinary people and were always very interesting. Unfortunately for Kannada literature, she died very young. Even now, after forty years, people continue to appreciate her novels.

One of her novels, called *Kashi Yatre*, was appearing as a serial in the Kannada weekly *Karmaveera* then. It is the story of an old lady and her ardent desire to go to Kashi or Varanasi. Most Hindus believe that going to Kashi and worshipping Lord Vishweshvara is the ultimate *punya*. This old lady also believed in this, and her struggle to go there was described in that novel. In the story there was also a young orphan girl who falls in love but there was no money for the wedding. In the end, the old lady gives away all her savings without going to Kashi. She says, 'The happiness of this orphan girl is more important than worshipping Lord Vishweshwara at Kashi.'

My grandmother, Krishtakka, never went to school so she could not read. Every Wednesday, the magazine would come and I would read the next episode of this story to her. During that time she would forget all her work and listen with the greatest concentration. Later, she could repeat the entire text by heart. My grandmother too never went to Kashi, and she identified herself with the novel's protagonist. So more

than anybody else she was the one most interested in knowing what happened next in the story and used to insist that I read the serial out to her.

After hearing what happened next in *Kashi Yatre*, she would join her friends at the temple courtyard, where we children would also gather to play hide-and-seek. She would discuss the latest episode with her friends. At that time, I never understood why there was so much of debate about the story.

Once I went for a wedding with my cousins to the neighbouring village. In those days, a wedding was a great event. We children enjoyed ourselves thoroughly. We would eat and play endlessly, savouring the freedom because all the elders were busy. I went for a couple of days but ended up staying there for a week.

When I came back to my village, I saw my grandmother in tears. I was surprised, for I had never seen her cry even in the most difficult situations. What had happened? I was worried.

'Avva, is everything all right? Are you ok?'

I used to call her Avva, which means mother in the Kannada spoken in north Karnataka.

She nodded but did not reply. I did not understand and forgot about it. In the night, after dinner, we were sleeping in the open terrace of the house. It was a summer night and there was a full moon. Avva came and sat next to me. Her affectionate hands touched my forehead. I realized she wanted to speak. I asked her, 'What is the matter?'

'When I was a young girl I lost my mother. There was nobody to look after and guide me. My father was a busy man and got married again. In those days people did not consider education essential for girls, so I never went to school. I got married very young and had children. I became very busy. Later I had grandchildren and always felt so much happiness in cooking and feeding all of you. At times I used to regret not going to school, so I made sure that my children and grandchildren studied well ...'

I could not understand why my sixty-two-year-old grandmother was telling me, a twelve-year-old, the story of her life in the middle of the night. But I knew I loved her immensely and there had to be some reason why she was talking to me. I looked at her face. It was unhappy and her eyes were filled with tears. She was a good-looking lady who was usually always smiling. Even today I cannot forget the worried expression on her face. I leaned forward and held her hand.

'Avva, don't cry. What is the matter? Can I help you in any way?'

'Yes, I need your help. You know when you were away, *Karmaveera* came as usual. I opened the magazine. I saw the picture that accompanies the story of *Kashi Yatre* and I could not understand anything that was written. Many times I rubbed my hands over the pages wishing they could understand what was written. But I knew it was not possible. If only I was educated enough. I waited eagerly for you to return. I felt you would come early and read for me. I even thought of going to the village and asking you to read for me. I could have asked somebody in this village but I was too embarrassed to do so. I felt so very dependent and helpless. We are well-off, but what use is money when I cannot be independent?'

I did not know what to answer. Avva continued.

'I have decided I want to learn the Kannada alphabet from tomorrow onwards. I will work very hard. I will keep Saraswati Pooja day during Dassara as the deadline. That day I should be able to read a novel on my own. I want to be independent.'

I saw the determination on her face. Yet I laughed at her.

'Avva, at this age of sixty-two you want to learn the alphabet? All your hair is grey, your hands are wrinkled, you wear spectacles and you work so much in the kitchen...' Childishly I made fun of the old lady. But she just smiled.

'For a good cause if you are determined, you can overcome any obstacle. I will work harder than anybody, but I will do it. For learning there is no age bar.'

The next day onwards I started my tuition. Avva was a wonderful student. The amount of homework she did was amazing. She would read, repeat, write and recite. I was her only teacher and she was my first student. Little did I know then that one day I would become a teacher in computer science and teach hundreds of students.

The Dassara festival came as usual. Secretly I bought *Kashi Yatre* which had been published as a novel by that time. My grandmother called me to the puja place and made me sit down on a stool. She gave me the gift of a frock material. Then she did something unusual. She bent down and touched my feet. I was surprised and taken aback. Elders never touch the feet of youngsters. We have always touched the feet of God, elders and teachers. We consider that as a mark of respect. It is a great tradition but today the reverse had happened. It was not correct.

She said, 'I am touching the feet of a teacher, not my granddaughter; a teacher who taught me so well, with so much of affection that I can read any novel confidently in such a short period. Now I am independent. It is my duty to respect a teacher. Is it not written in our scriptures that a teacher should be respected, irrespective of gender and age?'

I did return namaskara to her by touching her feet and gave my gift to my first student. She opened it and read immediately the title *Kashi Yatre* by Triveni and the publisher's name.

I knew then that my student had passed with flying colours.

Books for 'At Least One Library'

I come from a middle-class teacher's family. In my family, as with many other families of teachers, books and knowledge were considered to be more important than money.

In our village, I still remember the way people respected my grandfather. He was certainly not the richest man. He used to sit in front of our house, on a mat below a shady banyan tree. He always held a book in his hand. In the evening people would come to him for his advice. Even the richest man, when passing by, would greet him respectfully. I asked him once, 'Why should the teacher be respected?'

He smiled and told me a story. 'It seems, some friends of Arjuna, the mighty warrior in the Mahabharata, asked him why he gave so much of respect to his teacher Dronacharya. Drona was old, not as rich as Arjuna, and had never ruled any kingdom. But Arjuna would always sit at his feet respectfully. When asked why, it seems Arjuna replied, "In this life everything perishes over a period of time. Whether it be diamond, beauty, gold or even land. Only one thing withstands this destruction. It is knowledge. The more you give the more you get." A teacher gives knowledge to students and I consider him the richest person. That is the reason a teacher is respected; not for his riches but because he is the source of knowledge.'

As a child, the first expedition I ever made outside my home was to the village library building with my grandfather. The library was situated in a small two-storied structure. There was a shop on the ground floor and on the first floor was the library. A big banyan tree stood next to the building. There was a cement platform under it. In Kannada we call it *katte*. In the evening, all the elders of the village would sit here. My grandfather was one of them. I would accompany him and he would go and sit on the platform after dropping me at the first floor.

It was the first of the many libraries I was to enter. There were cupboards with glass panes so that one could read the titles of the books easily. Newspapers and weeklies were piled up neatly. Tables and chairs were laid for people to sit and read. There was absolute silence. I started reading children's books there and used to be absorbed in them until my grandfather would call me to go home.

Years passed and I became a girl of twelve years. By that time, I had finished reading almost all the books in that little village library. At times I used to feel bored going to the library as there were not many new books. But still I accompanied my old grandfather to the banyan tree.

One such evening, we were coming back after our outing. I was feeling particularly bored with the library that day. It was dark and the street lights were blinking. My grandfather could not see too well so I was leading him by his hand.

Suddenly he asked me, 'I will recite half a poem, will you complete it? This is a well-known poem.'

I said I would try. We often played this game and I had learnt many poems like this. He said, 'If I have wings . . .'

I immediately answered without blinking my eyes, 'I will go to the neighbouring village library and read many more books.'

My grandfather stopped in surprise. He said, 'Will you repeat it?'

I repeated, 'I will go to the neighbouring village library and read many more books.'

He laughed and said, 'What an unusual way to complete the poem! Do you know what the original poem is?'

'Yes, I know.

"If I have wings

I will fly in the vast blue sky

I will see beautiful places

I will meet great people

I will search for hidden treasures."'

My grandfather kept quiet. When we reached home he sat down on a mat and called me. He was tired but looked very happy. He took my little hand into his and said, 'Do you know, there was a great man called Andrew Carnegie in USA. He was a billionaire who lived a century back. He willed all his wealth not to his children, but to build library buildings in as many villages as possible. I have not seen America, but it seems any library you see in any village was invariably built using Andrew Carnegie's money.

'I do not know how long I will live, but today I realized how much you love books from the way you completed the poem. Promise me, when you grow up, if you have more money than you need, you will buy books for at least one library.'

It was a cold winter night. I still remember the warmth of his large hand in mine. He was old, and his hands had become hard and wrinkled writing thousands of lines on the blackboard with chalk every day. We were not rich like Carnegie, but certainly my grandfather had the richness of experience and knowledge.

Later in my life, I became well-off. I remembered my promise of buying books for a library. Today, through Infosys Foundation, we have given books to ten thousand such libraries.

Salaam Abdul Kalam

Ihave been writing columns for a number of newspapers and magazines for a while now. One of them was the Week magazine. Writing columns is not an easy job. One has to keep coming up with interesting anecdotes to write about. Sometimes the incident is so nice you feel like writing more but you have to be careful about the word limit. Sometimes you don't get any ideas at all, though the deadline may be nearing. Only very few gifted people can write regular columns for a long time.

Once I wrote a column for the *Week* on the role of Information Technology in people's lives. It was called 'IT Divide'. It was based on a true incident that once happened to me.

Soon after the column appeared, one morning I got a call from Delhi. The operator said, 'Shri Abdul Kalam wants to talk to you.'

That time Abdul Kalam was Principal Scientific Secretary to the Government of India. I had never met him in person till then. I had only read about him in the papers and seen him on TV. Of course, I started wondering why a person of his stature would want to talk to an ordinary person like me. We had nothing in common. It would be like a meeting between a Himalayan peak and the peak of Unkal Hill, which is in the small town of Hubli in north Karnataka.

When Abdul Kalam came on the line I said, 'Sir, there is a mistake by the operator. Perhaps you want to speak to my husband, Narayana Murthy?' I knew Murthy knew Mr Kalam. From the other end a soft, affectionate voice replied, '*Vanakkam*, there is absolutely no mistake. I told the operator to connect to you only.'

I was thrilled.

'Sir, you don't know me but I know a lot about you. I have read about your life in the book *Wings of Fire*.'

'But I too know about you by reading your columns. I read *Ananda Vikatan* regularly, where you talk about your dreams and your struggles. Today when I read 'IT Divide' in the *Week*, I laughed and laughed. You have written on a tough topic in such a humorous way! I called my colleagues in the office and told them to read the column. Normally whenever your column appears, I read the last paragraph first because it contains the gist. Then I read the remaining portion as and when I get time.'

That was the best compliment I had ever received. When I write, I always think of the end first and then the beginning. Kalam seemed to have guessed that in no time.

I had heard from many people that he is extremely simple, wears only white and blue shirts and slippers. Soon I got to know that this was not an exaggeration. After our talk on the phone I met him several times. Till today, the more often I meet him, the more I am convinced about the essential simplicity of the man. Any interaction with him is a joy and I always look forward to it.

I met him for the first time in Bangalore. He sent me word that he wanted to see me though he had a packed schedule. I was waiting for him in a room

when he came in, looking cool inspite of a long tough day. For a while we talked about literature and human qualities. He asked me in chaste Tamil, 'How come you know such good Tamil?'

'No sir,' I replied, 'I can't speak Tamil but I can understand. My translator, Mr Arokia Velu is an excellent translator. The credit for what appears in *Ananda Vikatan* should go to him.'

As we chatted, a man without a prior appointment wanted to enter. Kalam's security personnel were reluctant to let him enter. Finally Mr Kalam said, 'Please allow him. It does not matter. He might have come from a long distance.'

A middle-aged man entered the room along with a photographer. He was holding a huge album and a bag. He told Kalam, 'Sir, I own this institution,' and kept the album in front of him. 'Please come for our Prize Distribution Day. It will be a great honour for all of us.'

Kalam looked at a few pages of the album and said, 'I am short of time so I will not be able to make it. May God bless the children.'

Then the man requested for a photograph with Kalam, to which he agreed immediately. The gentleman took a pink-coloured shawl from his bag and told the photographer to take his photo while he was laying the shawl on Kalam's shoulder.

The photograph was duly taken and Kalam thanked him and continued talking to me. But my attention was still on the man. I noticed that he took back the shawl and walked out of the room. I could not control my anger.

'Sir, he has taken the shawl which he presented to you.'

Kalam smiled at me and said, 'It does not matter. I don't need any one of them. Probably he needs it.'

Each time I meet him, I am amazed at his straightforward behaviour and his secular outlook. He has a compassionate heart which particularly loves all children.

After that meeting, whenever I was in Chennai, I would see him in his chamber in Anna University where he was teaching. We would talk about many issues, the main one being about education, particularly in the rural areas. He is extremely grateful to his teachers and holds them in the highest respect.

Once I was sharing my experiences in Chandipur, Orissa and a lesson I learnt from a young fisherboy called Javed. He was a poor schoolboy who helped his mother sell red crabs. For an entire day's work he received only Rs 5. Yet he was happy and enthusiastic. When I asked him how he could always remain so optimistic, he said, 'It is better to be worn out than to be rusted.'

As soon as I told this story to him, Kalam wrote Javed's words down on a piece of paper and exclaimed what a great piece of advice it was. He told me that he liked Orissa immensely, as he had spent many years in that state doing missile tests.

'If you are doing something in Orissa I will definitely come. I know you work there and that state is very dear to your heart too.'

Once, I decided to visit Rameshwaram, along with a group of friends. When Kalam got to know, he was very eager to go with us as it is his birthplace. He said he would join us at the Madurai railway station. He had made all the arrangements when his nomination for the post of President of India was announced. He told me, 'We will keep the plan open for Rameshwaram.'

By this time I was sure he was going to be the President of India irrespective of the election. We could not ask him to join us as it could be a major security problem for him. Sadly I had to tell him, 'No sir, please do not come. We will go on our own.'

By the time we returned from the trip, he had, as I had predicted, been elected President. He invited me to his swearing-in ceremony in the central hall of Parliament. What I saw when I stepped into the hall amazed me. It was filled with children, teachers, his family members, odd people like me and Father George, who used to be my student in Bangalore and then was doing his research under Kalam in Anna University.

It was a most unusual oath-taking ceremony. Everyone seemed to be close to Kalam. Normally, such ceremonies are attended by industrialists, politicians and other VIPs. But here there were students, teachers, scientists, ordinary middle-class people and friends of Kalam. I saw Mrinalini Sarabhai, whose husband the late Dr Vikram Sarabhai, was also a great scientist and knew Kalam well. Her sister, Captain Laxmi, had contested against Kalam for the post of President. She, too, was present in the audience.

I came away from the function feeling deeply moved by the love I saw everyone showering on Kalam. After a few months, I asked my son, who is a teenager, to meet Kalam.

My son said, 'Amma, he is the President of our country. He is a learned and well-respected scientist.

He is a very busy man. What will he talk about to a person like me?'

'Child, please understand. I knew him before he became the President and I have met him after he became President. There is absolutely no change. He loves talking to people of your age. That is his mission. He interacts with children through email and chat. That is the reason I want you to meet him. Learn from him those qualities which you will never learn in any university.'

Somehow my son was not very convinced. 'He is too big a man for me,' he muttered.

Nevertheless, he was there when we had dinner with Kalam. For the next two hours they hijacked the entire conversation. Murthy and I could only sit and listen. They discussed the best operating systems for computers, the great Tamil saint Thiruvalluvar and his teachings, the future of the children of India, teaching methodologies in America, etc. After he left, my son told me, 'Amma, I never felt that I was talking to the President of India. Rather, it was like talking to my grandfather whom I loved so much and lost four years back. Amma, what you said was true and not at all an exaggeration.'

When Kalam went by train on a tour of Bihar, he invited me to go with him along with five other friends. There I saw another face of Kalam. He would work more than all of us. His schedule would start at 6.30 or 7 a.m. and end at 10.30 or 11 p.m. At seventy-one years, he was tireless and the most enthusiastic person in the team, all of whom were much younger than him.

He would regularly address large groups of students, followed by question-answer sessions. He would take individual questions and answer them. Then he would make the children recite some of the important lines after him. He reminded me of a loving schoolteacher or a doting grandfather or an excellent friend to these children irrespective of the difference in age.

During Bangalore's IT.Com I watched him taking an internet class for thousand students. He held their complete attention and was excellently prepared.

When we built a 150-bed Paediatric Hospital in Bhubaneshwar, Orissa for poor children, I was very keen that he should come and inaugurate it. I remembered his promise made to me in Chennai that he would come to Orissa if I invited him. But now he was the President of India, and there were many people like me inviting him to similar functions. He was no longer a professor at Anna University whom I could approach on telephone or send an email and convey my message. However, remembering his promise, I sent him an email assuming it might not reach. But within a few days, I got a reply from his secretary saying that he had agreed to inaugurate the hospital. Coincidentally, it was the eve of Buddha Poornima, 15 May 2003. I have heard many stories about Buddha who was born 2500 years ago. I was fortunate that this great teacher and lover of children could at least inaugurate and appreciate our effort.

Hassan's Attendance Problem

For many years now, I have been teaching computer science to students studying for their Master's in Computer Applications at a college in Bangalore. I have interacted with many students, and though it is not possible to remember all of them now, the memories of some are etched in my mind. That is not because they were all brilliant, but rather because something in them was very different from the others.

In my first batch, there was a very bright boy called Hassan. He was tall, handsome, with a very good memory. He came from an affluent family where he was the only son. Initially I did not come to know of his existence at all, mainly because he was hardly ever present. I normally take the first class of the day, which is scheduled at 9 a.m., or the one after that at 10 a.m. I prefer this time as this is when students are fresh and very attentive. Once in a while Hassan would turn up, particularly if there was a class test or during examinations. I met him more often in attendance shortage meetings. He would beg for attendance in such a manner that it was very difficult for me to say 'no'. Sometimes I would get upset and tell him, 'No, I can't give you attendance. There should be discipline.'

'Yes Madam,' he would reply apologetically, 'pardon me. From the next semester onwards I will definitely attend your class. Can you not pardon me this time? "To err is human; to forgive, divine". You have only taught us this.'

I could not remain angry for long. Teachers do get upset with students who are not regular, but if the attendance shortage affects their appearance in the final examination, then one tends to melt like snow against the sun. A good teacher will always wish for the best for her student, though I do agree discipline is very important too.

As he was very bright, Hassan would invariably get a first class in the exam. However, before the exams started, every semester this drama with Hassan would be repeated. I would get upset, threaten and ultimately give in. Each time, Hassan would promise to improve his attendance record, and for one week would attend all classes, then the same old story would follow. Each time, he had a different reason for his absences. Unfortunately, they always seemed genuine to me.

Once I got tired of his stories and called his parents. 'Your son is a bright boy, he is not arrogant but he is indisciplined. If only he came to class regularly and attended the lab, I am sure he could get a rank. I have failed to convince him. I will be happy if you could look into the matter more seriously, because this is going to affect his life,' I said to them.

Hassan's father was a busy man and did not take my words very seriously. He said, 'As long as he does well that is fine with me because after a certain age children do not listen to their parents. Only life will teach them.'

But his mother was in tears.

'Madam, I have failed as a mother. He does not listen to me at all. He spends all night listening to music, and chatting with his friends. He sleeps at six in the morning. How can he come to any class? He does not pay any attention to what I say and tells me I repeat the same thing always.'

The meeting ended in an argument between his parents. His father said, 'You are the mother. It is your duty to correct him. You spend more time with him. I am so busy. You have failed.'

His mother said, 'You are the father. It is difficult to control boys. You can speak to him man to man. Earning money is not the only thing in life.'

This continued for a while and the meeting ended fruitlessly. Hassan continued in his ways till he passed out of his course, as usual in first class. He was a nice boy. He came and thanked me.

'Madam, thank you for teaching me for the last three years. Because of your kind heart I could get all my attendance. I wish all teachers were like you in the college.'

I laughed.

'God willing, we will meet again.'

But I did not meet Hassan for a long time and forgot all about him. Years passed. I taught many students. Some of them became very good human beings, some became famous, some became rich and some remained ordinary. As far as I was concerned, they were like my children. Some remember me still and send invitations to weddings, naming ceremonies, house-warmings, etc. If I am in town I definitely try and attend, because for me their immense love is my strength.

One Monday morning, my secretary told me a person wanting to sell the latest software in high-school teaching wanted to meet me. I was extremely busy and the piles of unanswered letters were looking at me accusingly. I had no time to talk to a sales person. So I told her, 'He can meet someone else. I don't have time.'

But my secretary said he was insisting he wanted to meet only me and that he was my student. She knew how fond I was of all my students, so she had been unable to say 'no' to him.

'In that case let him see me at 2 p.m.'

In the afternoon, a man of about thirty-five, plump, with a bald head, and moderately dressed was waiting for me in the office. In his hand was the CD with the software. I could not place him though he seemed familiar. He smiled at me and said, 'Madam, can you recognize me? You may not, because how could you remember all your students? From a window you can see the outside world but from the outside you cannot see all that is inside.'

I liked his analogy and was sure he was my student because I often used this phrase in my class. Still, I could not guess who he was.

'Madam, I was the perpetual latecomer of your class.'

That's when the coin dropped. 'Hi Hassan. How are you? It's been a long time since I last met you.' I was very happy to see him.

'Madam, I am fine and remember many of your lessons.'

'Is it database management? Or C? Or pascal?'

'None of the software, Madam, I remember the moral lessons.'

I didn't know what moral lessons I had taught, though I do tell some stories during my lectures on computer software.

'Hassan, what are you doing now?'

Now his face became a little pale.

'Madam, I am selling this software which is useful in teaching maths, physics and chemistry. It is of help to both teachers and students. I know your foundation helps a lot in education at the high-school level. I thought it may be of some interest to you.'

'Hassan, what did you do for so many years?'

I knew all his classmates by this time were in very high positions in the software industry. Hassan being a bright student, should have definitely done well. Yet, on the contrary, he seemed to be doing a small job of selling high-school software door-to-door.

'Madam, you know I was very irregular in college. The same habit continued even after my graduation. I would get up late and was very lazy. My mother would lose her temper and peace of mind. I did not bother. I took her for granted. After a lot of pressure from my parents I took up a job. But I continued with the same habits of going late to office, not keeping appointments and not being responsible. I did not have the proper knowledge also. In college, I hardly studied. Getting a first class in the examination is not an index of the amount of knowledge one has. I would study just before the exams, guess the probable questions, and skip the chapters. I always thought I could somehow make it later. But without proper knowledge it is difficult to work. I always laughed at those people who were hard workers. I used to make fun of them and called them "nerds". Today those "nerds" have become millionaires. Nobody liked me in my office because of my behaviour. No employer would keep such an employee, and I lost whatever job

I took up. In my frustration I started quarrelling at office as well as at home. Finally, my father got so fed up he told me to stay separately. He always gave me a lot of freedom but I never picked up any good habits. My state today is the result of my own habits.'

I felt sorry for Hassan, who with all his intelligence and good nature, could not make it.

'Hassan, you knew your faults, you could have improved and made a better life for yourself. There is always a start at any age. Don't get disappointed. You may have lost a battle but you can still win the war.'

'Madam, old habits die hard.'

'But Hassan it is possible to change your habits. There is nothing which is impossible. You only require will power. You are yourself not aware of all your potential. Please remember when elders say something they do so because they want you to lead a better life than them. Excellence does not come by accident but by practice.'

I could see a twinkle in his eyes. I thought I saw a glimpse of the bright young Hassan. 'I will try my best, Madam,' he promised, as he rose to leave.

I have not met Hassan since that day. I hope to bump into him unexpectedly once again, and this time find him happy and successful.

The Red Rice Granary

Every year, our country has to face natural disasters in some form. It may be an earthquake in Gujarat, floods in Orissa or a drought in Karnataka. In a poor country, these calamities create havoc.

In the course of my work, I have found that after such calamities, many people like to donate money or materials to relief funds. We assume that most donations come from rich people, but that is not true. On the contrary, people from the middle class and the lower middle class, help more. Rarely do rich people participate wholeheartedly.

A few years back, I was invited to a reputed company in Bangalore to deliver a lecture on

Corporate Social Responsibility. Giving a speech is easy. But I was not sure how many people in the audience would really understand the speech and change themselves.

After my talk was over, I met many young girls and boys. It was an affluent company and the employees were well-off and well-dressed. They were all very emotional after the lecture.

'Madam, we buy so many clothes every month. Can we donate our old clothes to those people who are affected by the earthquake? Can you coordinate and send them?'

Some of them offered other things.

'We have grown-up children, we would like to give their old toys and some vessels.'

I was very pleased at the reaction. It reminded me of the incident in the Ramayana where, during the construction of the bridge between India and Lanka, every squirrel helped Sri Rama by bringing a handful of sand.

'Please send your bags to my office. I will see that they reach the right persons.'

Within a week, my office was flooded with hundreds of bags. I was proud that my lecture had proven so effective.

One Sunday, along with my assistants, I opened the bags. What we saw left us amazed and shocked. The bags were brimming over with all kinds of junk! Piles of high-heeled slippers (some of them without the pair), torn undergarments, unwashed shirts, cheap, transparent saris, toys which had neither shape nor colour, unusable bedsheets, aluminium vessels and broken cassettes were soon piled in front of us like a mountain. There were only a few good shirts, saris and usable materials. It was apparent that instead of sending the material to a garbage dump or the kabariwala, these people had transferred them to my office in the name of donation. The men and women I had met that day were bright, well-travelled, well-off people. If educated people like them behaved like this, what would uneducated people do?

But then I was reminded of an incident from my childhood. I was born and brought up in a village in Karnataka's Haveri District, called Shiggaon. My grandfather was a retired schoolteacher and my grandmother, Krishtakka, never went to school. Both of them hardly travelled and had never stepped out of Karnataka. Yet, they were hard-working people, who did their work wholeheartedly without expecting anything from anybody in their life. Their photographs never appeared in any paper, nor did they go up on stage to receive a prize for the work they did. They lived like flowers with fragrance in the forest, enchanting everyone around them, but hardly noticed by the outside world.

In the village we had paddy fields and we used to store the paddy in granaries. There were two granaries. One was in the front and the other at the back of our house. The better quality rice which was white, was always stored in the front granary and the inferior quality, which was a little thick and red, was stored in the granary at the back.

In those days, there was no communal divide in the village. People from different communities lived together in peace. Many would come to our house to ask for alms. There were Muslim fakirs, Hindu Dasaiahs who roamed the countryside singing devotional songs, Yellamma Jogathis who appeared holding the image of Goddess Yellamma over their heads, poor students and invalid people.

We never had too much cash in the house and the only help my grandfather could give these people was in the form of rice. People who receive help do not talk too much. They would receive the rice, smile and raise their right hand to bless us. Irrespective

of their religion, the blessing was always 'May God bless you.' My grandfather always looked happy after giving them alms.

I was a little girl then and not too tall. Since the entrance to the front granary was low, it was difficult for grown-ups to enter. So I would be given a small bucket and sent inside. There I used to fill up the bucket with rice and give it to them. They would tell me how many measures they wanted.

In the evening, my grandmother used to cook for everybody. That time she would send me to the granary at the back of the house where the red rice was stored. I would again fill up the bucket with as much rice as she wanted and get it for her to cook our dinner.

This went on for many years. When I was a little older, I asked my grandparents a question that had been bothering me for long.

'Why should we eat the red rice always at night when it is not so good, and give those poor people the better quality rice?'

My grandmother Krishtakka smiled and told me something I will never forget in my life.

'Child, whenever you want to give something to somebody, give the best in you, never the second best. That is what I have learned from life. God is not there in the temple, mosque or church. He is with the people. If you serve them with whatever you have, you have served God.'

My grandfather answered my question in a different way.

'Our ancestors have taught us in the Vedas that one should,

Donate with kind words.

Donate with happiness.

Donate with sincerity.

Donate only to the needy.

Donate without expectation because it is not a gift. It is a duty.

Donate with your wife's consent.

Donate to other people without making your dependents helpless.

Donate without caring for caste, creed and religion.

Donate so that the receiver prospers.'

This lesson from my grandparents, told to me when I was just a little girl, has stayed with me ever since. If at all I am helping anyone today, it is because of the teachings of those simple souls. I did not learn them in any school or college.

The Real Jewels

The district of South Canara in Karnataka is very different from any other. The literacy rate here is high, people are enterprising and hard-working. They have travelled all over the world in search of employment. If you see any Udupi vegetarian restaurant in India or any part of the globe, it is sure to have been started by a person from South Canara.

The Infosys Foundation has a project called 'A Library for Every School'. We donate books mainly to government school libraries, so that children have easy access to a variey of books. For this, I travel extensively in rural areas and donate books written in Kannada on various subjects. All the travelling has helped me to understand what children want to read in different places. During my travels, I frequently stay in the houses of people I meet, as often, there are no hotels in the small towns and villages I visit. Most of the time I stay with the family of a teacher from the school I am visiting. Some times I stay with people I had never met earlier.

In India, a guest is always treated with a lot of love, affection and respect. An old Sanskrit saying is '*Atithi Devo Bhava*', meaning God comes in the form of a guest.

I have felt this to be so true, especially during my stay in villages. The poorest of the poor have treated me with so much love and affection. They have given me the best hospitality possible without knowing who I am or expecting anything in return.

In 1998, I went to a village in South Canara for a school function. It was the rainy season and the small village was on the coast of the Arabian Sea. It was pouring and there were no hotels in the village. The schoolteacher was a bachelor and lived in a rented room. He told me, 'Madam, the chairman of this school is a fine gentleman. He has asked me to tell you that you could stay tonight with his family.

You cannot travel today because of this rain. Even the bridge has gone under water.'

I did not have much option. I felt a little uncomfortable staying with someone I had never even met. By that time the chairman, Mr Aithappa, came with an umbrella to call me. He had been caught up in some important work and not been able to attend the function.

His house was huge. It was functional without much decoration. There was a big granary room and a storage place for coconuts and vegetables. It had red oxide flooring and was like many traditional houses of South Canara where there was an inside courtyard. Water had to be drawn from a well at the side of the kitchen. There were a few bedrooms on the ground floor and the first floor. There was a cowshed at the back, along with a large vegetable garden. That was all I could see as it was already dark and the raindrops were hitting me like pebbles hard on my feet.

As soon as I entered, the lady of the house came with a warm smile and towels to wipe myself. Her smile put me instantly at ease. Without much ceremony she said, 'Please feel comfortable. Dinner will be ready in half an hour.'

I changed my dress and came to the dining hall. In the huge hall there were only four people including me, the couple and their elderly mother. Plantain leaves were laid on the floor and the cook was serving. There were innumerable food items and I did not know where to start. The old lady of the house was very gracious. She reminded me of my large-hearted grandmother. After dinner I wanted to chat with her. When I told her, she said, 'If you want, you can stay in my room so that we can talk.' I preferred that, rather than staying all alone in the first floor guest room.

I have always wondered why people in South Canara are so much more educated, compared to any other district of Karnataka. I asked Kuttamma, 'Did you study when you were young?'

Kuttamma sighed as if she was in pain.

'No, unfortunately I did not go to school. When I was young we were extremely poor and I was a coolie in the garden of a schoolteacher. I always felt education is essential. If you can read and write you can secure a better job. In my case it was not possible. So I was determined that my only son, Aithappa, should study as much as he could and I would work hard for that. My husband also felt the same way,

but he was killed by a snakebite when my son was only five years old. It was my promise to him that I would educate my son.'

I tried to imagine life six decades back—the social pressures, the great poverty, and no help from the government. I have met many women of that age group who have told me more or less the same story. Kuttamma continued.

'My son did not disappoint me. He went to Bombay as a hotel boy. He cleaned the plates in the morning, and in the evenings, went to Moghaveera Night School and studied there.'

'Yes, I know this school. It is in Worli and is the oldest Kannada school in Bombay. Many children have studied there.'

'Once he finished his schooling, he became a clerk at the counter of a hotel and went to night college. He got his degree and started his own hotel in Bombay. He became very successful.'

'Then why is he here now?'

Kuttamma smiled. I could see she was proud.

'He started many hotels in Bombay but I remained in my village. I never felt comfortable in Bombay in spite of all the money he had because nobody spoke my language there and I love this village.'

'Yes, I know there is a saying in Sanskrit:
Janani Janmabhoomischa
Swargadapi gariyasi
It means your motherland is always a heaven.'

'You are a learned lady so you can recite all this in Sanskrit but my intuition told me to stay here and do something for our own people. My son became very wealthy and handed over his business to his son. He is now sixty-five years old and ten years back he returned to his village.'

'How does he spend his time?'

I could understand the old lady not wanting to move out of her home but I was unable to understand how a busy, successful person like Aithappa could retire to this godforsaken sleepy village.

'When he became rich, my son asked me, "Amma, I have earned so much wealth. I want to know what you want. I remember you sold all your jewellery for my fees in college, you had only one meal so that I could have two. Now I want to buy lots of jewellery for you."'

'What did you answer?'

'I told my son that in life, the real jewellery is education. The schoolteacher for whom I worked when I was young used to tell everything will perish over a period of time—flowers, beauty, food. No person looks beautiful forever. But education brings confidence to your face and that is the real beauty. I have crossed the age to wear jewellery. If you respect my wishes, build as many free schools as possible, in as many villages in South Canara. My son understood my feelings. He himself shifted to this village and has, till today, built ten such schools. He remains very busy managing these schools.'

Now I understood the reason behind the high literacy rate of the area. Women like Kuttamma had never studied but they had understood the importance of good education. They had insisted their children go to school. It is certainly true that if one man studies, only one person is educated whereas if one lady studies, the entire family is educated.

A History Lesson on Teachers' Day

The date was 5th September 2003, or Teachers' Day. In Bangalore, on that day, I have a great time with my students. If, for some reason, I am out of Bangalore, I miss all the celebrations. On Teachers' Day, my students take me out and we all have lunch together and also watch a movie. They pool in their money and refuse to let me pay for anything. It shows me how close they are to me and that they remember me. It is an act of love and affection for their teacher. Each of them will go their different ways after they complete the course, but love, affection and concern for each other will always bind us together.

Last year, on Teachers' day, I was out of station on some work and feeling depressed. A friend of mine realized that and said, 'Let us go watch a film, you will feel better.'

We went to the theatre. There was a big queue. I was surprised because there were only students from schools and colleges in the queue. As my friend was getting the tickets, I remembered my students and started chatting with the youngsters.

'How come you people are here? Is there no celebration in your college or school?'

They were a group of girls. One of them replied.

'Why should there be a celebration in the school?'

'Is it not Teachers' Day?'

'So what? We knew there was a holiday, we did not even ask for what. Today being Saturday, we are very happy that we are getting two days of holidays.'

'Why? Does your school not celebrate Teachers' Day? Do you know why 5th September is known as Teachers' Day?'

Another girl replied. 'Our school may be celebrating Teachers' Day but we don't want to go. We see the same teachers every day. Why see them even on a holiday?'

That provoked the teacher in me. I asked, 'Tell me, what do we celebrate on November 14th, October 2nd, August 15th and January 26th?'

'We know they are holidays but not sure for what.'

One of them shyly said, 'I know October 2nd is Gandhi's birthday.'

At least they knew one answer! 'How come you know only that day?'

'Because it is my birthday. My grandfather was a freedom fighter. He named me Mohini and he told me Gandhiji's name was Mohandas.'

'So Mohini, do you like your name?'

'No, I don't like it. It is very old-fashioned. It sounds like it belongs to someone living a century ago. I have changed my name to Monica.'

Some other girl told me, 'I get confused with August 15th and January 26th. One of them is Independence Day and the other one is something connected with independence.'

I refused to give up. 'Tell me, when did we get independence?'

That started off a discussion in the group. I could make out a number of opinions were being debated. One said 1950, some others said 1942 and the third group said 1947. In fact the 1942-group was very

sure they were right as they had watched the movie *1942: A Love Story*.

'Do you know who was India's President then?'

'We know it is Abdul Kalam.'

'No, I am asking you before him.'

They were blank.

'Have you heard of Dr Sarvapalli Radhakrishnan?'

'We know about Radhakrishna. Their statues in marble are very beautiful. I have seen them in the Hare Rama Hare Krishna temple. I went with my parents,' one of them replied.

I told them, 'Dr Sarvapalli Radhakrishnan was a famous philosopher and a great teacher. He taught in Calcutta, Mysore and Banaras. When he left Mysore, it seems it was the students who pulled the carriage to the station, and not the horses. For his lectures, students from other colleges would come and listen, irrespective of the subjects they were studying. He was acknowledged as the best teacher wherever he taught. Later he became the President of India. Hence his birthday was declared as Teachers' Day. There are many stories about him. Please read any book or see on the Internet.'

The group looked ashamed now. I felt bad and realized it was not their fault alone. We give holidays to children but do not tell them the reason behind the holiday. Every year we prepare the same boring speech and deliver it to a handful of children. Most of us take the day off and do not make any effort so that children look forward to the day. We could make them plant trees and teach them about the environment; or we could take them out for a picnic and get close to them outside the classroom. It is our duty to make sure that days like Teachers' Day are utilized properly. We have to work hard for that, which we don't do. Children should be led by example and teachers are the best examples. What we preach, we should practise.

'Appro J.R.D.'

There are two photographs that hang on my office wall. Every day when I enter my office I look at them and start my day. They are pictures of two old people. One is of a gentleman in a blue suit and the other one is a black and white photograph of an old man with dreamy eyes and a white beard.

Many people have asked me if they are related to me. Some people have even asked me, 'Is this black and white photo that of a Sufi saint or a religious guru?'

I smile and reply 'No, nor are they related to me.'

'Then why do you look at them and start the day?'

'These people made an impact on my life. I am grateful to them.'

'Who are these people?'

'The man in the blue suit is Bharat Ratna J.R.D.Tata and the black and white photo is of Sir Jamsetji Tata.'

'But why do you have their photos in your office?'

'You can call it gratitude.'

Then, invariably, I have to tell the person the following story. It happened a long time ago. I was young and bright, bold and idealistic. I was studying in the final year for my Master's degree in computer science at Indian Institute of Science, Bangalore, which was then known as the Tata Institute. For me, life was full of fun and joy. I did not know what helplessness or injustice meant.

It was probably the April of 1974. Bangalore was just becoming warm. Red Gulmohars were blooming at the IISc campus. I was the only girl in my postgraduate department in Engineering, and was staying in the ladies' hostel. Other girls were pursuing their research in different departments of science.

After completing my postgraduation, I was keen to go abroad to do my doctorate in computer science and had already been offered scholarships from universities in USA. I had not thought of taking up a job in India.

One day, while on the way to my hostel from the lecture hall, I saw an advertisement on the noticeboard.

It was a standard job-requirement notice from the famous automobile company TELCO. It stated that the company required young, bright engineers, hard-working with excellent academic background, etc.

At the bottom there was a small line: 'Lady candidates need not apply'.

I read it and was very upset. For the first time, I was faced with gender discrimination.

Though I was not keen on taking up a job, I took it as a challenge and decided to apply. I had done extremely well in my studies, probably better than most of the boys. Little did I know then that in real life, to be successful, academic excellence is not a necessary condition.

After reading the notice, I went fuming to my room. There I decided not only to apply for the job, but also to inform the topmost person of the management of TELCO about the injustice. I got a postcard and started to write. But there was a problem. Who was the head of TELCO? I did not know. I was so ignorant that I thought it must be one of the Tatas. I knew JRD Tata was the head of the Tata Group. I had seen his pictures in newspapers. Actually, Sumant Mulgoankar was then its chairman, which I was not aware of.

I took the postcard and started writing. Even now, I clearly remember what I had written to JRD.

'Tatas have always been pioneers. They are the people who started the basic infrastructure industries in India like iron and steel, chemicals, textiles, locomotives, etc. They have cared for higher education in India since 1900, and are responsible for the establishment of the Indian Institute of Science! Fortunately I study there. But I am surprised that in such a company you can make a distinction between men and women.'

I posted the letter that was written in anger, and after a few days forgot about it.

Within ten days, I received a telegram stating that I had to appear for an interview at TELCO Pune, at their expense. I was taken aback. But my hostel-mates told me I had to use the opportunity to go to Pune free of cost. And the reason? Pune saris were cheap! I was told to buy saris for them. I even collected thirty rupees per head for each of their saris. Now, when

I look back, I feel like laughing at the reasons, but then they seemed good ones to make a trip.

This was my first visit to Pune. I fell in love with the city and even to this date it is very dear to my heart. I feel as much at home in Pune as I do at Hubli. The city changed my life in so many ways.

As directed, I went to TELCO's Pimpri office for the interview. There were six people on the panel and it was only then that I realized this was serious business.

'This is the girl who wrote to JRD,' I heard them whisper to each other as soon as I entered. By then I knew for sure that I would not get a job. And when I wouldn't get a job, why should I be scared? So I was rather cool for the interview.

Even before they started the interview I knew they were biased, so I told them, rather rudely, 'I hope this is only a technical interview.'

They were taken aback by my rudeness, and even today I am ashamed of my attitude.

During the interview they asked many technical questions and I answered all of them. Then one elderly gentleman with an affectionate voice told me, 'Do you know why we said that lady candidates need not apply? The reason is that to this day we have not employed any ladies on the shop floor of the factory. This is an automobile industry. Trainees may have to work in shifts. For training, we may have to send them to Jamshedpur in Bihar. All our plants have men and machinery. Our trainees may have to drive. We have a trainee's hostel and a guest house for them. If a lady enters, then how can we accommodate her? We do not know how men on the shop floor will accept her. How will she come for shifts? We care for our employees, particularly if she is a lady. It is not a college where there is no gender difference. This is a factory. When it comes to academics, you are a first ranker throughout. We appreciate that. People like you should work more in research laboratories.'

I was a young girl from small-town Hubli. My world was very small. I did not know the ways of large corporate houses and their difficulties. So I answered, 'But somewhere you must start. Otherwise a lady will never be able to work in the factories. You are pioneers in many aspects of life. When I look at your industries, you are far ahead of other people. If you think this way, then how will any lady ever enter this so-called man's domain?'

'Training a candidate costs a lot to our company. You are of a marriageable age. After your training you

will leave this company and shift to wherever your husband works. Is it not a waste of money for us?'

I thought for a moment and replied, 'I definitely agree with what you say. I am sure when many of you married, your wives came along with you. That has been our tradition. But is it also not true that many men undergo training, and just for a few more hundred rupees, they shift their jobs. You don't have any rule for them. You can't stop them.'

Finally, after a long interview, I was told I had been successful in securing a job at TELCO. On the way back, I got down at Hubli, my home town. I was eager to meet my father, always my best friend, and tell him my adventure. I was sure he would be happy and praise me.

But I was in for a shock. He was very upset. He said, 'You should have basic manners when addressing elderly people like JRD Tata. You should have written the letter more politely and put it in an envelope, instead of sending a postcard. Now you have to take up this job because you are morally responsible.'

That is what my future had in store for me. Never ever had I thought I would take up a job at Pune. There I met a shy young man from Karnataka, we became good friends and got married.

The elderly gentleman who interviewed me was Dr Sathya Murty, who was an excellent technocrat and human being. I worked with him for some years. After joining TELCO, I realized who JRD was. He was the uncrowned king of Indian industry. I did not get to meet him until I was transferred to Bombay. JRD had an office at Bombay House, the headquarters of Tata Industries.

One day, I was supposed to show some reports to our chairman Mr Mulgoankar, whom everyone always referred to as SM. So I went to his office on the first floor of Bombay House.

While I was in SM's room, JRD walked in. That was the first time I saw 'Appro JRD'. 'Appro' means 'ours' in Gujarati. In Bombay House, people used to affectionately call him 'Appro JRD'.

By this time, I knew who he was and was feeling very nervous, remembering my rude postcard to him.

SM introduced me very nicely, 'Jeh look, this young girl is an engineer and that too a postgraduate. She has worked on the shopfloor at TELCO. Is it not unusual? She was the first girl in our TELCO shopfloor.'

JRD looked at me. I was praying he would not ask me any questions regarding my interview or the postcard. Thankfully he didn't ask me anything about that. Instead he remarked, 'It is nice that in our country girls are getting into engineering. By the way, what is your name?'

'When I joined TELCO, I was Sudha Kulkarni, Sir. Now I am Sudha Murty.'

'Where do you work?'

'At Nanavati Mahalaya,' I replied.

He smiled at me nodding his head and the two men started their discussion. I just ran out of the room.

After that I used to see JRD on and off. He was the chairman of a large group of companies and I was only an engineer in one of those companies. There was nothing we had in common. I used to look at him with awe.

One day I was waiting for Murthy to come and pick me up after office hours. To my surprise, I saw JRD standing next to me. I did not know how to react. I was feeling uneasy. Again I started worrying about the postcard. Now when I look back, I realize JRD must have forgotten about it. It must have been a very small incident to him but not so for me.

He asked me, 'Young lady, why are you here? Office time is over.' I said, 'Sir, I am waiting for my husband to come and pick me up'.

JRD said, 'It is getting dark. There's no one in the corridor. I will wait with you until your husband comes.'

I was quite used to waiting for Murthy so I was not bothered much by having to wait in the dark. But having JRD waiting along with me made me very uncomfortable. Out of the corner of my eye, I looked at him.

He wore a simple white pant and shirt. He was old yet his face was glowing, without any air of superiority.

I was thinking, 'Look at this person. He is the chairman, a well-respected man in our country and he is waiting for the sake of an ordinary lady employee.'

As soon as I saw Murthy, I rushed out.

JRD called and said, 'Young lady, tell your husband never to be late and make his wife wait.'

In 1982, I had to resign from my job at TELCO. I was very reluctant to resign but did not have a choice. Even now, my love and respect for the House of Tatas is the same. I always looked up to JRD as my role model for his simplicity, generosity, kindness and the care he took of his employees.

After I had made my final settlements with the company, I was coming down the steps of Bombay

House when I saw JRD coming up. He was absorbed in some thought. I wanted to say goodbye to him. So I stopped. He saw me and he also stopped.

Gently he said, 'So what are you doing Ms Kulkarni?' (That was the way he always addressed me.)

'Sir I am leaving TELCO.'

'Where are you going?'

'Pune, Sir. My husband is starting a company called Infosys. So I have to shift to Pune.'

'Oh! What will you do when you are successful?'

'Sir I do not know whether we will be successful or not.'

'Never start with diffidence. Always start with confidence. When you are successful, you must give back to society. Society gives us so much, we must return it. I wish you all the best.'

Then JRD continued walking up the stairs. I stood for a while, watching him. That was the last time I saw him alive.

Many years later, I met Ratan Tata in the same Bombay office occupying the same chair as JRD. I told him many of my sweet memories of working with TELCO. I said, 'I cannot call you Mr Tata like Murthy calls you. You are occupying "Appro

JRD's" seat. You will always be "Chairman Sir" to me.'

Later, he wrote to me, 'It was nice listening about Jeh from you. The sad part is that he is not alive today to see you.'

I consider JRD a great man because, in spite of being an extremely busy person, he valued one postcard written by a young girl, who was asking for justice and questioning him. He must have received thousands of letters everyday. He could have thrown mine away in a dustbin. But he didn't do that. He respected the intentions of that unknown girl, who had neither influence nor money and gave her an opportunity to work in his company. He did not merely give her a job, but also changed her life and mindset forever.

Today, in any engineering college I see that forty to fifty per cent of the students are girls. On the shop floor of many mechanical industries we see so many ladies working. That time I think of JRD fondly.

If at all time stops and asks me what I want from life, I would say I wish JRD were alive today to see how the company we started has grown. He would have enjoyed it wholeheartedly.

Heart of Gold

This is a true story. I heard it on the radio during one of my visits to the US. It happened in one of the biggest cities in the world, New York.

It was winter. One evening, a worried mother stood shivering by the road, wearing an old coat. With her was a little girl, thin, sick-looking with a shaven head. She was wearing an oversized dress which somebody had probably given to her out of mercy. It was apparent that they were homeless and poor. The child had a cardboard placard in her hand which said, 'I am suffering from cancer. Please help me.'

The mother was carrying a begging bowl. Whenever the traffic lights turned red they would approach people, stopping them on the road and asking for help.

America is a rich country, but if you are sick and don't have insurance, then you are lost. Nobody can support you. People give small amounts of money when they see such pleas for help. This kind of a scene is not uncommon in India. We see lots of beggars with small infants in one hand and a begging bowl in another. But in America it is not so common. People felt bad for this unfortunate mother and child.

One day, a policeman was passing by and saw them. He asked them a few questions and noticed that the child indeed looked very sick, with her swollen eyes and shaven head. He wanted to help, so he opened his purse. He saw a bundle of notes which he had just drawn from the bank. He had received a good bonus for the excellent work he had done. He thought, 'I have a warm home, a caring wife and a loving son. God has been very kind to me. But these unfortunate people don't have any of these things. It is not their mistake that God has not been kind to them.' He remembered the many things he had promised his wife and son he would buy when he got his bonus. For a while he was in two minds. Then he decided and gave all the cash which he had

drawn from the bank to the woman and said, 'Please take good care of the child.'

When he reached home, his son met him at the doorstep as usual and hugged him. The house was warm and nice. He sat in front of his wife, and looking at the snow falling outside, he narrated the whole incident. After listening to him for a while his wife was silent, then she smiled. But the son was angry. He said, 'Dad, how are you sure that they have not cheated you? And even though you wanted to give some money you could have given some portion. Why did you give everything?'

The policeman laughed at his son and said, 'Son, you do not know what poverty is. I come across such unfortunate people in my work.'

The days passed and everybody forgot about it.

One day a news item in the paper caught the son's attention: 'Mother and child caught cheating.' With great interest he read:

'A greedy mother used her healthy child to pose as a cancer patient. She shaved the child's head, starved her and dressed her shabbily so that anybody would feel the child was suffering from cancer. Using this tactic she duped many people. The mother has been arrested.'

The son realized who these people were and was very upset. When his father came home, he told him as soon as he entered the house, 'Dad, you were cheated by that lady and her child who you thought was a cancer patient. The child is healthy and you gave away your entire bonus to that child.'

His father did not reply. He sat down, and looked out of the window. There were children playing outside. Winter was over and summer was setting in. In a calm voice he said, 'Son, I am very happy. The child is healthy.'

The boy was surprised. He thought being a policeman, his father would pick up the phone and talk to the police station or he would be depressed that he had been cheated and had given away so much of money to a healthy child. But there were no traces of such emotions.

He asked, 'Dad, tell me, are you not upset?'

His father again gave him the same answer, 'I am happy that the child is healthy.'

By that time his wife came with a mug of coffee in her hand. She had heard the entire conversation. With happiness in her voice she told her son. 'Son, you are very fortunate. You have an extraordinary father, who is not angry even though he has lost a lot of money. You should be proud that your father is happy thinking somebody's child is healthy, rather than worrying about his own big bonus. Learn from him. Help people without expecting anything in return.'

A Wedding in Russia

A wedding is a great event in everyone's life. In India, it is done with a great deal of ceremony. In our films, a large number of stories are based on weddings.

If you look at Indian history, you will see many wars have been fought for the sake of a marriage. People have always spent a lot of money and effort on these. In the olden days, the wedding celebrations used to carry on for a week. Later it came down to three days, then two days and now it is for a day. The amount of money spent sometimes constitutes the entire life's savings of a person. At times, people take such huge loans for this celebration that they have to go on repaying throughout their lives. In my experience, whenever I have talked to bonded labourers, I have found that a majority of them have got into that state because of the wedding expenses they had incurred.

In a marriage, the couple and their parents are worried about various things. Is she looking pretty? Are the guests being looked after? Will he keep her happy? People like you and me are worried about the wedding lunch. It is an occasion where young boys get to meet young girls, old people talk about their ailments and women exhibit their finest jewellery and silk saris.

Recently I was in Moscow, Russia. Moscow City has many war memorials. Russia has won three great wars in its history, which is a source of pride for them. They have built war memorials and erected many statues of the generals who were responsible for the victories. The first war was between Peter the Great and Sweden. The second was between Tsar Alexander I and Napoleon of France. The third one was against Hitler in World War II in 1945.

There is a huge park in Moscow, known as Peace Park. In the middle of this Peace Park there is a large monument. There is a pillar, and on the pillar the different battles fought by Russia have been mentioned along with dates and places. The park has beautiful fountains. In the summer, flowers of many colours bloom and the place is a feast for the eyes. In the night it is decorated with lights. Every Russian is proud of this park and it is a spot visited by all tourists.

The day I went to the park was a Sunday. It was drizzling and cold, though it was summer. I was standing under an umbrella and enjoying the beauty. Suddenly, my eyes fell on a young couple. It was apparent that they had just got married. The girl was in her mid-twenties, slim with blond hair and blue eyes. She was very beautiful. The boy was almost of the same age and very handsome. He was in a military uniform. The bride was wearing a white satin dress, decorated with pearls and pretty laces. It was very long, so two young girls were standing behind her holding up the ends of the gown, so it wouldn't be dirtied. One young boy was holding an umbrella over their heads so that the couple would not get drenched. The girl was holding a bouquet and the two were standing with their arms linked. It was a beautiful sight. I started wondering why they had come to this park in this rain soon after getting

married. They could have surely gone to a merrier place. I watched as they walked together to the dais near the memorial, kept the bouquet, bowed their heads in silence and slowly walked back.

By now I was very curious to know what was going on. I could not ask the couple because they probably could not speak English and I didn't know the Russian language. There was an old man standing with them. He looked at me, my sari and asked, 'Are you an Indian?'

I replied, 'Yes, I am an Indian.'

'I have seen Raj Kapoor's movies. They were great. Raj Kapoor had visited Russia. I know one Hindi song, *Main awara hoon*. Do you know Moscow City has statues of three great Indians?'

'Who are they?'

'Jawaharlal Nehru, Mahatma Gandhi and Indira Gandhi.'

Since we were chatting quite amicably now, I decided to use the opportunity to ask some questions.

'How come you know English?'

'Oh, I worked abroad.'

'Will you tell me why that young couple visited the war memorial on their wedding day?'

'Oh, that is the custom in Russia. The wedding takes place normally on a Saturday or a Sunday. Irrespective of the season, after signing the register at the marriage office, married couples must visit the important national monuments near by. Every boy in this country has to serve in the military for a couple of years at least. Regardless of his position, he must wear his service uniform for the wedding.'

'Why is that?'

'This is a mark of gratitude. Our forefathers have given their lives in the various wars Russia has fought. Some of them we won, and some we lost, but their sacrifice was always for the country. The newly-married couple needs to remember they are living in a peaceful, independent Russia because of their ancestors' sacrifices. They must ask for their blessings. Love for the country is more important than wedding celebrations. We elders insist on continuing with this tradition whether it be in Moscow, St Petersburg or any other part of Russia. On the wedding day they have to visit the nearest war memorial.'

This set me wondering about what we teach our children. Do we tell them about the sacrifices of the 1857 War of Independence? Do we talk about the 1942 Quit India Movement, or ask newly-weds to visit the Andaman Cellular Jail where thousands lived in solitude and were sent to the gallows? Do we remember Bhagat Singh, Chandrashekhar Azad, Shivaji, Rana Pratap, Lakshmi Bai who gave their lives to save our country?

These men and women never lived to see an independent India. But do we have the courtesy to remember them on the most important day of our lives? We are busy shopping for saris, buying jewellery and preparing elaborate menus and partying in discos.

My eyes filled with tears at the thought and I wished we could learn a lesson from the Russians.

'Amma, What Is Your Duty?'

At that time, my daughter Akshata was a teenager. By nature she was very sensitive. On her own, she started reading for blind children at Ramana Maharshi Academy for the Blind at Bangalore. She was a scriber too. She used to come home and tell me about the world of blind people. Later she wrote an essay on them, called 'I Saw the World through the Blind Eyes of Mary'. Mary was a student at the academy who was about to appear for the pre-university exam. Once, Akshata took Mary to Lalbagh for a change. The conversation between them was quite unusual.

'Mary, there are different types of red roses in this park,' Akshata told her.

Mary was surprised. 'Akshata, what do you mean by red?'

Akshata did not know how to explain what was red. She took a rose and a jasmine, and gave them to Mary.

'Mary, smell these two flowers in your hand. They have different smells. The first one is a rose. It is red in colour. The second one is jasmine. It is white. Mary, it is difficult to explain what is red and what is white. But I can tell you that in this world there are many colours, which can be seen and differentiated only through the eyes and not by touch. I am sorry.'

After that incident Akshata told me, 'Amma, never talk about colours when you talk to blind people. They feel frustrated. I felt so helpless when I was trying to explain to Mary. Now I always describe the world to them by describing smells and sounds which they understand easily.'

Akshata also used to help a blind boy called Anand Sharma at this school. He was the only child of a schoolteacher from Bihar. He was bright and jolly. He was about to appear for his second pre-university exam.

One day, I was heading for an examination committee meeting. At that time, I was head of the department of computer science at a local college. It was almost the end of February. Winter was slowly ending and there was a trace of summer setting in. Bangalore is blessed with beautiful weather. The many trees lining the roads were flowering and the city was swathed in different shades of violet, yellow and red.

I was busy getting ready to attend the meeting, hence I was collecting old syllabi, question papers and reference books. Akshata came upstairs to my room. She looked worried and tired. She was then studying in class ten. I thought she was tired preparing for her exams. As a mother, I have never insisted they study too much. My parents never did that. They always believed the child has to be responsible. A responsible child will sit down to study on her own.

I told Akshata, 'Don't worry about the exams. Trying is in your hands. The results are not with you.' She was annoyed and irritated by my advice. 'Amma, I didn't talk about any examination. Why are you reminding me of that?'

I was surprised at her irritation. But I was also busy gathering old question papers so did not say anything. Absently, I looked at her face. Was there a trace of sadness on it? Or was it my imagination?

'Amma, you know Anand Sharma. He came to our house once. He is a bright boy. I am confident that he will do very well in his final examination. He is also confident about it. He wants to study further.'

She stopped. By this time I had found the old question papers I had been looking for, but not the syllabus. My search was on. Akshata stood facing me and continued, 'Amma, he wants to study at St Stephens in Delhi. He does not have anybody. He is poor. It is an expensive place. What should he do? Who will support him? I am worried.'

It was getting late for my meeting so casually I remarked, 'Akshata, why don't you support him?'

'Amma, where do I have the money to support a boy in a Delhi hostel?'

My search was still on.

'You can forfeit your birthday party and save money and sponsor him.'

At home, even now both our children do not get pocket money. Whenever they want to buy anything they ask me and I give the money. We don't have big birthday parties. Akshata's birthday party would mean calling a few of her friends to the house and ordering food from the nearby fast food joint, Shanthi Sagar.

'Amma, when an educated person like you, well-travelled, well-read and without love for money does not help poor people, then don't expect anyone else to do. Is it not your duty to give back to those unfortunate people? What are you looking for in life? Are you looking for glamour or fame? You are the daughter of a doctor, granddaughter of a schoolteacher and come from a distinguished teaching family. If you cannot help poor people then don't expect anyone else to do it.'

Her words made me abandon my search. I turned around and looked at my daughter. I saw a sensitive young girl pleading for the future of a poor blind boy. Or was she someone reminding me of my duty towards society? I had received so much from that society and country but in what way was I returning it? For a minute I was frozen. Then I realized I was holding the syllabus I was looking for in my hand and it was getting late for the meeting.

Akshata went away with anger and sadness in her eyes. I too left for college in a confused state of mind.

When I reached, I saw that as usual the meeting was delayed. Now I was all alone. I settled down in my chair in one of the lofty rooms of the college.

There is a difference between loneliness and solitude. Loneliness is boring, whereas in solitude you can inspect and examine your deeds and your thoughts.

I sat and recollected what had happened that afternoon. Akshata's words were still ringing in my mind.

I was forty-five years old. What was my duty at this age? What was I looking for in life?

I did not start out in life with a lot of money. A great deal of hard work had been put in to get where we were today. What had I learnt from the hard journey that was my life? Did I work for money, fame or glamour? No, I did not work for those; they came accidentally to me. Initially I worked for myself, excelling in studies. After that I was devoted to Infosys and my family. Should not the remaining part of my life be used to help those people who were suffering for no fault of theirs? Was that not my duty? Suddenly I remembered JRD's parting advice to me: 'Give back to society.'

I decided that was what I was going to do for the rest of my life. I felt relieved and years younger.

I firmly believe no decision should be taken emotionally. It should be taken with a cool mind and when you are aware of the consequences. After a week I wrote my resignation letter as head of the department and opted only for a teacher's post.

I am ever grateful to Akshata for helping bring this happiness and satisfaction in my work and life. It means more to me than the good ranks I got in school, and my wealth.

When I see hope in the eyes of a destitute, see the warm smile on the faces of once helpless people, I feel so satisfied. They tell me that I am making a difference.

I joined Infosys Foundation as a Founder Trustee. The Foundation took up a number of philanthropic projects for the benefit of the poor in different states of India.

I received many awards on various occasions. One of them was the Economic Times Award given to Infosys Foundation. As a trustee I was invited to receive this award. At that time I remembered my guru. Now she was a student in USA. I told her, 'At least for one day you must come for this award ceremony in Bombay. If you had not woken me up at the right time, I would not have been receiving it today. I want you to be present.'

I will remain indebted to Akshata forever for the way she made me change my life and the lesson she taught me.

The Story of Two Doctors

My sister is a doctor in a government hospital. She works very long hours. Often she has to do night duty which can be very exhausting. Our government hospitals may not have too many facilities, but at least the poor can get treatment here almost for free.

Once, during one of her night duties, she had to perform many operations and came home very late. Just as she reached home there was a call from the hospital for her to come and perform another emergency operation. She was about to leave immediately. Seeing her tired face, I made a comment. 'I agree patients are very important to doctors. But for the last twenty-four hours you were in the hospital. You are also a human being; you too require rest. You can tell somebody else to do this operation. Why don't you rest now?'

She smiled at me and said, 'It is not me alone. There are many doctors along with me who are working equally hard. They also require rest. I am the seniormost doctor, so I must lead the team. In the larger interest of the people you must sacrifice your personal pain. Don't you remember the story of anaesthesia?' Saying this she went away.

I then remembered the story she had mentioned. My sister had narrated it to me some years ago. To what extent this story is true I don't know. But it is a remarkable one.

Many years ago, in England, there was a father-and-son pair who were doctors. The father was very famous and innovative, and the son was young and enthusiastic. In those days there was no concept of anaesthesia and whenever a patient was to be operated on, chloroform was given.

The senior doctor did many experiments in this field and developed a medicine, which when injected in the area where the operation was to be done, made only that part numb. There was no need to make the patient unconscious. Today we call this local anaesthesia.

He performed several experiments and was convinced by adding different chemicals that his medicine was effective. But there was one problem. No one would offer himself for the experiment. Without experimenting on a human being this medicine could not be officially released in the market.

Now, the doctor's son had six fingers on his left hand. One day, he suggested to his father, 'Father, I know your medicine is very good. Inject it to my sixth finger and operate and remove the finger. Anyway I wanted to get rid of that finger. Let us perform this operation in front of other doctors. No man can stand the pain of surgery without anaesthesia. When they look at my face they will come to know that your medicine has made the area numb and I am not experiencing any pain.'

The suggestion was very good. The father conveyed a message to the members of the Academy of Medical Science, who were the final authority for allowing this medicine to be used in public.

The day of the operation came and several scientists, doctors and other public figures assembled to watch the effect of this miracle injection. The father exhibited his son's sixth finger, and injected the medicine. He said, 'Now I will start the operation. You can observe the patient's face.'

There was a smile on the young man's face. The operation was performed and was a success. Throughout, the smile remained on the son's face. Everybody was amazed by what they saw and congratulated the senior doctor for his work.

After they left, the young doctor was dressing his wound. His father had tears in his eyes. He embraced his son and started sobbing uncontrollably.

'Sorry, my son, I knew what pain you were undergoing during the operation, you never showed it to the public.'

The injection had to be prepared by adding four chemicals, but in his hurry and tension before the operation, the father forgot to add the fourth. Because of that the injection was not at all effective. There was uncontrollable pain during the operation. However, the son realized there was something his father had forgotten. If he showed his pain his father's experiment would fail. He knew how hard his father had worked to develop this medicine. He himself was aware that it was effective. It was

unfortunate that something was not making it work now. In the middle of the operation the father too realized the fourth chemical was missing and the medicine was not working. But he was unable to tell this in public. He knew what agony his son was undergoing in spite of the smile on his face. That was why, when everyone left, he broke down crying.

The son consoled his father. 'Father, don't worry. For the welfare of others, I controlled my own pain.'

I don't know how true this story is, but in my sister's and her colleagues' dedication to their work, I thought I saw a glimpse of the sacrifices people in the medical profession make.

A Journey Through the Desert

Till a few years back, I did not have a driver, and used to drive everywhere myself. The petrol bunk where I filled petrol from had a service station beside it. Some Saturdays, I would take my car to that service station and stay there until it was serviced. There were two boys, perhaps fourteen years of age, who worked there. They were identical twins. One was called Ram and the other one was Gopal. They were very poor and did not go to school, yet they could speak many languages.

Though Bangalore is the capital of Karnataka, Kannada is not the only language spoken here. There are many people who have come from outside the state and settled in this beautiful city, hence Bangalore has become very cosmopolitan. These boys had met many people during their work in the station and so could speak Kannada, which was their mother tongue, and also Tamil, Telugu and Hindi. Ram and Gopal worked as errand boys. They were always very cheerful and everyone liked them.

The servicing of my car used to take about two hours. The boys would bring a chair for me and I would sit under the shade of a tree and read some books.

Over a period of time I became friendly with them and they told me about their life. They did not have a father. Their mother worked as a labourer. They stayed in a nearby slum with their uncle. They had studied up to class four but then had to drop out as they were too poor. There was nobody who could guide and teach them at home. Though the salary at the service station was not much, they got free breakfast and lunch and sometimes some small tips from the car owners. They had no fixed working hours. They came around eight in the morning and went home only by 8 p.m. Sunday was the only holiday they got.

In spite of all the difficulties they faced, these kids were always smiling. They never said no or grumbled about any work they were told to do. I have seen children in many well-off families with grumpy faces and no happiness. If you ask them to do any work they give hundreds of reasons to avoid it. I suppose happiness does not depend on the amount of money in the bank.

I used to really like these two boys for their enthusiasm. Once in a while I took snacks and some old shirts for them. They took the clothes with great joy, as if they were made of silk. But I never saw them wear those clothes. If I asked, they said, 'Madam, we always wear dirty clothes to work, because at the station they become greasy.'

Once I took some storybooks for them, thinking they could read them at night. After all, while other children of their age were studying in schools and attending hockey matches and chess tournaments, these boys were slogging to make both ends meet. But when I gave them the story books, their faces became pale and for the first time ever I saw a trace of unhappiness on their faces. They said, 'Madam, it takes a lot of time for us to read as we are not used to reading. Will you tell us the story?'

'How can I tell the story here, when you are working all the time?'

'We get some free time at about four o'clock. If you come to service your car then we can sit with you and listen to the story.' Their two pairs of eyes were begging me for the stories and I could not say no. I remembered how my own children always insisted I tell them stories in the night. I agreed.

So it became a routine for me to tell stories on Saturday evenings. I went there even if my car did not need to be serviced. They were very attentive when I told my stories and waited eagerly for more. This went on for many months. Then I decided to get a driver and stopped driving myself. My driver took the car for servicing after that and I did not meet Ram and Gopal for a long time.

Time flows like water. After almost a decade, one day my driver was complaining about some problem the car was giving him. I told him to get it repaired. My old car had outlived its life but was still working. When my driver came back from the garage he said, 'After looking at the car, the car mechanic asked about you. Do you know the owner of the Good Luck Garage?'

'I have not heard this name. Is it a new garage?'

'It is relatively new. I always prefer to go to garages owned by youngsters. This young man is

very sincere. It seems he has known you for a long time. He asked if you are still teaching in the college.'

I could not think of anyone I knew who could be owning a garage now. Since my driver did not even know his name, I was unable to place him and assumed it was some old student of mine, though since I teach computer science, I could not figure out how this person had shifted to Automobile Engineering. When my driver told me a second time that the owner of the garage had asked about me, I felt I should go and meet this man who was so concerned about me.

The next day, I went to the Good Luck Garage. It was a fairly modern garage and well equipped. There was a glass cabin where I assumed the owner was sitting. As soon as I entered, a handsome young man in blue overalls greeted me. He was holding a spanner and a screwdriver in his hand.

'Madam, please come and sit down in the cabin. I will wash my hands and come in a minute.'

I sat on the sofa in his office. It was a nice functional office. The young man looked vaguely familiar to me. I knew I had met him somewhere but could not place where. I wondered, did I teach this boy in pre-university? That time, boys are sixteen or seventeen years old, adolescents with a lot of energy. When I meet them after they have grown up, I often fail to recognize them. They look so different and mature. By that time the man had returned with a coffee mug and a glass of water.

'Madam, you have changed a lot. You look old and tired.'

'I am sorry, I am unable to recollect your name. You should excuse me and tell me your name. As you said, I am growing old.'

He smiled at me. There was a dimple on his cheek. And then I knew who he was. He was one of those kids who used to work in the garage a decade back. Was he Ram or Gopal? Even in those days I used to get confused. I asked him, 'Are you Ram or Gopal?'

'I am Ram, Madam.'

'Please sit down. I am very happy to see you like this.'

Now I could understand why Ram had enquired about me after recognizing the car.

'Madam, I am very grateful to you for your help in those days.'

'What help did I give? I used to give some old shirts and eatables and told some stories.'

'Madam, you do not know how your stories changed my life. Do you remember the stories you told us?'

I didn't. From the ocean of stories in my head I had told them a few.

'No, I don't remember.'

He sat down opposite me, closed his eyes and started telling his own story.

'Madam, our life was very difficult. You were aware of it. The only thing we looked forward to was your visit every Saturday when we listened to your stories. We used to stay with our uncle, and whatever we earned he would take. The stories you told us were our only escape from the drudgery of our lives. Our working hours were long. I felt I should go to school and continue my studies. But the night schools were all quite far from where we stayed. With no financial help or support from home, it seemed studying would always remain a dream, till we heard one of your stories. It made a big difference in our lives.'

Now I was keen to know what happened next.

'Tell me which story that was?' The roles had got reversed. I was the listener and he, the storyteller.

'Once, in a village there were many poor people. They all wanted to cross a desert to go to the next village where life was better and the future more promising.

'Many boys wanted to go. The elders in the village had said to them, "If you want to do something in life you must go to that town. You pick up stones from the desert and carry to that town. Some buyer will pay money for those rare stones."

'One morning, two boys started their journey. They carried food and water with them. In the beginning, the sand was still cold and the sun not yet hot. Their journey was great. They did not feel tired and strode on. After sometime the sun rose over their heads and the sand started getting hot. After walking for a long time they thought they must have reached the edge of the desert. So they ate all their food and drank the water. But soon they realized they had walked only half the way.

'They also started collecting stones to sell in the town. After some time their bags were full of stones and very heavy. One boy felt it was too much to carry so he threw the stones and decided to go back. The other boy said, "Let us listen to our elders. Come what may, let us cross this desert and go to the next town."

'The first boy did not listen and went back. The second boy continued to walk towards the other town. It was a difficult journey, collecting the stones and travelling all alone, with no water to drink. Sometimes he felt his friend was right. There was no guarantee what was in that town. It was better to stop and go back to the village. But faith and hope kept him going. After walking for a long, long time he reached the town. Much to his disappointment, he saw it was like any other town. There was a dharamshala near by. It was getting dark and he was tired. So he decided to spend the night there.

'Next morning, when he got up he wanted to throw away the heavy stones he had collected and return to his village. He opened his bag. What he saw surprised him. All the stones had become big diamonds! In a minute's time he had become a millionaire.

'Do you remember Madam, you also told us the meaning of the story? A student's life is like the desert, examinations are the hot sun, difficulties are like the warm sand and study is like hunger and thirst. As a student, you have to travel all alone, collecting knowledge and skill the way the boy in the story collected stones. The more you collect, the better is the life you lead later.

'After hearing the story, I decided to study in spite of all the odds I had to face. With a lot of determination and after facing many difficulties, I managed to finish school. The service station owner was also helpful. When I got good marks, he helped me pay my fees for an Automobile Diploma. I continued to work while I learnt. Later, I took a loan from the bank and started this work. By the grace of God, I am successful and have repaid my loan. I am a free person now.

'Madam, rich people are usually scared to start a new venture. They feel if the venture fails they will lose their money. I never had anything to lose.'

I had learnt this from my own experience too.

'Where is Gopal now?'

'He followed another story of yours.'

Ram looked sad.

'What happened?'

'Gopal's state can also be explained by another story you told us. It seems there was a jackal in the desert. One morning he walked out and faced the sun. He saw his shadow was larger than him. It was so huge that he decided he would hunt a camel for his afternoon meal. He spent the whole day searching for a camel and did not pay attention to the smaller animals he could have caught. He did not find one till the evening. By then his shadow was even smaller than him. So he started hunting for a mouse.

'Gopal was the same. He always tried to do things beyond his capacity and failed miserably. He doesn't even want to work with me. Now, he is a peon in an office.'

I was dumbstruck to hear how a small story I had told brought about so much of change. I had never imagined while telling them that such a thing was possible. I am not even the original writer of these stories. I could only silently salute the person who thought of these stories first. Did he or she realize the effect they would have on two children after so many years?

Dead Man's Riddle

Often, when there are two or more brothers in a family, they want to divide their parents' property between them and get into arguments and court cases over this.

In the villages, the panchayat decides how the property should be divided. In my childhood, I used to attend meetings of the panchayat with my grandfather where the division of some villager's property would be discussed. The elders would assemble and call the brothers who were fighting over the property. If there were three brothers, they would make three divisions of the property, each of approximately the same value. For example, each part would contain a little bit of gold, some silver and vessels. The values of all the articles in each group would be approximately fixed by the elders of the villages. It was difficult to always make the value of each part equal to the others. In such a situation, the youngest brother would get to choose his part first. The logic behind it was that he had stayed the least number of days with his parents. In those days, in villages, staying with parents was also considered an asset.

The village elders were all well-respected and everyone knew they were impartial. Their decisions were final and no one went to court against them. Going to court for such matters was considered a waste of time and energy. There is a saying in the village that if two feuding parties approach the court, both parties lose money, only the advocate becomes rich.

Once, there was such a disagreement in the division of property of a certain family. The Sarpanch tried his best to make the brothers agree to a certain division but they just would not accept the decision. Finally, Sarpanch Som Gowda told a story which everyone listened to carefully.

It seems, a long time back, in our village itself, there lived a rich man. He had three sons who never agreed with their father about anything. The rich man had a friend called Sumanth, who was well-educated and very wise. He would say, time will teach them everything, don't be in a hurry.

One day, the old man died. He left seventeen horses, lots of gold and land for his sons. He wrote a will which was very strange. He divided the land and gold into three parts but for the division of horses there was a riddle. Nobody could understand the riddle. It said, 'The half of the total horses should be given to the elder son, in the remaining half two-third should be given to the second son and what remains out of that two-third should be given to the third son.'

Seventeen was the total number of horses. Half of it meant eight and a half horses to the elder son. That meant one had to kill a horse to divide it. Subsequently, two-thirds of eight would mean one more horse had to be killed. The old man loved his horses immensely and would never have wanted any of them killed. So what did he mean? The brothers scratched their heads for a few days over the will. When they could not come up with a solution, they showed the will to their father's friend. Sumanth read it and smiled.

He replied, 'It is very easy. Tomorrow morning I will come and divide the horses.'

The next day, everybody assembled in the ground. All seventeen horses were standing in a row. Sumanth came on his own horse. He made his horse stand along with the other horses.

He said, 'Now there are eighteen horses. I am as good as your father. Let us divide the horses as per the will.'

But the sons objected. 'You have added your horse to our horses, that was not our father's wish.'

Sumanth said, 'Don't worry, wait until the division is over. I will take my horse back. Out of these eighteen horses as per the will, half will go the elder son. Half of eighteen is nine, so the elder one gets nine horses. Now there are nine remaining, out of nine two-thirds means six horses will go to the second son. Now there are three remaining. Two-thirds of three means two horses out of three, will go to the third son. One horse is left, which was any way not yours. It is mine and I am taking it and going home.'

All the people who had assembled were puzzled. The three sons did not know how the division took place without killing a horse. They went to Sumanth and asked, 'Uncle, how did you manage without killing any horse?'

Sumanth smiled and said, 'Experience has taught me many things in life. Your father also knew it. Many a times, a work may look impossible. But if someone gives the smallest suggestion, you can work on it. That is the reason your father wrote his will in such a way that you were forced to take somebody's advice. You may think you know everything, but please remember you are still a student. Life is an eternal teacher, provided you have an open mind.'

Som Gowda concluded, 'That's the way elders have taught us lessons. Experience is the best teacher in life. Elders have seen many ups and downs in their lives and interacted with many people. During the process they have acquired knowledge which can't be taught in a school or college. It has to be learnt over a period of time. Now it is left to you people to make the decision.'

The three brothers, after listening to the story, agreed to the panchayat's division of their property.

'I Will Do It'

He was short. He was sharp. He was the brightest boy in his class. His seniors used to ask him to solve their difficulties in science. He could have gone unnoticed in a crowd, but once you asked him a question related to physics or maths, there was a spark in his eyes. He could grasp theories of science faster than the speed of light.

He came from a poor but educated family. His father was a high-school teacher and an avid reader of English literature. He, like all the boys in his class, was trying to get admission into some engineering college. The brighter ones wanted to study in the Indian Institutes of Technology, or the IITs. There was an entrance test for IIT. This boy, along with his friends, applied to appear for the test. They did not have any special books or coaching. All these IIT aspirants would sit below the shade of a stone mandap close to Chamundi Hills in the sleepy town of Mysore. He was the guide for the others. While the others struggled to solve the problems in the question paper, he would smile shyly and solve them in no time. He sat alone below a tree and dreamt of studying at IIT. It was the ultimate aim for any bright boy at that age, as it still is today. He was then only sixteen years old.

D-Day came. He came to Bangalore, stayed with some relatives and appeared for the entrance test. He did very well but would only say 'ok' when asked. It was the opposite when it came to food. When he said 'ok' it implied 'bad', when he said 'good' it implied 'ok', when he said 'excellent' it implied 'good'. His principle was never to hurt anyone.

The IIT entrance results came. He had passed with a high rank. What a delight for any student! He was thrilled. He went to his father who was reading a newspaper.

'Anna, I passed the exam.'

'Well done, my boy.'

'I want to join IIT.'

His father stopped reading the paper. He lifted his head, looked at the boy and said with a heavy voice, 'My son, you are a bright boy. You know our financial position. I have five daughters to be married off and three sons to educate. I am a salaried person. I cannot afford your expenses at IIT. You can stay in Mysore and study as much as you want.'

Indeed it was a difficult situation for any father to say 'no' to his bright son. But circumstances were like that. It was common then for the man to be the single earning member with a large family dependent on him.

His father was sad that he had to tell the bitter truth to his son. But it could not be helped. The boy had to understand reality.

The teenager was disappointed. It seemed his dreams had burnt to ashes. He was so near to fulfilling his fondest hope, yet so far. His heart sank in sorrow.

He did not reply. He never shared his unhappiness or helplessness with anybody. He was an introvert by nature. His heart was bleeding but he did not get angry with anybody.

The day came. His classmates were leaving for Madras, (now Chennai). They were taking a train

from Mysore to Madras. They had shared good years in school and college together. He went to the station to say goodbye and good luck to them for their future life.

At the station, his friends were already there. They were excited and talking loudly. The noise was like the chirping of birds. They were all excited and discussing their new hostels, new courses etc. He was not part of it. So he stood there silently. One of them noticed and said, 'You should have made it.'

He did not reply. He only wished all of them. They waved at him as the train slowly left the platform.

He stood there even after he could no longer see the train or the waving hands. It was the June of 1962 in Mysore city. Monsoon had set in and it was getting dark. It had started to drizzle. Yet he stood there motionless.

He said to himself, without anger or jealousy, 'All students from the IITs study well and do big things in life. But it is not the institution, ultimately it is you and you alone who can change your life by hard work.'

Probably he was not aware that he was following the philosophy of the Bhagavad Gita: 'Your best friend is yourself and your worst enemy is yourself.'

Later he worked very hard, and focused on one thing, never bothering about his personal life or comforts. He shared his wealth with others. He never used the help of any caste, community or political connections to go up in life.

A son of a schoolteacher showed other Indians it was possible to earn wealth legally and ethically. He built a team of people who were equally good.

He became a pioneer of India's software industry and started the Information Technology wave. Today he has become an icon of simplicity, uncompromising quality and fairness, apart from being a philanthropist. He really believes in the motto, 'Powered by intellect and driven by values'.

He is none other than Infosys founder and present chairman, Nagavara Ramarao Narayana Murthy.

The Rainy Day

When I was young, before a girl got married, her mother would give her some words of advice. They were usually like: 'You must adjust to your new house and in-laws, try to learn how they eat and cook their food, go out of your way to be friendly and helpful to everybody,' etc.

My mother, Vimala Kulkarni, told me similar words when I got married. But along with this, she said something which helped me immensely in later life. She said, 'In life, we never know when a rainy day will come and you might fall short of money. In order to be prepared for such a situation, you should always save some money from your salary, and if you are not earning, then from your husband's salary. If your salary is one thousand rupees take fifty or hundred rupees and keep it separately. This money should not be used for buying ornaments or silk saris. When you are young, you want to spend money and buy many things but remember, when you are in difficulty only few things will come to your help. Your courage, your ability to adjust to new situations and the money which you have saved. Nobody will come and help you.'

When I heard her advice, I laughed. I felt it was impossible that such a 'rainy day' would ever come in my life. I was young and thought every day was a sunny day. But I always listened to my mother, so I started saving slowly. The money was kept in a safe place in my kitchen cupboard and I never counted it.

After my marriage, for a while life was smooth in Bombay. We had a daughter and were happy like any other middle-class family. We used to stay in a flat in Bandra. I used to work for TELCO at Fort and Murthy for PCS at Nariman Point.

One day, my husband returned from office looking very worried. By nature he is not talkative and is reluctant to share his emotions, but that day he was different. I was making some chapattis in the kitchen.

'Why are you looking so worried?' I asked him.

He replied, 'Software is going to be the biggest new business in the years to come. We have no dearth of intelligent people in our country. Writing software requires a logical mind and hard work, which we can find plenty of in India. I feel I should harness this talent. I want to start a software company.'

I was shocked. I had never imagined we would ever think of starting our own company. Both, in my family and Murthy's, there was not a single person who was an entrepreneur. I had thought Murthy would work in PCS and I would work in TELCO forever and we would lead a quiet and contented life. My immediate reaction was 'No'.

Murthy started explaining his plans and vision for the business to me. 'You are fond of history. You must appreciate my reasoning. You know we Indians missed the Industrial Revolution. That time we were ruled by foreigners. Now the world is on the threshold of an intellectual revolution. We must make full use of this. We have to bring this revolution to our country. If we miss this we shall never get a chance to do well in life. I want to take this step not for money alone. This is one desire that I have had for a while now. Let me do it now. It is now or never.'

My mind went back to my childhood days. One of our relatives had started something on his 'own'. He ended up incurring heavy losses. Finally he had to sell his family property. So for me, starting our own business was synonymous with loss. I was afraid the same thing would happen to us. We did not even have any property to sell in order to cover our loss. Apart from that, we had a daughter now. I was confused.

Probably Murthy read my mind. He said, 'This is a new kind of industry. It is driven by intellect and does not require large capital. I need your wholehearted support.'

There was sincerity and honesty in his voice. I have always respected and appreciated his honesty.

As I sat there wondering what was right, I smelt the chapattis burning in the kitchen. The smell reminded me that we would have to have our dinner without chapattis that day.

Still I sat and measured the odds and consequences of the problem. Murthy had a large family and they were dependent on him. He had unmarried sisters. In such a situation, if he started a new company, our financial stability would be severely affected. I was worried, but I also had a lot of faith in him. I felt that unless I supported him wholeheartedly, he would feel uncomfortable starting a new venture like this. In business there is always profit and loss. If we went into a loss, we would lose our precious savings of many years. Yet, when I thought about it, in my heart, I was also sure that we would survive somehow.

I asked him, 'Are you alone in this?'

Murthy rarely smiles. This time he smiled and replied, 'No, six of my young colleagues are joining me. This is our one chance to earn money legally and ethically. I have a dream that India should be a leader in this industry which will bring pride and revenue to our country. You have to help me. Can you give me some money? If you don't help me now, my dream will remain unfulfilled.'

I knew that if I did not give him the money he would not be able to start his company. At that moment I remembered my mother's words. 'Save some money and use it only in extremely essential situations.' This was one of those situations. Finally, I came to a decision. I went inside the kitchen and opened my rainy day saving box. I took out the money I had deposited in it every month and counted. There were ten thousand rupees. I took it, offered up a brief prayer to God and gave it to Murthy.

'All the best Murthy, that's all I can give you. With happiness I will bear all the responsibilities of this new enterprise. By the way, what are you going to name this company?'

'Infosys, and thank you for your support and the seed money. Be ready for the most bumpy ride in your life for the next few years.'

When I look back now, I realize that our lives changed completely because I had listened to my mother's valuable lesson.

I often tell this story to my children and students. One never knows when a rainy day will come. And when it does, my mother's words will always stay true.

Doing What You Like Is Freedom

One day, I was travelling by train from Bangalore to Belgaum. It is an overnight train and the only rail link between Bangalore and north Karnataka. I was travelling by second class as that's where one can meet lots of people who are eager to talk. I have noticed, the more expensive the ticket, the lesser the co-travellers speak.

As I settled down in my seat, I glanced at the opposite berth. There was a small family of husband, wife and son. The son was about eighteen or nineteen years old and probably going to college. The family was obviously quite well-off. I sat and watched them. The parents were giving numerous instructions to their son.

'It is very cold, why don't you wear a sweater?'

'Are you hungry? Shall I serve food?'

'We have got three berths, lower, middle and upper, which one would you want to take?'

'Have you brought your bathroom slippers? If you are going to the bathroom please use them...' and so on.

The young boy looked ill at ease at all their attention, particularly in front of a stranger, but was obeying and answering them reluctantly.

Then the father asked the mother, 'Did you bring some old cloth? I want to clean these seats. They look dirty.'

The mother answered, 'How many times have I told you to make reservations early. But you never listen to me. If you had booked the tickets earlier, we could have gone by first class or second AC. People like us travel in those compartments and they are maintained better, not like this second class where every Tom, Dick and Harry travels.'

The father bowed his head and answered, 'Nowadays there's so much rush for tickets for the higher classes. I did not realize that. Normally we travel by air so I underestimated the situation. Unfortunately, this Belgaum does not have an air connection.'

By now, since I knew they were also travelling up to Belgaum and we were going to be together till eight o'clock the next morning, I struck up a conversation with them.

'Are you going to Belgaum for the first time?'

They looked at me with some surprise, but the woman was eager to talk.

'Yes, we have never gone there before. My son has got admission in the Belgaum Medical College. We have heard it is a good college. Do you know anything about it?'

'Yes, it is a good college.'

'How do you know?'

'Because I belong to that area.'

After this they were eager to talk to me as they wanted to know more about the town.

The man introduced himself. 'I am Rao. I am a CA in Bangalore. This is my wife Ragini. She is an MA in Home Science. That's my son Puneet, who is going to be a medical student.' He gave me his card.

By now the train had started moving. Even before it left Bangalore city, they had opened their dinner box. It was a huge tiffin carrier and many items were placed in it. The mother laid table mats on the berth and placed steel plates. It was as if she was serving dinner at home. There were two subjis, two kinds of dal, roti, rice and a dessert. It was an eight-course meal! I watched them in amazement. The son sat down quietly for his meal but before he could touch his plate his mother said, 'Take the Dettol soap, wear your bathroom slippers, carry this towel, wash your hands and come for dinner.'

When he left, his father explained to me, 'Puneet is our only son. We have brought him up very well. We wanted him to study medicine in some college in Bangalore but unfortunately he got admission in Belgaum. We have never sent him alone anywhere. This is the first time we are leaving him. We were thinking, if the hostel does not suit him, my wife will shift to Belgaum and we will rent a small house there for the next five years. I will stay in Bangalore and meet them once a week. For children's sake parents have to make sacrifices.' His voice broke and I could see tears in the lady's eyes.

I could understand their pain at their only son leaving home. It is always a difficult time for parents, but it is also inevitable. How long can you keep birds in cages when their wings are strong and they are ready to fly? We can give our children only two things in life which are essential. Strong roots and powerful wings. Then they may fly anywhere and live independently. Of all the luxuries in life, the greatest luxury is getting freedom of the right kind.

Now the mother joined in. They were clearly very upset and worried. They wanted to share their grief with somebody, even though I was unknown to them.

'Our son is very dear to us. I was a lecturer in a college, but I left my job after his birth. Many of my colleagues have become Principals in other colleges but I was determined to bring up my son very well.'

The husband said, 'I had a good practice in Tumkur district and I own plenty of land there but I decided to shift to Bangalore for Puneet's studies. I visit my farm once in a while. I bought an apartment next to his school. I don't go anywhere without my family.'

'I take his lunch to school every day. Then I talk to his teacher regarding his performance. I have also enrolled him in different evening classes. He learns chess as it is good for the brain, karate to protect himself and cricket which is a well-respected game.'

I could not control my laughter. I felt pity for the child. I asked, 'What about music, general knowledge and debating?'

'Oh, we don't require all these. When he was born, we decided he should become a doctor.'

'What is his choice?'

'Our choice is his choice. He is only a child. What does he know about the outside world?'

By that time the 'child' came back and they started eating their dinner. After finishing, the parents decided he should sleep on the lower berth. Immediately, a bed was made by the father. He spread a snow-white bedsheet, an air pillow and the boy was made to lie down and was covered with a Kashmiri shawl.

'I hope you don't mind, we want to switch off the lights. My son cannot sleep with the lights on.'

The gentleman switched off the light without even waiting for my reply. I was left sitting alone without dinner and not feeling in the least sleepy.

I was wondering what Puneet's mother would do when he got married. They seemed to have forgotten that he was an independent person who could take his own decisions with some love and guidance. Instead, they were bombarding him with their own ideas and opinions. Too much of affection can become a golden noose around the neck. Puneet will never be a confident person.

It was only ten in the night. I never sleep that early. Even in the partial darkness, I spotted an old friend walking down the passage. We were delighted to meet each other so unexpectedly.

'Come on, why are you sitting in the dark?' she asked. 'Are you planning to steal somebody's purse? How can you sleep at ten o'clock? Come to my compartment. It is the next one. Let us talk for some time. It is very hard to catch you in Bangalore.' She started laughing loudly at her own joke.

A quiet conversation in north Karnataka would mean a high-pitched talk in sophisticated society.

'I have reservation only for this compartment.'

'Don't worry, we will tell the ticket collector. In my compartment, one berth is vacant.' My loyalty switched immediately and I followed her.

There was loud laughter and joking going on in the other compartment. Some other friends of mine were also there. We sat and remembered our college days and made fun of each other.

In the midst of us middle-aged people, there was a young boy sitting. He, too, was very jolly with enormous energy. When all of us opened our tiffin boxes, the boy offered everyone bananas from his bag. Though he did not know any of us, he looked confident and happy.

I asked him, 'What is your name? Where are you going?'

'My name is Sharad. I am going to Belgaum.'

'Why are you going there?'

'I have got a seat in the medical college there and I am going to join my class.'

'Are you going for the first time? Do you have anybody with you?'

'Yes, I am going for the first time and I am alone.'

I forgot my tiffin box. Suddenly I thought of Puneet who was of the same age as this boy.

'Where are your parents?'

'My father is a postman and my mother is a schoolteacher. I come from a village near Kolar.'

'How many siblings do you have?'

'I am the only child.'

'Did you never get lonely?'

'No. Since both my parents were working, I knew all the neighbours. After school I would visit one house every day. All those children I used to visit became like my brothers and sisters.'

I wanted to know what all subjects he studied in school.

'My father being a postman, I learnt cycling at a very young age. In the evenings, I did some extracurricular activities. My father always told me "In life, extremes are bad". It is better if one takes the middle path so one should know a little bit of music, sports, social activities. This helped me a lot. Now I can travel anywhere without a problem because I know four languages: English, Kannada, Hindi and Telugu. I can swim and sing. I was in NCC, so I travelled to many places with my batch.'

'How did you do in your exam?'

'I think I did fairly well. I got a seat in Belgaum Medical College, didn't I.'

'Is it not very expensive?'

'It is expensive. My parents have sacrificed a lot and I have taken a bank loan. I am confident I will repay the loan once I start working.'

'Tell me, for a young person, what do you think is the most important thing?'

'It is freedom. Freedom to choose your own life; freedom to pursue your own interest; freedom to enjoy your own likes, provided they are not harmful to you and the society. I feel I was very fortunate to grow up with so much of freedom, like a tree in the forest.'

Somehow, I felt I had seen a stunted bonsai plant in the previous compartment.

Gowramma's Letter

In India, particularly in villages, even a few decades back, women without children were looked down upon. Such women were not invited for naming ceremonies, and were taunted as barren women. Nobody understood the hurt and trauma they underwent.

When I was a child, I had a teacher called Gowramma. She was kind and warm. She was also tall, beautiful and always cheerful. She used to teach us Sanskrit. She was a great teacher and would tell lots of stories in the class. Students usually took Sanskrit as an optional language, in order to score marks like maths. They were not interested in the

story. They only wanted to get good grades and were not interested in Gowramma's old epics. As soon as the class was over, students used to run to escape from her elaborate stories. But I always loved listening to stories, so I would sit with her for hours.

Storytelling is an art which not everyone is good at. There are many ways to tell a story. You have to change your voice depending on the circumstance, and describe people you have never seen.

Gowramma described Lord Krishna as a tall, handsome person with a dark complexion, a mischievous smile and a kind heart. Later when I saw the Mahabharata on TV, the actor who was playing Krishna's role was exactly how she had described. Whereas when I saw the Ramayana on TV, the actor looked very different from what I had imagined Lord Rama to be like. The storyteller influences your imagination of what the characters in the story look like.

Gowramma would pick up many stories from Katha Sarithsagara, literally meaning the ocean of stories, and recreate the scenes for me. For us, time would stop and we would be immersed in the story until the peon of the school would come and harshly tell us, 'Time is up. Except you two, only the school ghost is here. You may not be scared of the ghost but I am. Kindly vacate the room.'

Then Gowramma and I would get up and depart with a heavy heart.

This went on till I was in class seven. Then I joined another school. For a few days I missed Gowramma, but soon I forgot her in my new activities. Once in a while, I met her at the marketplace and she would affectionately ask about my studies.

At home, whenever I got lost in a storybook, I would be teased as Gowramma's only true student. My mother would tell me sadly, 'Poor Gowramma, she is so beautiful, so good-natured but luck is not on her side. Her husband has left her because she cannot bear a child. He has married another woman. That woman has produced children but in no other way is she a match to Gowramma.' Then I would understand the reason behind the sadness in Gowramma's eyes.

Time flew by as swift and light as straw. I did my engineering, got married, had children and later became the Chairperson of Infosys Foundation. I toured the length and breadth of the country, met many celebrities and many poor people. My life became public.

I was often invited to colleges and universities to deliver lectures. Once, I went to a university to deliver a lecture. After it was over, students gathered to ask some questions. Though it was getting late for my next programme, since I love talking to students, I remained there answering their questions. I feel students are like my young friends, brighter than me but with less experience.

Students also ask me a lot of questions about my young days, so that they can relate to my life.

One bright girl in the crowd asked me a question which left me dazed. It was a very difficult question. 'When you are faced with some difficulty, how do you solve it? Do you avoid it?'

I did not know how to answer her and was tempted to ignore her, but my heart would not let me do that. She was a girl of twenty, bright and simple, direct and bold with no hesitation or shyness. When she saw me looking at her blankly, she repeated the same question. Somehow, looking at her, I felt I was looking at myself when I was twenty years old.

In a fraction of a second an answer came to my mind. 'Children, in answer to this question, I will tell you a story. It is a story from the Ramayana.

In the battlefield at Lanka, during the battle between Rama, Lakshmana and Ravana, Lakshmana became unconscious. He needed the medicine plant Sanjeevini to revive. Sanjeevini was only available in the Dhrona mountains. These mountains were huge and far away. The only person who could do this job was Hanumana. Hanumana flew to Dhrona mountains, but alas, he was unable to recognize which was the Sanjeevini plant. Time was running short. The only way out was to take the entire mountain along with the plants to Rama. The mountain was huge, how could he lift it? But Hanumana had the gift to increase his body size. He became higher than the mountain, till it was like a pebble for him. Then he put the mountain on his palm and flew back to Lanka. The rest of the story, all of you know.'

The girl was impatient and restless.

She said, 'I asked you a different question but you told me an old story which everyone knows.'

I smiled at her and said, 'Have patience. I have not yet completed my answer. When you come across difficulties, you have to grow bigger than the problem. You have that capacity within you, but you are not aware of it. If you become bigger, difficulties will look smaller than you, and you can solve them easily. If you become smaller than the difficulties, they will look like mountains and crush you. This is the theory I have followed in life.'

The students were pleased with my answer and there was a lot of applause. I stopped them in the middle of the clapping, with moist eyes and a heavy voice, 'The credit for this answer should go to my teacher, Gowramma. When I was young, she taught me this lesson. She used to tell me many ancient stories which are priceless in their wisdom. To understand them we need great storytellers like Gowramma. It was she who taught me to love stories when I was young.'

The function got over and I returned to Bangalore. As usual I became busier than ever. I forgot about the whole thing.

One day there was a letter. My secretary came up to me and said, 'Madam, it seems to be from somebody who knows you well. Probably this is a personal letter, so I did not read it.' She placed the letter in front of me and left. I was wondering who it could be from. It was written in a shaky handwriting. I looked closely at the name at the bottom and was surprised. It was from Gowramma.

It said, 'I think you know my husband left me long back and everyone used to make fun of me and call me a "barren woman". Everyone looked down on me and called me story teacher rather than Sanskrit teacher. Sometimes people used to tell me that instead of telling stories to children, I should make money by giving private tuition classes. I did not, because I believed in my work. I was always humiliated because I could not bear any children. You know my husband married a second time and had his own children. These children got into bad habits and brought shame and debt to him. He used to come and cry at my doorstep. At that time I helped him with my savings . . .'

I could not understand why Gowramma had written this personal story to me. I was aware of her situation. But why had she written it all to me now? But patience is one quality I have acquired along with my grey hair. It told me to complete reading the letter.

'Today, my husband brought me the newspaper and showed it to me. He said that you mentioned my name in public and contributed your success to my storytelling. For a minute I froze. I am not your biological mother but you behaved as if you were my child. People have children, but they fight and bring disgrace and shame to their parents. My husband felt ashamed about his own children, whereas I felt proud about my child whom I taught selflessly and who listened wholeheartedly. You made me proud. Now I don't have any complaint with God.'

Tears welled up in my eyes and fell on the letter mingling with the ink. I was unable to read further.

Who Is Great?

Whenever I teach my class, I make sure that everyone participates in the question-answer session. I normally teach for forty minutes and the last twenty minutes I keep open for debates, questions and answers. This way, students learn to express their opinions in front of others and the teacher also understands how much the students have learnt. Many times I have learnt a lot from my students during these sessions. Sometimes their questions are so difficult I am not able to answer. Then I tell them that I will refer to my books and answer the next day.

Frequently, after the class I tell a story which leads to debates. Once, I made a statement, 'Many a times there is no perfect solution for a given problem. No solution is also a solution. Everything depends upon how you look at it. We make judgements on others depending upon what we think of them.'

My students immediately objected to this statement. 'Convince us,' they said.

'Okay, I will tell you a simple story. This happened many centuries back. There was a beautiful girl called Rathnaprabha who was rich and bright. She completed her studies and asked her teacher, "What shall I pay you as *gurudakshina*?"'

'Her teacher replied, "Your father has already paid me. You don't have to worry."'

'Rathnaprabha insisted and the teacher was upset. He said to himself, "I want to test the courage of this girl. Let me put a difficult condition which she will not be able to fulfil. Then she will not trouble me any more."'

'So he said, "Rathnaprabha, on a moonless night you should deck yourself with lots of jewellery and come to my house all alone."'

'There was a forest between Rathnaprabha's house and the teacher's. The road was very bad. There were many animals in the forest and a river too. Rathnaprabha thought for a minute and went away. The teacher was very happy that he had silenced his student.

'Finally it was a moonless night. Rathnaprabha decked herself with expensive jewellery and was about to set out to her teacher's house. Her father saw this and was very upset. He asked her where she was going, so Rathnaprabha narrated the story. Her father was taken aback.

'He said, "Your teacher is a nice person, you must have troubled him, which is why he told you to do this, just to teach you a lesson. I know him well, I will explain to him tomorrow. Don't go. He will understand and he will pardon you. You are like a daughter to him."

'Rathnaprabha did not listen. She insisted on going all alone as she had promised she would. There were many animals in the forest but she had made up her mind and kept walking.

'Suddenly, she was stopped by a young thief. He had never seen so many expensive ornaments and was delighted by the amount of money he would make that night. He stopped her and told her his intentions.

'Rathnaprabha was unperturbed. She said, "I promised my teacher I would go to him wearing

all these ornaments. I will give them to you when I come back from my teacher's house. I always keep my word."

'The thief was surprised and let her go. But he followed her secretly to know what happened next. Rathnaprabha knocked on the door of the teacher's house. He opened the door and was surprised and sad to see her.

'"I thought you would take it as a joke. It was only to discourage you. I never thought you would come here against all the odds. Please go back home. I will bless you my child. You are a woman of your word."

'Rathnaprabha turned to go back when the thief appeared before her. She said to him, "I promised to give you all my ornaments. Please take them."

'The thief smiled and said, "You are an unusual woman. I don't want anything from you. It is difficult to meet people like you."

'Rathnaprabha came home. Her father was waiting at the doorstep. She described everything to him. Her father was proud and happy. He said, "You are courageous and you kept your word. Come inside and take rest. You have travelled a lot today."'

When I completed the story, my students were not impressed. They said, 'What is great in this story? There is a headstrong girl, a foolish teacher, an impractical thief and an irresponsible father. What do we have to learn from this story?'

I told them, 'That is how you view things. I understand the story in a different way. Courageous Rathnaprabha, kind-hearted teacher, generous thief and a responsible father who values his daughter's words. Who do you think was the greatest person in the story?'

A lot of noise broke out in the classroom. The students started debating and arguing amongst themselves. I was smiling and looking at them.

One group got up and said, 'Madam, we think Rathnaprabha was great because she was aware of all the difficulties and yet did not change her mind. She was opposed by her father, scared by the thief, worried about the animals in the forest, but still she believed that *gurudakshina* should be given to her teacher. We only hope Madam, you will not ask such a *gurudakshina* from us.' The whole class burst into laughter. I did not answer.

Another group immediately got up and argued, 'We don't agree. There was nothing great about

Rathnaprabha. She was a headstrong girl. The thief was the greatest person because a thief usually robs people without asking their victims or worrying about what happened to them afterwards. There is some bond between the teacher and Rathnaprabha and between Rathnaprabha and her father. They had some commitment to each other, whereas the thief was not a part of the system. So we think the thief was the greatest personality.'

Before they could complete, another group got up and argued for the teacher. 'The teacher was the greatest. He told Rathnaprabha not to worry about the fees. But when she was adamant, he put forth a difficult condition. When she came, he was surprised and worried. He did not ask anything else. He blessed her wholeheartedly.'

The last group did not agree, because they believed the father was the greatest. They argued, 'The father allowed Rathnaprabha to take her own decision. How many fathers even today allow their daughters to do that? Madam, in this class how many girls can take independent decisions?'

Things became too noisy after this because the debate had now become personal. I realized it was time for me to interfere.

I said, 'There is no one person in this story who was great. It is the way we look at it. Similarly, whenever any problem arises we should view it from different angles. The decisions each of us arrives at will be different. Whenever we blame somebody, for a minute we should enter into that person's mind and try to understand why he did what he did. Only then should we take a decision.'

Now my entire class agreed with me.

Balu's Story

Balu is my cousin. In no way is he extraordinary, yet he is very special to me. That is because he can always see the lighter side of any situation, however difficult. When I talk to him I feel life is so simple, and I have been complicating it unnecessarily.

Once, a friend of mine who was working in a bank, was transferred to a small village in a forest area. He was worried about his family, children, their education, etc. He could not resign, as he would not have got another job at that age. One day, while he had come to my house and was telling me his worries, Balu arrived. He heard the problem and started laughing.

'If I were you I would have accepted this happily. You can leave your children with your parents. Grandparents always look after children very well and also teach them better lessons. Is it not true, Sudha?' Without waiting for my answer, he continued, 'Of late, your health has not been good. In this city it is difficult to go for a walk. The congestion and traffic chokes your throat. The best cure for your problems is to go for a five-kilometre walk every day. How will you do that here? That is why a village is the best place for you. There are trees everywhere and the air is fresh. Take advantage of this situation and enjoy it. Your wife can visit you once a month and you can come here once, that means you will meet your family twice a month. Sometimes it is better to be away from the family for a while, as you get a lot more respect. This is my personal experience.' Balu finished in a hushed tone.

My friend certainly looked more at ease after listening to Balu's speech. That is the way Balu speaks. If somebody fails in the exam, Balu has a ready-made consolation.

'In life, some failures are essential. Repeated success makes a person arrogant, whereas occasional failures are essential to become mature. Have you not heard the famous words, "Try and try and try again, you will succeed at last." Don't fail next time. Start studying now.'

Parents don't always like this advice of his but it goes down very well with the students.

Another cousin of mine, Prasad, is always complaining, 'People cheat me a lot. I want to help everybody, but people take advantage of me.'

Balu was ready with a clever answer, 'There was a person who used to complain the whole day, from morning to evening, that he had a headache, a stomach ache or a leg pain. I asked him, "Show me where you are aching." He pointed all over his body with a finger. Then I told him, "You have a pain in your finger and not in the other parts of the body." Prasad, when you say everyone is cheating you and taking advantage of you, then you have a problem, not others.'

Balu is a good narrator and once he starts describing something he forgets the time. That is the reason why he is very popular with children.

He exaggerates his stories, is never punctual, but still I enjoy his company. He is not cunning and would never hurt anyone. He can live without food but not without talking.

His children have all grown up now and done well in life. Balu jokes about this too. 'They have done well because I did not help them in studies.' He can laugh as much at himself as at others.

Balu has travelled to many places. He has a story to tell about every place he has visited, but I usually take them with a pinch of salt. His son works in the US. When he had a baby, he invited his parents to the US for a year. Before Balu left, the whole village knew he was going abroad. After he came back, he summoned everyone in the village under the big banyan tree and said, 'I want to describe my experiences in the US.'

Today, going abroad is not anything great. But not too many people from our village had gone. The ones who had gone did not describe their stay there in too many details. They just said, 'That is a different country with a different value system.'

But Balu was not like that. He started describing his stay endlessly from the day he arrived. I knew Balu's nature, so before he went to tell all the villagers his stories under the banyan tree, I said to him, 'You don't have control on your tongue. Anybody can make out that you are telling a lie. There is a method to describe and a limit to exaggeration. If you want to say some boy is tall you can say he is perhaps six feet four inches in height. But you will say, the boy is ten feet tall, which is not possible. People make fun of you. Do not underestimate villagers. They know about America. They have seen it on TV.'

Balu did not argue. He said, 'I agree. But when I start talking I lose control over my tongue. Exaggeration has become a habit with me. Will you do me a favour? When I start exaggerating, you pull my shirt. Then I will understand and I will correct myself immediately.'

We agreed. Balu started describing New York City with its tall buildings. But one of the villagers got up and said, 'We have seen this city many times on TV after 11th September. Don't exaggerate. Tell us something about their methods of agriculture, their fodder, grass etc. Then we can compare them to our ways.'

Balu said, 'Oh, I saw their fields and the grass. The grass was almost five feet tall.'

I pulled his shirt.

He realized he was talking too much. Immediately, he said, 'No, no, the grass is very thin.'

Somebody asked, 'What do you mean very thin?'

'It was as thin as a hair's width.'

Again I pulled his shirt. But I was so exasperated that I pulled it very hard and it tore. Balu, for once, did not know what to say. But I could hear people talking, 'After all, it is Balu's version of America. The real America must be different.'

Balu's wife is very quiet, which is understandable. If two people talk too much it can get difficult to live together. Once, she was unwell and had a very high fever. Balu talks a lot, but in such a situation he gets scared easily. He was very worried and called me up.

'Get a doctor immediately. My wife is running a very high temperature.'

'What do you mean by very high temperature. How much is it?'

'Oh, it must be about five hundred degrees.'

'Then you should not call a doctor, you better call a firefighter. Kindly check with the thermometer. It must not be more than 106 degrees.'

Once, we were sitting and chatting when a stranger entered. Many people are aware that Infosys Foundation helps students to study further if they do not have the funds. With help from the Foundation, many children have graduated and stood on their own feet. Whenever I am in villages, parents of such children come and see me. After talking to them, if I feel the case is genuine, we help them. This stranger had come with a similar request.

I had a detailed talk with him and was convinced his son needed help.

I told him, 'After I go back to my office I will send you the cheque.'

Balu called me aside and said, 'How can you say that? Do you know what may happen tomorrow? Will you remember your promise? There is a gap between today evening and tomorrow morning. Life is uncertain; anything can happen. If you want to give anything, you must give him immediately. Time is never in your hands. On the contrary, all of us are living at the mercy of time.'

'Balu, I don't have a chequebook with me.'

'That is your mistake. You must carry a chequebook and cash when you travel for this purpose. Many times poor people may not even have an account in the post office or bank.'

I always thought Balu was only an uneducated, hilarious, comic man. But I was wrong. He taught me a great lesson. When donating, don't think twice or put it off for another day. Nobody has conquered time. Time is not in anybody's hand.

'A' for Honesty

The American education system at the university level is different from ours. There, the final marks are based on the average marks of three examinations held earlier in the semester. As a result, students have to study and do well consistently, and there is not much pressure during the final exam. There is also greater student-teacher interaction in that system.

As a teacher, I have seen that sometimes even a bright student may not do well because of the pressures of the final test. There are other ways to examine the depth of knowledge of the student, like surprise exams, open book exams, oral exams, etc. The examination should not scare the students, instead it should measure their knowledge fairly and give marks accordingly. This kind of system requires more number of teachers for students. However, this is difficult to achieve in India, where there are large numbers of students. There is also great pressure on students from the parents and society to perform well.

My son is studying in a college in the US. He loves computer science immensely and always puts in a lot of hard work when he studies it. One day, he called me after his midterm exams. I could make out from his voice that he was very sad. He told me, 'I did not do my exams well. It is not that I did not know the answers, but instead of digit eight I assumed the digit as six and did the entire calculation based on that. I prepared so well and now I know I will not do well. I'm feeling very depressed.'

As a teacher, I don't give too much of importance to marks because I am aware of such situations. Many a time I have seen children who are really good in subjects unable to answer questions due to various factors. So I consoled him.

'Don't worry. So what? You have lost the battle but you will win the war. Examinations are not the only index in life. Keep courage, face reality and don't be negligent while reading the questions. Good luck for next time.'

He was not at all pleased to hear my words. 'You talk like a moral science teacher, Amma. It is very competitive here and difficult to achieve anything in such an atmosphere. You are a teacher and you only give grades. You don't sit for the exams. So you do not know the difficulties of students.'

I knew he was sad. My consolation did not help him. But he had forgotten that once upon a time I had also been a student and had passed through the same passage.

After a few days, I got another call from him. There was joy and great enthusiasm in his voice. Suddenly the dark winter days had turned into bright sunny days.

'Amma, you know I got grade "A" in that subject, which I did not do well in.'

'How come?' I was very surprised.

'It is a very funny thing. After the exam, I was talking to the professor and we were discussing various topics. When I got my papers, I saw I had got good marks for the question which I had answered wrongly. My other friends said the professor must have made a mistake, don't tell him, keep quiet. Getting a good grade is more important in this competitive world.'

'What did you do?' I asked anxiously.

'I thought for a while, then I realized, grades are important but honesty is even more important. You taught me that when I was a little boy. Do you remember, Amma? Once, the shopkeeper mistook fifty rupees for one hundred rupees and gave change for one hundred. At that time we did not have much money, but still you sent me back to the shop to return the extra money. At that age, I was so reluctant to go and return the change but you were strict with me and said if I didn't, I would have to go without dinner. Somehow I was unable to keep quiet about the professor's mistake. I wrote an email to him saying I did not deserve those marks. But his reply was more surprising.'

'What was that?'

'He replied, "I have not given the marks by mistake. It was deliberate. After the exams I was talking to you, and my constant interaction with you throughout the semester had convinced me of the depth of your knowledge and your passion for the subject. Mistakes do happen by oversight or due to

tension. That is the reason I gave you some marks for that question. After all, exams should also measure the depth of your knowledge.'"

My eyes filled with tears on hearing this story. I was happy, not because he had got an 'A' grade but because he had practised what he believed in. Many of my own students have behaved in a similar way in different situations, though they may have lost a lot in the process. To some people it may seem to be stupidity. But I am sure the good values they have learnt will help them in any crisis.

A Lesson in Ingratitude

I was attending a seminar on how to eliminate poverty. For some reason, such seminars always seem to be held in five-star hotels. I really do not know why they have to be organized in the most expensive places.

After attending the seminar, I was standing in the lobby of the hotel, when I saw a middle-aged person in an Armani suit with a pipe in his hand. His perfume was expensive and very strong. I could smell it from a considerable distance. He was talking on his mobile and was probably waiting for his car. I looked at him and felt sure I had seen him somewhere earlier. He finished his call and stared

at me. Both of us were trying to place each other. Suddenly I realized he was my classmate from thirty years back. His name was Suresh. I said, 'Are you Suresh? Who was my classmate ...'

He said, 'I was wondering, are you Sudha?'

We started laughing. It had been thirty years since we had last met. Both of us had put on weight and become different to look at from our college days. Suresh and I had gone to the same college, where we knew each other fairly well for four years. We had attended many lab classes together where he was my lab partner.

I asked him, 'I have not met you for a long time. The last I heard you were in Bombay. What are you doing here?'

'Yes, I live in Bombay. I have my own business there. By the grace of God, I am doing very well. Why don't we meet up sometime and talk about the old days? By the way, where are you going? Can I drop you?'

I agreed immediately because my driver was on leave. By then his Mercedes Benz had arrived at the hotel door and we got into the car.

Suresh started explaining. 'I own a few companies in Bombay and Bangalore. I am into Medical Transcription. I also train people and send them abroad for software jobs. Now there is a dearth of teachers in the UK. I want to train teachers and send them. This is a very lucrative job as there are not many overheads... I heard from many people you have become a teacher and a social worker. I felt sad for you. You would have done well in business. You were one of the brightest in the class.'

He looked genuinely sad at my choice of profession. To console him I said, 'Don't look so sad. I took up this profession out of choice not compulsion. Do you know Suresh, "Doing what you like is freedom, liking what you do is happiness." If you look at it that way, I am very happy.'

By then, we had reached my office. Before I got off the car, Suresh gave me his visiting card and insisted I come to his house for dinner or breakfast.

One Sunday, I was free and I remembered Suresh's invitation. I called up his home and his secretary told me he was in Bombay. She fixed up a breakfast for the next Sunday. She also said she would send a car to pick me up as it was difficult to locate the house.

That Sunday morning, a driver came with a Toyota car and I got into it. I started chatting with the driver after some time. He was very talkative as he knew I was his boss's classmate. Suresh's house was sixty kilometres away from Bangalore city. It was a farmhouse on the banks of the river Cauvery. It was inside a forest and spread over twenty acres of land. There they grew fruits and vegetables without using chemical fertilizers. Madam, the driver told me, is very conscious about health and has got a special gym and a swimming pool made. Suresh had another house in Indiranagar, in the heart of Bangalore city. They visited this farm only on weekends and invited special guests there.

I asked him, 'How long have you been working for Suresh?'

'Oh, I have been with him for the last twenty years. Actually I was his father-in-law's driver. He was a businessman in Bombay, and Madam, his only daughter. I can call Madam by her first name if I want to, I have known them for that long, but I don't do that.'

I could make out a sense of belonging and a shade of pride on the driver's face.

When I reached the house, I realized the driver had not exaggerated in his description of the place. It was like entering a palace. There were five or six guest rooms, a huge hall, a large dining room, spacious courtyards, all built in the traditional

Indian style. There were many servants in uniform. Now I could understand how zamindars and petty kings lived in the olden days.

Suresh came in two minutes. He was dressed in silk. He looked very pleased to see me. 'Welcome to our small abode. I am very happy you could make it. Let us go to the living room.'

His living room was full of statues, paintings, Persian carpets and chandeliers. There were silk-covered sofas made out of sandalwood. I felt I had entered a museum and not someone's home.

'Tell me Suresh, how you made your journey from college to this place.'

I remembered Suresh came from a very poor family. His father was a cook and the family had many children. He was unable to educate his son. A kind-hearted gentleman knew Suresh's father. He offered a room and food for Suresh in his own house. His son was also studying with us. Our college provided Suresh a full scholarship. We all knew his financial situation and we would help him in as many small ways as possible. We used to contribute money for him to buy books. Even the librarian went out of his way to give special concessions to him. Suresh was a fairly good student, hard-working and very shy.

He hardly spoke with us. So I wanted to know how he had become this affluent, talkative Suresh.

'You know, after college I went to Bombay in search of work. I got a small job. I worked very hard as I knew then that to come up in life you require talent, hard work, aggression and connections. I had the first two but had to build up the latter two qualities. Later I met Veena, my wife, whose father helped me a lot and we started a different business. Today I am well-off. I helped out my family in various ways. You know I came from a poor family. I bought lands, shops, built houses which I gave to my parents, brothers and sisters. Everyone now owns two cars and is well-off. I am very happy that I have done my duty towards my family.'

'What about your children?'

'I have two daughters. Both of them are studying in England, one is studying Indian culture and the other one is doing home science. Do you know any good boys who are well-off and handsome for my daughters? But they should not want to stay with their parents. They must be either independent or live with us. You must be knowing some eligible men, you meet so many people.'

'Suresh, the people I meet are poor, helpless, destitute. Or I meet students. I don't know the kind of people you are talking about.'

By that time his wife called us for breakfast. The food was served in silver plates. Veena looked very beautiful and young. Only when she came near me, did I realize she was as old as I was. She had hidden her age with a lot of clever make-up.

Suddenly I remembered the gentleman with whom Suresh stayed, our college librarian, and the rest of the students in our college.

'Suresh, did you ever go to college after you left? Do you remember our librarian, the Principal, our batchmates?'

With a grim look on his face Suresh replied, 'No, I never went to college, nor have I met any one of them. Some classmates I have bumped into accidentally. I have invited them here. I never felt like going back to the college.'

'What about Mr Rao? You stayed in his house, did you not meet him any time?'

'No. I feel everyone in college helped me because they wanted to feel better about themselves. After all I was a very good student. I am convinced people help others only with a selfish motive. They want to say, "I brought up a person". That is the reason why I never felt like meeting any one of them.'

Still I persisted, 'I heard Mr Rao's financial condition is not good.'

Suresh replied emotionlessly, 'Yes, that was bound to happen. He fed so many unwanted students who were not good in studies or hard-working. How long could he continue like that?'

I remembered the institution which gave him free scholarship, the librarian who helped him, Mr Rao who was his host for five years. They were all good, kind people, but Suresh refused to recognize that. What was great about helping your own sisters and brothers? Giving them two cars and a few houses is not philanthropy. Helping somebody who is needy and without expecting anything from them in return is real philanthropy. In life, you must help others so that they can live independently.

Gratitude is the highest form of education, but Suresh never learnt that. Without receiving any help from others he could not have reached the position he was in that day. When climbing the ladder it is very easy to kick those below, but one must not forget that you cannot stay at the top forever. The higher you go, the longer is the fall.

I did not feel like eating breakfast from a silver plate that day.

My Biggest Mistake

In my computer science class, once I gave a very tough problem to my students. Programming is an art to some extent. When the same problem is given, different students use different methodologies to arrive at the same result.

I never insist on a single method and allow my students their freedom. This problem was very difficult and I myself took almost a week to solve it. When I brought my solution to class, my students wanted to check it. I gave my diskette to one of them, Nalini, and said, 'Please copy this program on your diskette and return mine. This is the only copy I have, so be careful.'

Everyone gathered around. Nalini inserted the diskette into the computer drive. While she was talking to me, by mistake she formatted the floppy. Formatting is nothing but clearing all the information on the diskette. Everybody was stunned. Then they looked at me. Nalini was in tears. They were aware that I had spent one whole week trying to find a solution to this problem.

For a while I was very upset. But after five minutes I cooled down and smiled. A smile can make tension disappear and is the best medicine in a friendship. After all, my students are my young friends. When I smiled, the bubble of tension broke. I got up from my chair.

Nalini was sobbing 'Madam, I am very sorry. I did not do it purposely. Please forgive me.'

'I know you did not do it on purpose, Nalini. None of my students can do such a thing. Accidents do not require an invitation. Anybody can commit mistakes. If someone says he has never ever committed a mistake then he must be a robot, not a human being. Even our gods and our great rishis committed mistakes. Let us put our heads together and see if we can redo the program.'

Somebody asked me, 'Madam, how can you be so cool, when you have spent so much of time on that?'

'Yes, I am aware of it. I will somehow steal some time and try to write the program again. I am cool because I also committed a similar mistake when I was young.'

My students immediately switched the topic from computer science to storytelling. I told them my story.

'When I was young, I was very sensitive about what people said about girls. If they said "Girls cannot do that", immediately I used to feel I should do it just to prove them wrong. I wanted to show to the world that girls can do everything. Today, I laugh at this logic. Men can do certain things well and women other things. Men and women are complementary to each other. One need not prove one's strength.

'That time, I was working in a computer software firm as a systems analyst. It was way back when computer hardware was not advanced. Today you have a tiny floppy of three and half inches. At my time, a huge fifteen kg heavy Tandon Disc Drive was used.

'Casually my boss made a comment one day, "This disc is very heavy, only men can carry it."

'That remark upset me a lot. I told him, "I will carry it and show you."

'The disc was a bit like a gramophone but very heavy and large. It contained vital information about the company like its finances, employee details, etc. I took the disc and walked to the boss's room. It was really very heavy but I did not show it on my face. I believed strongly that showing emotions on your face is a sign of weakness. Today I feel one should be as transparent as possible.

'Seeing me walk in with the disc, my boss was surprised. "How did you manage to bring this?" he asked.

'Without thinking, in my happiness at having proved him wrong, I lifted my hand and let go the disc.

'In a fraction of a second it fell and broke into pieces. The noise could be heard throughout the office. Everyone turned to look at me. It was the biggest mistake anyone had ever committed in the history of the company. It was an unforgivable error. The company's entire vital data was wiped out in a minute.

'I stood there dumbstruck. Because of my foolish behaviour the whole company was going to suffer. An employee should always work for the betterment of the company. But what had I done? I was so numb I could not even cry. I went back to my desk and sat quietly. After thinking for a while I knew what I should do.

I took a blank sheet of paper and wrote my resignation on it. That was the only way I felt I could atone for my mistake. I went to my boss's chamber and gave him the letter. Then I stood there, my head bowed in shame.

'He read the letter carefully. Then he tore it up. He said, "Everybody commits mistakes. I took a backup of the information on the disc before you lifted it. The data is still intact in the storeroom. You don't have to worry. Repentance itself is a punishment and you have repented enough. You should not be so sensitive. Sensitive people suffer a lot in life. Go and do your work."

'I did not have any words to say to him.'

Now I looked at Nalini and told her, 'It was also my mistake. I should have made a copy of such an important program. Please do not worry. I will rewrite the program. I still have some notes at home.

'That incident taught me that when you become a leader you should be kind and forgiving to your subordinates. It is not fear that binds you to your boss. Affection, openness and the appreciation of your qualities builds a long-lasting relationship. We spend most of our time at our work places. This time should be spent in happiness, not in blaming each other.'

My students broke into applause.

The Secret

In my class, about forty per cent of the students are girls and sixty per cent boys. When I studied engineering thirty-five years back, I was the only girl in the course. I could only see boys and more boys everywhere. Today that trend has changed. People often ask me how I managed. But when I look back I feel it was not very difficult. Having a girl in the class was unusual for the boys, and initially I was the target for a lot of teasing. But over a period of time, they became my best friends.

One day, in the class I was teaching, the students got into an argument. This happens often and I always allow them to speak. Normally this happens in the last class of the semester. I call it a free day, and there are no studies that day.

An argument had broken out between the girls and the boys about who was better. This is a very juicy topic and there is absolutely no end to the arguments. Suddenly the class was divided into two groups and the debate became emotionally charged. I sat back and enjoyed their arguments.

The girls said, 'It is ultimately the woman who makes the man. She is more powerful, has great endurance for pain and is a better manager than a man. All successful men have been backed by supportive women. Without her help, man cannot achieve anything.'

The boys laughed at this, 'The woman will always be behind, never in the front. How many women have got the Nobel Prize? A woman's brain weighs less than a man's.'

I had to interfere here to say that there is absolutely no co-relation between the weight of the brain and its functions. The boys looked quite upset at my comment.

'Men start wars.'

'Wars happen because of women. Look at what happened because of Helen of Troy, Draupadi or Sita.'

The foolish arguments continued for a long time. Neither of the two groups was ready to accept the reality. Now I realized, I had to step in.

I said, 'I will tell you a story. Listen to it and decide who is great.'

Immediately there was pindrop silence.

A long time ago there were two kings. One ruled over Kashi, and the other over Kosala. They did not like each other. Once, both kings were travelling and they met. They were on their chariots. The road was small and only one chariot could pass at one time. Unfortunately, both chariots reached that spot at the same time. They stood facing each other. Which chariot would pass first? The kings refused to talk to each other, so their charioteers started talking.

The Kashi charioteer said, 'My king has ten thousand soldiers.'

The Kosala charioteer replied, 'My king also has ten thousand soldiers.'

'My king has two hundred elephants.'

'So does my king.'

'My king owns ten lakh acres of fertile land.'

'So does mine.'

The arguments carried on. It was very surprising that both kings had the same things.

Then the Kosala charioteer said, 'My king punishes bad people, dislikes lazy people and uses his money for the betterment of the kingdom.'

The Kashi charioteer replied, 'My king helps bad people become better human beings, makes a lazy person work hard and uses his money for the betterment of poor people.'

When the king of Kosala heard this, he told his charioteer, 'He is a better human being than me, I must become his friend. Give way to their chariot first.'

When the king of Kashi heard this, he got down and embraced the king of Kosala. Thus their enmity ended and they became friends.

I looked at my students and said, 'Today I will tell you a secret. I usually tell this at the end of the course in the last class. In real life, men and women are not opponents, they are the two wheels of a chariot. There is nothing good about one and bad about another. Both should possess good qualities.

'A person gets known by the qualities he or she possesses, not by the gender. That is decided by God.

'I am teaching you computer science today, but you will learn more in real life. Technology changes every day and good books are always there in the market. What I am teaching is also how to be a good human being. These values have not been prescribed in any syllabus nor will they appear in any examination. But these are the essential qualities you need, to do well in life. When you become older you should remember that there was a teacher who taught you the values of life along with your first knowledge of computer science. You must then teach your children these same values with as much love and affection.'

The class ended that day with my students gathered around me and all of us trying to hold back our tears.

BOOK II

Grandma's Bag of Stories

The Beginning of the Stories

Summer holidays! Ajji smiled to herself as she waited for two more of her grandchildren to arrive. Raghu and Meenu would be here soon. Anand and Krishna had already arrived with their mother the previous evening. They had been waiting restlessly for their cousins to arrive ever since. Even though Ajji told them Raghu and Meenu would be here the next morning, these two kids just would not listen. They went to the railway station with their grandfather, Ajja, to receive them. The train must have pulled into the tiny railway station of Shiggaon by now, and their grandfather would have hired a taxi to bring them home along with their mother and the stacks of luggage.

Ajji hurried through her bath. She had finished cooking their favourite dishes, and was now wearing a nice, soft cotton sari before going to the veranda to wait for them.

There! There they came! What a noise the children were making! They all nearly tumbled out of the car and came leaping and shouting to her, each wanting to be the first to be hugged by her. Each one wanted to be closest to Ajji.

Soon the children settled down. A visit to Ajji and Ajja's house meant first inspecting the garden to see how much the plants had grown since they last came. Then they went to check on the cows, calves, dog, pups, cats and kittens. Then they all ate huge quantities of Ajji's delicious food. Finally, while their mothers went off to chat and rest, the children gathered around their grandmother for the best part of the holidays—listening to her wonderful stories, particularly in the late afternoon.

Let us, too, gather under the fast revolving fan, on a mat on the floor, fighting to be nearest to her, and listen in.

'Doctor, Doctor'

The first day, the children asked, 'Ajji, how do you know so many stories?'

Ajji smiled and answered, 'My grandmother told me many stories. Some I read in books. A few I learnt from youngsters like you, and the rest from your Ajja.' Then Ajji paused and said, 'I see all of you have grown a lot since the last time I saw you. So before I start telling any stories, I want to know what each of you want to be when you grow up.'

Raghu, who was eleven years old, and the oldest of all, said immediately, 'I want to be an environment scientist.' Meenu, who was nine, said, 'I have not decided, maybe a computer person like my dad.' Anand, who was ten, said, 'I want to be an astronaut,' and his twin sister Krishna firmly said, 'I want to become a fashion designer.' Ajji smiled. 'I am glad all of you have thought about this. We should always have some aim in life which we must try to achieve while being of help to others. Now let me tell you a story of a person who learnt just such a lesson.'

Shall we, too, join Ajji and her gang of young friends and hear the story?

On a blazing hot summer afternoon, an old man came walking down a narrow village path. He was tired and thirsty. Right by the road, he spotted a tiny grocery store. It had a tin roof and mud walls. The shopkeeper sat inside fanning himself and shooing away the flies that were buzzing around in the stifling heat. There was a little bench in front of the store where the villagers met when evening came and the land had cooled down. The old man flopped down on the bench. He was so tired that for a while he could not speak. Finally, he opened his mouth and uttered one word, 'Water!'

Now, this village had been facing a horrible problem for a long time. It was near a great desert and the rains came only once a year to fill its ponds and wells. But the rains had disappeared for the last two years, and the villagers had been making do with water from a faraway stream. Every morning groups of men and women walked a long distance, filled their pots from the little stream and used that the whole day. Naturally, no one wanted to waste even a drop of this precious water.

Yet how do you say no to a thirsty, tired old man when he asks for water? Without a second thought, the shopkeeper, Ravi, who was very kindhearted, poured out a tumbler of water from his pot and gave it to the old man. The man drank it up greedily. Then he said one more word: 'More!' And without waiting for Ravi to give it to him, he lunged for the pot, picked it up and lifting it to his lips drank up Ravi's entire day's supply of water!

Poor Ravi, what could he do? He just stared in dismay. Then he told himself, 'Never mind. After all, I did help someone in need.'

The stranger, meanwhile, now seemed to feel better. He handed the pot back to Ravi, gave a smile that filled Ravi's heart with warmth and said,

'My son, always be kind like this. Help everyone who comes to you like you helped me, and you will be blessed.' Then he picked up his stick and slowly hobbled down the road. Ravi watched the strange old man disappear into the distance, then returned to his shop.

The afternoon heat grew worse. After a while Ravi felt his head was about to burst with a headache. His lips were parched and his throat hurt, it was so dry. He really needed a drink of water. But the visitor had finished it all up! Hoping to coax a drop or two out of the pot, Ravi lifted it to his lips and tilted it. Imagine his surprise when a gush of water ran down his face! It was sweet, refreshing water which not only quenched his thirst, but wiped out his headache too.

Ravi was staring at the water pot, trying to figure out what had just happened, when Karim limped into his shop. Karim was a young man who had hurt his leg in an accident many years ago which had left him with a limp. When he was unwell or tired, his limp became worse. Karim, too, flopped down on the bench in front of the store and caught his breath, like the old man. Then he fished out a shopping list from his pocket and handed it to

Ravi. As Ravi started packing up the items listed on the paper, Karim opened a little bundle of food and ate his lunch sitting on the bench. Finally he wiped his mouth on his scarf and pointed to Ravi's pot of water. 'Mind if I take a little sip? It is so hot after all.'

Ravi was busy measuring out some dal. He said without looking up, 'I would be happy to offer you some, but someone's already had most of it. Then I was feeling unwell and I think I finished the last of it.'

'What are you saying, my friend? I can clearly see the pot brimming over with water!'

Ravi looked up and stared in disbelief. In front of his eyes, Karim poured out a tumblerful of water and drank it. Then he paid for all his groceries and left the store.

Did his limp look as if it was nearly gone? Ravi watched him for a while trying to figure out, then decided the heat was playing tricks on his mind and went back into the cool comfort of his shop and dozed off.

He woke with a start as someone was calling his name urgently. He opened his eyes to find Karim back. This time he was holding by the hand his little sister Fatima. 'Brother, wake up. We need your help,' Karim urged.

'Wh-what? Is something wrong?'

'Fatima is burning up with fever!'

'Then go to a doctor, why have you got her to a grocery shop?'

Karim stared at him and said, 'You mean you don't know how you just helped me? My leg, which has been troubling me for the last many years, healed up on its own as soon as I drank the water from your magic pitcher! Give Fatima a drink from it, too. I am sure her fever will disappear in no time.'

Ravi was astounded. Magic pitcher? Healing water? What *was* Karim going on about? Nonetheless he passed the pot to Fatima. She drank a bit, then sat down to rest. Within minutes she lifted her head and said, 'It is true, brothers! I am indeed cured of the fever!'

Soon the news spread in the village like wildfire. Ravi, the quiet, kind grocery storekeeper, was now the owner of a magic pitcher, the waters from which could heal anyone of any disease. Every night Ravi left the pitcher in the store, and in the morning it would be filled to the brim with sweet, cool water. Daily, a queue of sick people and their relatives collected in front of his shop. To each one Ravi gave a drink of the water, and they went away saying they were now better. The pot was never empty. Ravi realized the old man he had helped must have given him this gift in gratitude. Ravi understood what a great gift it was and thanked him daily in his mind.

Soon his little store turned into a hospital. Ravi did not charge a paisa for the water. People would leave some money, some gifts for him, and others did not pay him anything but he was still happy with that.

One day, a rich landlord's servant appeared at his doorstep and said, 'My master is unwell. Come with me and give him a drink of your water.'

Ravi replied, 'See the crowd of people behind you, waiting for their turn. How can I leave without helping them and go to your master? Do you think these sick people can stand in the sun for long? Tell your master to come to me instead and I will give him the water here.'

The servant said, 'Ravi, what will you get by helping these poor people? A few rupees? Some rice and dal? Come to my master's house. He will shower you with money and gifts. Your worries about making ends meet will be over for at least a month.'

Ravi was tempted. It was true, why not cure one rich man and get some help in buying his daily needs? Ravi told the people waiting outside to come back the next day and went with the servant to the landlord.

Slowly, in this way, Ravi changed. Where once he could not bear to see the pain and sadness of the sick and poor people, he now started each day hoping he would get one rich patient at least, who would pay him handsomely.

Days passed thus. Seasons changed and it was summer once more. Ravi was in his old store, writing up his accounts, when the voice of an old man quavered in his ear, 'Son, water!'

Startled, he looked up. Was it the same old man who had given him the gift of the magic pitcher? But right behind the visitor was none other than the king's messenger. 'Come quickly!' the messenger shouted. 'The queen has been bitten by a mosquito!'

'Water!' the old man repeated.

'The queen is unwell!' the messenger shouted again.

Ravi looked from one to the other. One was a grubby old man who may or may not be the same person who gave him the pitcher. On the other side a messenger from the king himself! He pictured the gold coins showering down on him once his healing water soothed the queen's mosquito bites. The choice was clear.

He picked up his pitcher and said to the stranger, 'Wait right here, Uncle, I'll be back soon.'

The king's swift-footed horses took him to the palace. There he rushed to the queen who was staring in dismay at the mosquito bites on her arm. He tilted the pitcher to pour some water into a tumbler, but nothing came! Again and again he tilted the pitcher. He turned it upside down and stared into its depths. It was dry as a bone.

'You cheat!' the king roared. 'So this is how you have been fooling the people of my kingdom! Get out, and never let me hear that you have acquired magical healing powers. If you claim such a thing again I will banish you forever from the village.' Then he turned to comfort his queen who was splashing tears on the bump on her arm.

Ravi slowly walked back to his village. He went to his shop. No one was there. He searched for the old man who had asked for water. He was nowhere to be seen. He called out, 'Uncle, I am sorry. I made a mistake. Please do come. I will give you water.'

But there was no reply. Now he realized this was the same old man whom he met a year back.

He remembered the people he had healed once out of kindness and compassion and how much they had blessed and loved him in return. He remembered their little acts of generosity, sparing him a few coins, a bundle of vegetables from their garden in return for the water. When did he become so selfish and greedy that he would neglect the people who had needed him the most? The old man had taken back his powers when he sensed Ravi had misused the gift.

Never mind, Ravi smiled to himself. He would use the money he had received for the water to help bring a real doctor to the village, someone who would help the people with his knowledge of medicines and diseases, so that they need not wait for a magician to cure them of their illnesses.

From that day onwards Ravi filled his pitcher with ordinary water from the stream and carried it back carefully to his little store and waited for the old man. Maybe one day he would be back, but till then, Ravi was determined to bring a real medicine man to his village.

Ajji finished her story and looked around at the four little faces around her. Raghu was deep in thought. Ajji smiled at him. Then the children shouted, 'Ajji, tell one more story!'

'Ah ha,' Ajji said, 'too many stories a day are not good either. One laddoo is very sweet, very delicious but if you eat laddoos all the time it's no fun. Go and play outside. Tomorrow I will tell you another story.' With that she got up and went to the kitchen to supervise the dinner.

Kavery and the Thief

The children had gone with their Ajja to the paddy fields that morning. They were all city kids and did not know a thing about farming! On the way, Anand was surprised to see a bird's nest on top of the tree. He said to Ajja, 'I wonder how birds decide where and how to make their nests!' Ajja said, 'The straw in the nest is from the paddy field. Do you know, farming helps human beings as well as birds?' Krishna replied, 'Ajja, I thought wheat and rice can be just plucked from trees, like mangoes. But today I realized there is so much work in farming.'

That afternoon, after lunch, when they gathered around Ajji for the day's story, she looked sharply at the children. They had enjoyed learning about farming activities like cleaning seeds and separating the straw from paddy. In the city everything came from the supermarket, but here they had seen how things were really produced.

Ajji said, 'Farming is very important. If farmers do not grow any food, what will we all eat?'

Anand said thoughtfully, 'If farmers do such important work, why are they so poor?'

'That's true, my dear,' Ajji sighed, fanning herself. 'Of course there are rich farmers too, people who own lots of land. But many in our country till small pieces of land, and so make less money.'

Then seeing the kids' crestfallen faces, she put down her fan, sat up and said, 'But I can tell you of a poor farmer woman who did not remain very poor. All due to her sharp wit!'

'Tell Ajji! Do tell!' the kids yelled. So Ajji started her story.

⁓

Kavery's lazy husband annoyed her no end. There she was working like a donkey in the fields, ploughing and watering and tending a hard, dry piece of land, while her husband snored away happily at home! Why, once when a stranger came asking for some food and water, he just pointed towards the kitchen and went back to sleep. The stranger, thankfully, was an honest man and took only enough for himself and his horse. Not that there was much to steal in Kavery's little house. They were poor farmers with only a patch of land where nothing seemed to grow. Somehow Kavery tilled the land, did some odd jobs in the neighbourhood, and made ends meet.

The land was right next to a temple. On some days her husband would come along with her on the pretext of helping her, but no sooner would her back be turned than she would find him stretched out near the temple courtyard gossiping with passing villagers.

One day, as she was working in the field, trying to dig up the ground so she could sow some seeds, a thin man with a big moustache appeared beside her. He was a thief, and up to no good. Kavery, of course, did not know this. She greeted him politely and went back to her work. Now the thief wanted to steal the coins that were given as offerings in the temple and perhaps even the ornaments on the idol. The only way into the temple was by digging his way in from Kavery's land. But how could he do anything there, with this tough, no-nonsense woman working away?

Guessing Kavery was hard up for money, he whispered to her, 'Sister, why are you working so hard on this barren land? I will give you one thousand rupees, sell it to me.'

Kavery raised her eyebrows; why did he want to buy the land for so much money? Surely something was wrong . . .

The thief sensed she was not about to sell it to him, so he raised his price: 'A thousand and fifty? No? Two thousand? No again? FIVE THOUSAND? No?'

Kavery kept shaking her head. She did not like this odd-looking man who was offering her so much money for the field. Clearly he had some evil plans. Finally, to keep him quiet, she made up a story. 'I will never sell this land. You see, it belonged to my ancestors. Now we are poor, but I am told that once our family was very rich. Though we lost a lot of our money, much of it was also buried here, in this field by one ancestor, to keep it safe from robbers. Then people forgot about it for years and years. My husband found a clue to the location of the hidden treasure just a few days back. Why do you think I am digging this hard earth? Not to sow seeds, oh no, that's just what everyone thinks. I am actually looking for hidden treasure!'

The thief was stunned. He felt this woman was really innocent, giving such important information to a stranger. He thought, why should I not take advantage of this situation? Here he was, hoping to steal a few coins from the temple, and this woman was telling him about hidden treasure! He replied in a very humble way, 'Yes sister, I understand; after all it is your family treasure. Only you should get it.' He pretended to walk away, and went and hid himself a little way down the road.

Night fell; Kavery packed up her tools and headed home. The temple, too, emptied out and the priest locked it up for the night. Then at midnight, when all was quiet and the night creatures were coming out of their homes, the thief crept into the field.

All night he dug and dug, looking for treasure, but of course there was no sign of it as there never had been any treasure to begin with! By the time dawn broke he realized Kavery had made a fool of him and all he could do now was get away from the field fast.

When Kavery reached the field she grinned to herself. Just as she had expected, the thief had spent the night digging up the land nicely for her. All she needed to do now was sow the seeds. She worked hard in the field for the next few months and managed to grow a good crop. She sold those and finally they had some money. With a part of this money Kavery bought some jewellery.

Many months later, the thief decided to show his face in the village again. He was careful to disguise himself, though. He trimmed his long moustaches, tied a colourful turban and pretended to be a travelling salesman. No sooner had he stepped into the village than he saw Kavery going about her work. But what is this . . . Instead of the simple, unadorned lady he saw last year, she was now wearing jewellery which looked as though it had been in the family for years! Surely she must have located that missing treasure finally! He was determined to look in her house and find the rest of her money and treasure.

That night, he appeared at Kavery's house and said to her husband, 'I am a traveller and don't have a place to spend the night. Please give me shelter for the night.'

Kavery's husband agreed immediately. Kavery, however, glimpsed the man from inside the house and saw through his disguise. She knew he must be planning some robbery, so she said in a loud voice, making sure the visitor heard her, 'Oh dear, your dear aunt is all alone at night and has asked us to come stay with her. You know how the dark scares her when your uncle is not there. Come, let us go there for the night.' Then lowering her voice a bit, yet making sure she was heard clearly, she continued, 'Don't worry about the jewels. I have hidden them in little holes in the house walls. No one will suspect the hiding spot.' Then she came out and in her normal voice told the thief, 'Brother, you can sleep in the veranda. The house will be locked. Here is some food and water for you. We will come tomorrow morning.' The thief smiled to himself at Kavery's foolishness.

Her husband, meanwhile, stared at her with an open mouth, wondering which aunt and what jewels she was talking about. When she firmly walked off, he followed obediently.

The thief could not believe his luck. He had the entire night to comb through the house, tap all the walls and look for the hidden stash of gold ornaments. So he started. Tap tap tap. Kick, punch and shove. He prowled and he tapped, he kicked and he pushed the walls, hoping to spot the jewels. Finally he tore down all the walls. But, of course, there was nothing he could find. Exhausted he fell asleep and woke only with the crowing of the cock as the sun rose. Quickly he found his little bundle of things and ran off. Within minutes Kavery and her husband returned.

'Oh Kavery, see what the bad man has done to our house! You gave him food and shelter and made me come with you leaving the man alone in the night,' her husband wailed. But Kavery was smiling! Then she broke into peals of laughter and said, 'Don't worry. I had planned this all along. You see, I saved money from our last crop to rebuild the house. I needed to call in some labourers to help tear it down, but our guest has done it for us! Now we can make a larger house for ourselves, just the way we always wanted.'

The whole village heard the story and started marvelling at her intelligence. Many months flew by. The thief was burning to take revenge. How dare that village woman trick him, that too not once but twice! He realized that she was very clever.

One day, he dressed up as a bangle seller and started wandering in the village. Kavery spotted him and knew who he was at once. She said to her friends who were crowding around the bangle seller, 'Oh dear, I would have loved to get some for myself. But ever since that good-for-nothing thief tried to steal all our money by tearing down our house, I have hidden everything in a little hole in a tree in the woods.'

'Which tree?' her friends asked.

'Oh no, I am not saying which tree, but it is at last safe and sound out in the forest.'

The thief looked at her. Yes Kavery was wearing an ordinary sari with no ornaments at all.

Her friends turned around in astonishment at the crash with which the bangle seller flung down his collection of bangles and made off for the forest. Only Kavery watched with a grin on her face.

Out in the forest, the thief searched high and low for the jewels. He climbed trees, poked around in bushes, got bitten, scratched and growled at, but he would not give up. The jewels were there somewhere and he had to find them.

So that is where we will leave him, prowling around in the forest, looking for money and gold that don't belong to him. Everyone praised Kavery for her quick wit in ridding the village of the thief. She continued to work hard and made more money from her farming and became a rich old lady. Even her husband was shamed into giving up his lazy ways and helping her. As for the thief, who knows, perhaps he is still in that forest, looking for what was never his. Now if only he had learnt to work hard like Kavery—he would have been as rich!

———

The children laughed and laughed when the story was over. 'The poor thief!' Meenu and Krishna giggled. 'Maybe he got eaten by a tiger!'

Ajji grinned. 'See,' she told Anand, 'sometimes with a bit of luck and lots of pluck, people can change any situation in which they find themselves!'

Who Was the
Happiest of Them All?

Meenu was upset. She pouted and sulked and would not talk to Ajji. But how can any child be angry with Ajji for very long? Their grandmother was just too loving and affectionate for anyone to not tell her what was wrong.

'Ajji, it's been three days, and you have not told a story about a king yet!' Meenu grumbled.

Ajji nodded. 'It's true, Meenu. That was my fault; I should have told you a story about a king right away!'

'And I want a good, nice king, who does good, nice things for his people—not horrible things like punishing them and jailing them,' Meenu sat straight and demanded.

'All right, dear. Here's a king, just as you wanted . . .'

And Ajji began her story.

———

King Amrit loved his people and looked after the affairs of his kingdom well. His minister, Chandan, was a wise man who helped the king in his work tirelessly.

One day, King Amrit and Chandan were taking a walk on the terrace of the palace. The terrace offered beautiful views of the surroundings, and they could see far into the distance. They spotted the weekly market from up there, with people in colourful clothes buying and selling all kinds of things. There was plenty to buy and people had money to buy, too. There were no poor people to be seen anywhere. The king watched with a smile on his face. He was delighted to see the prosperity of his kingdom. Like any good ruler he was happy when his people were happy.

He turned to Chandan and said, 'See how contented my people are. But I want to check this first-hand by talking to them. Tomorrow, summon people from all walks of life to the court, and I will ask them myself how they are doing.' Chandan was used to the king's strange requests, so he nodded and went off to carry out this order.

The next day, the king arrived in court humming a happy tune to himself. Seeing all the people gathered there waiting for him, he was even more pleased. He cleared his throat and said in a loud voice, 'I have called you here to ask you a very important question. As your king, I need to know if all of you are contented. Do you have enough for your needs? Do you know anyone who is not happy about anything?'

The citizens looked at each other, thought for a while and slowly one by one they came forward to answer. One after the other they all said how happy they were—their kitchens had enough food, their trades and businesses were doing well, the king had made them feel safe. The farmers had grown good crops and the rivers and ponds were full of fish. What more could they ask for?

The king became more and more pleased as he heard this. Only Chandan, his minister, watched and heard everything with a frown on his face. Why? What was wrong? Soon he walked up to the king and whispered something in his ear. King Amrit's eyebrows rose up in astonishment. Surely, Chandan could not be serious! But he looked at the minister's face and found no trace of this being a joke.

He turned back to the court and made a most unusual announcement. 'I am delighted that all of you have said you are happy. But I want to test this. Tomorrow, I want all the happy people of this kingdom to come and meet me in the royal gardens. But I have a condition. All of you will have to enter the garden from the main gate, walk across and meet me by the gate at the rear of the garden. I will wait for you there. When you enter the garden you will be given a sack each and you can pick whatever fruits or flowers your heart desires.'

An excited buzz broke out among the crowd. It sounded like a lot of fun. No one was usually allowed to enter the king's special garden. He had planted trees from all over the world in that garden and it was said to be filled with all kinds of beautiful and strange plants.

Right on time the next day, everyone gathered at the gate of the garden. At the time the king had told them, the guards opened the gates and handed out the sacks. Men, women and children started roaming around the beautiful garden. They spotted juicy apples and plump mangoes hanging from trees. They picked these till they saw ripe pomegranates bursting with juice, grapes and colourful flowers no one had seen before. People went about picking whatever they wished for and filling their sacks with them.

But as they walked further into the garden it became wilder, more like a forest, and there they saw trees laden with apples of gold, mangoes of silver and flowers studded with gems and jewels!

Everyone emptied their sacks of the fruits they had collected earlier and started madly filling them up with these precious fruits and flowers. They all forgot that they had said they had more than enough for their needs at home. Greed took over, their minds and all they could think about was adding more and more valuables to their sacks. The fruits which they had picked earlier, and had tasted to be as sweet as nectar, now lay in heaps around the garden— forgotten and left to rot.

Then with their sacks filled right to the top, the citizens made their way to the rear gate of the garden where the king was waiting. But what was this? To their astonishment they found a raging stream stopping their way. Water gushed down from behind some rocks and rushed over pebbles and big boulders through the garden. The stream was narrow, but the current was strong. There were no boats to take the people across. Clearly, the only way was to swim. But how could they swim with such heavy sacks filled with gold and silver fruits?

The people stood by the stream for a long time scratching their heads. Then one young man did what they all knew needed to be done. He simply abandoned his sack by the stream, waded into the water, then swam across to the other side. Slowly the others, too, followed suit. Sadly, some wailing in distress, they left their sacks filled with what they had thought was the riches of a lifetime, and dived into the stream. Then they walked up to their king—wet, unhappy and angry.

King Amrit and Chandan watched them trudge up in their soaking clothes. Chandan had a small smile on his lips, while the king looked sad. When they had assembled in front of him, he said, 'When

I asked you yesterday if you were happy with your lives, all of you said you were contented and did not need anything more. Yet, today I can see the sadness in your faces when you had to leave behind the riches you had gathered in my garden. If you were really happy with your lives, why did you gather the jewel fruits, and why are you so sad now?'

Everyone looked down, ashamed at their behaviour. Only the young man who was the first to cross the stream after leaving his sack behind seemed to be unconcerned. Chandan spotted his cheerful face in the crowd and beckoned him forward. Then he asked, 'Tell me, are you not sad you had to leave behind so much of wealth that suddenly came your way?'

The man said, 'I didn't pick the jewelled fruits and flowers. I had picked some of the lovely, tasty fruits and had eaten my fill of them. In my sack I had kept some others for my little daughter who is at home. I had thought she would enjoy these tasty apples and mangoes. But when I saw there was no other way to go across the stream, I did not think twice about leaving my sack by the river. My little girl can get tasty fruits from some other garden, too! But I am so happy the king let us all wander around his garden, looking at the trees and plants and animals. He is a great king for having created this place of beauty, and it was a pleasure walking around there.'

Finally a smile appeared on King Amrit's face. Chandan turned to him and said, 'Your Majesty, I hope you now realize that people's contentment does not end with having enough food or money. They also need to be truly happy inside. Only then will they not be swayed when they gain or lose wealth. That is a lesson that everyone—whether a king or a commoner—needs to remember.'

The king nodded, as did his subjects. This was a lesson they would not forget in a hurry!

⁓

'Did you like the story, Meenu?' Raghu asked.

'Oh yes,' Meenu nodded. 'But I liked the minister more than the king!'

'That's true, Meenu,' Ajji agreed. 'Kings did need intelligent ministers to show them the right path sometimes. Remember Akbar had Birbal, and Krishnadevaraya had Tenali Rama? Why just kings, we all need someone to tell us if what we are doing is wrong. It could be our parents, grandparents, teachers or even our best friend. The important thing is to listen to them and change our ways when needed.'

The Enchanted Scorpions

What an exciting morning the children had had that day! Ajja had asked for their help in cleaning up his old storeroom. Ajja loved to keep all kinds of old things in that room, much to Ajji's annoyance. She firmly believed the room was the principle attraction for all the cockroaches, mice, termites and other such bugs in the house. Every summer holiday the children spent a day clearing out the room, exclaiming over all the treasures they had unearthed. Ajja even let them keep some of the odds and ends they found. That didn't please their mothers too much though!

Today they had found an old wooden box. It was a big box, beautifully carved all over with flowers, and vines and leaves. Inside, it had little compartments to keep all manner of things. Now these compartments were empty, but Raghu, who had been reading *Treasure Island*, imagined that once these were full of gold and silver coins, gems as big as eggs and all kinds of fantastic jewels.

After examining the box thoroughly, the children decided that the day's story had to be about lost treasure. Ajji, who knew a story about anything under the sun, started right away.

———

Siddharth was a young, good-natured merchant. Looking for work, he arrived in a village. He liked the people of the village so much that he decided to use all his savings, buy a house and live there forever. While searching for a house, he met Uday.

Uday was a poor man. His family had once been extremely wealthy landowners but were now not so well off. Uday was looking to sell his old family mansion in order to pay off his family's loans.

Siddharth loved the house Uday showed him and bought it immediately. Then he set about repairing the mansion, which was in ruins. As he dug out the old flooring, he found a sealed box buried underground. When he opened it, to his surprise, he saw it was filled with scorpions. He flung the box away in fright.

That evening, he went to visit the wisest man in the village and asked him about the box of scorpions. The wise man thought for a while, then said, 'Perhaps Uday's ancestors hid some money in that box and buried it, to be used when someone in the family needed the money. Over the years they must have forgotten about the existence of the box.'

Siddharth was still puzzled. 'But the box contained scorpions,' he said, 'not money.'

The old man smiled. 'The box is protected by an old spell. If it is opened by anyone other than a family member, it will appear as if it is swarming with scorpions. Only a true family member will be able to see that the box contains money.'

Siddharth was sad to hear this story. He remembered the tears that had sprung up in Uday's eyes as he had looked back at his ancestral house for one last time before leaving the village. If only he had known about the hidden treasure, he would not have had to sell the house. When Siddharth reached home, he decided to keep the box safely till someone from Uday's family came to claim it. To make sure that the box was taken only by a true descendant of Uday's family, he took four scorpions from the box and hung them in four corners of his newly opened shop.

All his customers would comment when they entered the shop. 'Siddharth, are you mad? Why have you hung dangerous insects in your shop? Do you want to scare away shoppers?'

Siddharth would only smile. He knew his goods were the best for miles around, and people would come to shop at his store, scorpions or not. Gradually the shop came to be known as the Scorpion Shop and the villagers laughed at him behind his back. But Siddharth did not care.

Many years passed. Siddharth was now a middle-aged man with a wife and children and enough money. But he had one regret. No one had come to claim that box.

One day, a young boy walked into the shop and said, 'Sir, I have heard from many people in the village that you are wealthy and often help those in need. I had to stop going to school because I could no longer pay my fees. Could you please lend me some money so I can finish my studies?'

Siddharth shook his head sadly. 'The villagers have exaggerated about my wealth,' he said. 'Yes, I am earning enough, but not so much that I can help you or lend you money, though I would have loved to do so.'

The boy flared up in anger when he heard this. 'Sir, if you do not want to help me, please say so openly. Why do you lie? You have so much money that you don't know what to do with it. Why else have you hung gold coins in the four corners of your shop? Surely you can spare some coins to help a poor student like me.'

Siddharth stared at him in astonishment. 'Wh-what? What did you just say?' he asked, his eyes bulging in excitement.

'I said if you don't want to help . . .' the boy repeated.

'Yes, yes, I heard that,' Siddharth cut him short. 'But what did you say after that, about the gold coins in my shop?'

The boy now looked at Siddharth doubtfully, afraid that perhaps this excited old man was a bit mad. 'I said you are so wealthy that you have hung gold coins in the four corners of the shop. There they are, for the world to see!' And the boy pointed to what appeared to Siddharth as four writhing scorpions.

Siddharth gave a happy whoop of laughter. He rushed forward and hugged the boy.

'Are you related to Uday Kamalakar? Did your family ever live in this village?' he nearly shouted into the boy's ears.

The young man stepped back in alarm. Perhaps this rich man was mad and dangerous after all. 'Y-yes, my name is Uday. I was named after my grandfather. His family lived here for many generations. Then, when they fell on hard times, my grandfather sold his old house and moved. He never recovered from the grief of having to sell his ancestral property and died heartbroken.'

Siddharth wiped away the tears from his eyes. 'Wait here, my son,' he said. Rushing to his house, he came back with the old box and gave it to the young boy. 'Go on, open it and tell me what you see,' he chuckled.

The boy opened the box and his eyes nearly fell out of his head. For he held in his hands more treasure than he could dream about in his wildest fantasies. The box was filled with gold and silver coins and jewels!

He looked up in astonishment at Siddharth, who was grinning broadly. 'Yes, it belongs to you,' Siddharth explained. 'I have held it safe for many years, hoping someone from Uday's family will come to claim it. Your troubles are now over. Go home, use the wealth of your ancestors judiciously and do well in life.'

Then he told the boy the story of how he had found the box which appeared to be filled with scorpions to anyone who did not belong to Uday's family.

Uday was amazed when he heard the story. He offered Siddharth half his wealth in gratitude. But Siddharth would hear none of it. 'This is yours,' he insisted. 'Go, enjoy your life.'

Uday went away with the box, and all his life he remembered the funny, honest old man who had kept his wealth safely for him.

—

'How lovely, Ajji!' Krishna gasped. 'If only we had such a shopkeeper in this town!' All the children agreed that that would have been such fun. Ajji laughed at their dreamy faces. Then she shooed them out to play in the garden. And do you know what they played till late in the evening? Treasure hunt, of course!

The Horse Trap

The next day, there was a surprise summer shower. The land smelled beautiful. The thirsty earth had soaked in every drop of rainwater. The children had been very busy shifting the puppies and kittens, who were roaming in the back and front yards, into the house so that they did not get drenched in the rain. Their respective mothers were very busy shifting the pappadams left to dry on the terrace. Summer is the season when, under Ajji's leadership, pickles and pappadams were made.

Meenu started a calculation. 'Everyone needs at least five pappadams per day. For the next one month 600 pappadams will be needed. Tomorrow our neighbour Vishnu Kaka's three grandchildren are coming. They will also eat with us these tasty pappadams. We may have to keep five per head . . . That means Ajji has to prepare 600 + 50 pappadams.' When Ajji listened to Meenu's mathematics, she laughed and said, 'Don't calculate that way. It may be true today that we will all eat five pappadams a day, but this may not be true for every day. After eating pappadams for three days, one may get bored. There is a wedding in my brother's house and we all might go there. So we may not eat any pappadam those days. The way you are calculating, reminds me of the man who calculated the number of horses, once in England . . .'

All the children immediately gathered around her. 'Oh Ajji, you must tell us this story of how the horses were counted.'

So Ajji had to stop what she was doing right there and tell them the story.

———

Many many years ago, in England, there lived a great thinker and scholar called George Smith. He thought a lot about how it would be in the future, and advised the prime minister about many things. He researched how many people would live in the country in twenty years' time, he calculated how many schools, hospitals and roads needed to be built, or how much food needed to be grown or bought from other places to feed all these people.

His calculations helped the government immensely in planning for the future.

George often needed to visit the prime minister's office to talk to him about some new project and advise him. One day, the prime minister had invited him for a meeting, so he hopped into his horse carriage and set off for the office. Now George was always deep in thought and rarely noticed what was happening around him. Today, too, he sat in his carriage thinking about farms and ships and houses. But suddenly his carriage stopped with a jolt and he was shaken out of his thoughts. There was some commotion on the road and all carriages had stopped around him. Normally George would have just sunk back into his thoughts again, but today something stopped him. A horrible, strong smell. A smell that hung in the air and made you cover your nose with a hanky if you were not a scholar wrapped up in your own world.

Today, somehow, George was not able to disconnect himself from what was going on around him. The smell kept wafting into his nose and taking his mind away from the problem he was tackling. He called out to his coachman, 'Hi John, what is this extraordinary smell?'

John the coachman was used to his master's absent-minded ways, and he replied briefly, 'Horse dung.'

Horse dung! Now that was something George had never given a thought to. Somehow, he could now think of nothing else. Soon his carriage pulled up in front of the prime minister's office. But George kept sitting inside, lost in thought. Finally John tapped on the window to tell his master that they had reached their destination.

George walked to the visitor's room still thinking. He was sitting there, reflecting on horses and their dung, when the prime minister's secretary came to meet him. Now Adam, the secretary, was not as learned as George, but he was very sharp and intelligent. He greeted George and said to him apologetically, 'The PM had to make time for another important meeting, and will be late in seeing you. I hope you don't mind waiting.'

George kept staring out of the window, watching yet more horse-drawn carriages rushing up and down the road. Thinking he had perhaps not heard him, Adam cleared his throat and repeated loudly, 'Mr Smith, the PM . . .'

'Yes, I heard you, Adam,' George mumbled.

Worried that this great thinker of the country was in some trouble, Adam asked gingerly, 'Is something bothering you? Perhaps I could help . . .?'

George looked at him excitedly, 'You know, I just looked into the future and realized we will all die in about a hundred years. Our country will be destroyed, our way of life gone forever. And do you know why? All because of horses . . . and their dung!'

Adam stared at George, puzzled. Surely he could not be serious?

George continued, 'See, now we use horses as the principal mode of transport in the country. They are used to draw carriages, in the king's stables, even in the farms.'

Adam nodded. This was true.

'So how many horses are there now? Let's assume that there are 500 rich families who can afford to own a horse carriage. If each family has at least two children and all of them are rich enough to own carriages, that will mean a minimum of two more carriages in a few years. Each carriage would require two horses. So, each rich family would be using four horses at the least. So then there will be 2,000 horses. If you add our king's cavalry, and the number of horses in the farms, the numbers increase substantially.'

Adam nodded. Yes, this sounded true enough, but what was George's point?

'How do we get rid of the dung they generate now?'

Adam answered patiently, 'We dig pits and empty the dung into them.'

George nodded, 'Now that's my point. Imagine the scene a hundred years from now. 2,000 horses would have increased to 400,000, given the way the population is increasing. This will mean more dung! And what will we do with all this dung? Humans will need more space and houses and farming to sustain themselves. Where will we find open land to dig up and bury the dung? It will lie unattended everywhere and cause horrible diseases. If they make their way into the water sources it will be even worse. We will end up poisoning ourselves and our environment. We will become sick, and our country will become poor just by tending to so many sick people, and finally our way of life will just die out—as we all will. All because of horses!'

Adam sat and thought about this for some time. George's thoughts and the grim picture he had painted of the future was scary indeed. But . . . here Adam's practical thinking kicked in; what if things did not work exactly the way George was seeing it? He turned to his friend and said, 'Mr Smith, you are not taking into account one very important bit into your calculations—the ability humans have to innovate and adapt. Many years ago there were no carts or carriages, we went everywhere by foot. Then once we started domesticating animals we realized we could use them for transport too. But do you think humans will rest with this achievement? Who knows, in a hundred years what other modes of transport we would have invented so that we may not require horse for transport at all. Perhaps we will even be able to fly like birds!'

George never solved this problem in his lifetime. Neither did Adam live to see how true his thoughts about the future had been. Man went on to invent so many new ways of moving from place to place that horses are no longer used in the numbers they once were. James Watt invented the steam engine, which led to the invention of railways. Then cars were invented by Karl F. Benz and became widely used in cities for transport. Finally the Wright brothers showed that humans could fly—in aeroplanes! With all these great inventions, the horse and other animal-drawn carts and carriages are now a thing of the past.

Truly, if man did not innovate and experiment, our species would have died out—just like George had predicted!

—

Everyone was very happy this story. They all teased Meenu. 'You are the George Smith of our house. Who knows one day nobody will eat pappadams and Amma may not prepare that many pappadams. We may even buy directly from the shops if it is a small number.'

Meenu felt very embarrassed. She hid her face with a pillow. Ajji said, 'Don't make fun of her. Foresight is very important. If you don't have foresight, then you will land up in trouble like Ramu.'

'Who is Ramu?' the children immediately asked Ajji.

'I will tell the story of Ramu only tomorrow.' And Ajji bustled off. The children knew she would tell only one story a day, so they eagerly waited for the next day to hear Ramu's story.

A Treasure for Ramu

Vishnu Kaka's grandchildren had come to visit him. Vishnu Kaka was a very good friend of Ajja's. They had lived next door to each other for years. Unfortunately, his wife Vasanthi Kaki had died a few years back. Though there was a cook, his grandchildren—Sharan, Suma and Divya—always preferred to eat in Ajji's house, which Ajji also welcomed.

With seven hungry children to feed, Ajji realized telling a story would be a good way to keep them quiet till the food got cooked. Ajji started the story while peeling the cucumbers.

Did you know that sometimes even the gods in heaven can get into an argument? That's what happened once when Lakshmi, the goddess of wealth, found herself cornered by all the other gods. Together, they accused her of one thing—that she never stayed in one place for too long! 'No sooner are you comfortably settled in one house, do you decide to leave it, and off you go elsewhere!' they said to her.

Lakshmi sniffed and said, 'That's not true. I stay in a house as long as I am welcome. If people think ahead, work sincerely and spend money wisely, I stay with them forever. Unfortunately often when I am in one place for a while, people behave strangely, and I have no choice but to leave.'

The other gods pooh-poohed this and refused to believe her. Poor Lakshmi decided she needed to show them proof of what she had just said. Here is what she did to show that she was correct. Remember, many human years make only a second in god years. So what took years to happen on earth, the gods could see in only a few minutes.

Ramu and Rani were farmers. They worked hard in their fields and earned enough money to feed their children and meet their other needs. They were not rich and sometimes had to make do with fewer new clothes and not very nice food.

One day, Rani was digging a corner of her garden in order to plant a tree. As she dug deeper, there was a loud clang! Her shovel had hit something metallic hidden underground. Excited, she dug faster, till she pulled out a large metal box. When she opened it she could not believe her eyes. It was filled with gold and silver jewels! For a while Rani stood dumbstruck. Then she did a happy whoop and ran home with the box under her arm.

'Ramu, Ramu, see what I found buried in our garden!' she yelled.

Ramu was writing up the accounts for the month, and for a while paid no attention to his wife. Only when she came up to him and did a happy jig around him did he look up. Imagine how his mouth fell open in surprise when he saw the box of jewels.

Soon Ramu and Rani were the richest people in the village. They stopped going to work—after all, what was the need, they told each other. Why work in the hot sun when they had piles of money

at home? They left their small cottage and moved into the biggest house in the village. They had servants who worked day and night doing every small job, so the two did not need to lift even a finger. There was a cook who cooked delicious meals, a person to serve it, another just to clean shoes and one person to even fan Ramu as he sat on his bed the whole day and gossiped with his newfound friends.

Then Ramu decided village life was too boring and they moved to the big city. There they had another big house, more servants and lots of fun at various parties. Slowly they forgot the good things that had once made them a well-loved family. They forgot to work hard, to help others in their need, or to just be nice people. They thought that with money they could buy anything, including respect. They behaved rudely to others. They spent more and more money on clothes and parties, and as they did no work at all, the money started dwindling. They started borrowing from others which they soon could not pay back.

One day, Ramu looked sadly at his account book. It was now filled with numbers that showed he only needed to pay others; there was hardly anything left for himself. In a heavy voice he called out to his wife, 'Rani dear, the good days are over. I think we forgot to be the kind of people Goddess Lakshmi likes. She has gone elsewhere, and we are left with nothing.'

Rani stood silently for a while, then replied, 'Never mind, Ramu. We have learnt our lesson. I now think of the days when I would work all day long and go to sleep a tired person and sleep soundly. I would fall into a deep slumber as soon as I lay down on the bed. Now I lie awake all night, wondering which sari to wear the next day and what to do with our money. I am too fat to even dig, like I did when I found the treasure!'

Ramu smiled and hugged his wife. 'We'll go back to our village, and to our old ways. We will work hard like we did once, and we will help everyone around us. Maybe that will make Lakshmi come back to us one day. And even if she doesn't, we will try and be happy with what we have.'

So Ramu and his family went back to their old home. And do you know what? They did live happily ever after!

The gods watched what was happening with Ramu and Rani from the heavens as Lakshmi entered and then left their house. They had to agree with her—if the people of the house she entered became nasty, then what could she do except leave, and hope they saw the error of their ways?

The Donkey and the Stick

Ajji was on an outing with her daughter and daughter-in-law, Sumati and Subhadra. One lived in Bangalore and the other in Mumbai. They were returning the next day as they had used up all the leaves their offices had given. The children would remain at Shiggaon though, with their grandparents. Everyone was looking forward to this stage of the holidays. The children because there would be no parents telling them what to do, to Ajji's delicious food and to fun outings with Ajja. The grandparents, too, were looking forward to having the children to themselves. The rest of the year it was only the two of them in the house.

As Ajji walked with the two younger women, they talked about how difficult it was for them to manage their office work and the children. Ajji listened silently. Then Sumati said, 'But they are so good when they are with you, Amma. How do you manage them so well?' Subhadra nodded. 'I have read so many books and articles to find out about this, but nothing works the way it is written in books.'

Now Ajji said, 'Do not always go by what you read in books. Learn to use your life's experiences, read between the lines.' Then she grinned and said, 'Otherwise you will become like the people in the story about the donkey and the stick!'

Sumati and Subhadra forgot they were at the temple and clamoured together, 'What is this story? Tell us!' Ajji shook her head. 'Now you are behaving like children. But you are my children after all. All right, come join us at night when I tell today's story.'

That night the two mothers were the first to appear to listen to the stories. The children were surprised to see their mums, and Ajji started her story.

Aruna Marg was a busy road. It connected a number of villages to each other and many people, animals and carts used it every day. Walking along that road, a group of students discovered a rock which no one had bothered to look at in many years. 'Look!' they told each other in excitement, 'there is something written on the rock. What can it mean?'

They called out to their teacher. When they examined the rock carefully, they found the markings were actually little drawings. One showed a stick, and the other a donkey.

By now a large crowd had gathered. Everyone was puzzled. What could these strange drawings mean, they asked, scratching their heads. They decided to go to the ashram of a wise sage nearby and ask him. But when they trooped into the ashram, they found to their disappointment that the sage had gone on a long pilgrimage. Only his young disciple was there, looking after the cows and calves.

They asked the disciple if he could throw some light on the strange drawings. Now this young man was not very bright. But like many foolish people he loved to put on an air of learning and pretend to be very clever. He examined the drawings carefully and minutely. Then he proclaimed, 'It is very

simple. This is the drawing of a magic stick. The man with the stick is the hero of this place. He died protecting this village centuries back. Each person using this road must worship the rock and make an offering to it. The one who ignores it will become a donkey!'

The villagers were astonished to hear this strange explanation. But they were devout people and on that very day they set up a shrine around the rock. They installed the foolish disciple as head priest in charge of taking offerings from passing travellers. The disciple was pleased with his brainwave. Of course he did not know what the silly drawings meant, but he no longer had to run after calves and get kicked by angry cows in the ashram! He could sit by the rock the whole day, taking his pick of the offerings to the rock and mutter a few mumbo-jumbo prayers.

His happiness lasted a few months—till the wise old sage returned to the ashram. The old sage was annoyed to find his disciple missing and his beloved animals roaming around, uncared for. Then he looked into the distance and saw a large crowd gathered by the road. He went to investigate, and found his missing disciple there, looking happy and well fed, busy accepting offerings for a rock. He stood watching for a while. Then he walked up to the rock and closely examined the pictures. Without saying a word, he picked up a stout iron rod and, to the astonishment of the gathered crowd, started moving the rock. Many came forward to help him and when they had been able to move the rock, they found a pot of gold under it!

The sage said to the people gathered around him: 'The pictures meant you had to move the rock with an iron rod and find the hidden money. If you didn't, you were all like donkeys. You should not follow rituals and the words of others blindly. Think for yourselves and understand why you are doing what you do. If you had given this some thought, you would have recovered this treasure many months ago. Instead, you wasted your time and money making offerings to a rock and helping this greedy disciple of mine become fat and make fools of you. This treasure belongs to all of us. Let's use it to keep this road in good repair so everyone can use it and go about their work in peace.'

The villagers hung their heads in shame for they realized how foolish they had been. As for the disciple, he had to clean the cowsheds for many months to atone for his greed.

'What's in It for Me?'

Ajja told Anand, 'Will you go fetch my clothes from the dhobi?' Anand was reading a book, and said without looking up, 'Then what will you give me?' Ajja smiled and said, 'I will give you nothing. Why should I give you anything? You are a part of the family.' Anand looked up now. 'Oh! But that is not true in our house,' he declared. 'Whenever my dad tells me to do some work, I ask for a reward and he gives it to me.' Ajja was surprised. 'Let me talk to your father. The joy of helping someone itself is a reward. This is not right.'

'Dad is a big officer in a bank. Can he make mistakes?' asked Krishna with great surprise.

'He may be an officer in the bank but at home he is your father and my son, and I will talk to him. If you go on like this you will become like "Mushika".'

'What's a "Mushika"?' asked Sharan.

Ajja looked around. There was no sign of Ajji. Probably churning out some last-minute masala powder for the mothers to take back with them. He looked pleased. 'Today I will tell you a story. Of a Mushika and what happens if you want to be paid for every little thing.'

Mushika the mouse walked jauntily down the road, whistling a happy tune to himself. There had been a storm earlier in the day which had got rid of the summer heat. He had just eaten a big, juicy mango that had fallen in the storm, so his tummy was full and he was as pleased as Punch. On the road, he saw a twig, also fallen from the tree above in the storm. Now a mouse will store and keep anything, hoping it will be of use one day. So Mushika picked up the twig in his mouth and set off.

A little ahead he met a potter. The potter was sitting with his head in his hands. Why? Because his oven had been drenched in the rain and now he did not have enough dry wood to light it again. How would he bake his pots and sell them?

As the potter sat wailing in front of his house, Mushika walked up and watched him for some time. 'Wossh up, brother?' he asked with the twig still clutched in his mouth.

At first the potter paid no attention to the strange talking mouse. Then when Mushika asked him again and again, he told the little creature why he was crying. Mushika nodded, kept the twig aside and said, 'See, this twig has dried in the wind and can be used to light your kiln. I'll happily give it you, Brother Potter, but what's in it for me?'

The potter thought hard and, deciding that a little mouse could not ask for much, said, 'I will give whatever you ask for.'

In a flash Mushika replied, 'Then give me that large pumpkin that is lying in the corner of the room.'

The potter was astonished—how can a mouse carry a pumpkin? Besides, he had been looking forward to the lovely pumpkin curry his wife would make for him that night. 'Choose something else, little mouse,' he urged. But Mushika was stubborn— the pumpkin for the twig or nothing.

So the potter gave Mushika the pumpkin. The mouse was delighted. He had made a mighty human do what he wanted! He left the pumpkin near the potter's house saying he would collect it soon and set off down the road again.

Further ahead, a milkman was sitting by his cows, shaking his head.

'What's up, Brother Milkman?' asked a tiny voice. To his astonishment the man saw a mouse with bright eyes peeping up at him.

Sadly he shook his head some more, then said, 'The storm scared my cows and they are refusing to give me milk. What will I sell today and what will my family eat?'

'Spicy pumpkin curry—if you want!'

'Surely you are joking, my friend. I have ten people at home. Where will I get a pumpkin large enough to feed everyone?'

'Just walk back the way I came. You will reach a potter's house. Right beside that I have left a pumpkin. That's mine, and you can have it. But what's in it for me, Brother?'

The milkman shrugged and said, 'Whatever you want.' Like the potter he thought, what can a mouse want?

Mushika said, 'Then give me a cow.'

'Are you mad? A pumpkin for a cow? Whoever has heard such a thing?'

'It's that or nothing, my friend,' replied Mushika firmly. So the milkman went and got the large pumpkin and gave one cow to the mouse.

A big cow with large horns that listened to what he commanded! Mushika the mouse could not believe his luck. Off he went, seated on the cow, whistling another happy tune, when he stopped in front of a marriage hall. Why were people standing around looking sad and worried? They should be busy preparing for the marriage feast! Even the bride and groom were standing, with long faces.

'What's up, Brother Groom?' called Mushika, sitting atop his cow.

The groom replied gloomily, 'There's no milk to prepare the wedding kheer. How will the wedding feast be complete without the dessert?'

Mushika grinned. 'Worry not. Here, take this cow, she is now happy and will give you milk. But what's in it for me, Brother?'

The groom was very happy and said, 'Why, you can have whatever you want! You can eat your fill of the feast—sweets, pulao, fruits, whatever your heart desires.' The mouse kept quiet and gave the cow to the wedding party. They milked the cow and had plenty of milk. There was a great wedding feast. After the party was over, the mouse replied in a flash, 'Give me your bride!'

The groom and everyone in the marriage party were astonished at the mouse's cheek. The groom was about to give him a good whack, when his newly wedded bride stopped him. 'You had given him your word that he could have whatever he wants. Let me go with him. I'll teach him such a lesson that he will never try to carry off another human bride again!'

Her husband agreed, so off she went with the mouse.

Mushika scampered ahead, eager to show the bride his home. But what was this, why was she walking so slowly?

'Hurry up, Bride,' he called. 'It's about to rain again.'

The bride replied, 'I am a human, I can't run as fast as you.'

So Mushika had to slow down. By the time they reached his home, which was a little hole under a tree, he was very hungry.

'Cook me a nice meal with lots of grain,' he commanded.

The bride nodded and said, 'Of course, but where is the kitchen, the spices, the oil and the vessels? I am a human after all. I can't cook only grains.'

The mouse realized he was in a real fix having got this useless human back with him. 'Never mind,' he sighed. 'At least come inside the house.'

'Oh, but how will I do that?' wailed the bride. 'I cannot set even a toe inside that hole, it is so small. Where will I sleep tonight?'

'Err, how about under that tree?' Mushika suggested, pointing to another big tree nearby.

'No way,' sniffed the bride. 'It will rain and I will get wet and I will catch a cold, then a fever, and I will need a doctor, who will give me bitter medicines . . .' Now she started wailing even louder.

'Shush shush,' Mushika comforted her, thinking he should have agreed to eat his fill of the wedding feast instead of bringing this strange whiny woman back home with him. 'How about you stay in that temple veranda for the night?' he suggested, pointing to a big temple across the road.

'Oh, but thieves and robbers will come there, and try to snatch away my lovely jewels,' cried the woman. Then suddenly she dried her tears and said, 'What if I call my friends Ram and Shyam to protect me?'

Before Mushika could say anything, she whistled loudly and called, 'Ramu, Shyamu!'

From nowhere a big dog and cat appeared next to her and made as if to eat up Mushika. Oh, how he ran and saved his life by jumping into the safety of his hole.

The bride grinned and went back to her wedding feast with her faithful pets. As for Mushika, he had to go to sleep on an empty stomach that night. 'Tomorrow,' he sighed, 'perhaps there will be another storm,' and went off to sleep.

The Princess's New Clothes

After their mothers went back, Ajji took all the children on a shopping spree. They went to the biggest clothes store in the town. Ajji had filled her purse with notes and told all the seven children, 'Each of you can buy one dress. It is our gift to you. Remember, I have Rs 500 for each of you to buy one dress.'

At the store she chose a nice comfortable chair. The children were allowed to decide which clothes they wanted and in which colour. They could go into the trial room and try them out before buying. After an hour, everybody had whatever they wanted, except Krishna. She had tried on many many dresses but found fault with all of them. She told Ajii, 'This store does not have anything nice for me. Shall we go to another one?'

'What is wrong with this one? It is a well-known store,' Ajji remarked. But Krishna pouted and complained that she already had the colours and cuts available here, so everyone trooped off to the next shop. There, too, after a lot of thought, finally, Krishna chose her dress. Ajji had been watching all this with her typical soft smile. On the way back, as they piled into the taxi, she whispered to Krishna, 'It's good you chose a dress finally. But beware, or else you may turn out to be like that princess . . .'

'Which princess, Ajji?' the children asked.

'The one in the story.' Ajji was now looking out of the window.

'Tell us, oh tell us!'

So Ajji told them the story of the princess who never liked any of her clothes.

———

The king and queen of Ullas were very sad. No one was attacking them, the subjects were happy, the farmers had grown a bumper crop . . . then why were they so sad? Because they longed for a child and did not have one.

One day, they learnt of a place in the forests in the kingdom, where if you prayed hard and well, you were granted your wish. They went there and for many days prayed to the goddess of the forest. Finally their prayers were heard and the goddess appeared before them and asked what they wished for.

The king and queen bowed low and said, 'We wish to have a child.'

'So be it, you will soon have a little girl,' said the goddess, shimmering in the greenery. 'But remember, though she will be a loving child, she will have one flaw. She will love new clothes too much and it will make life difficult for you. Do you still want such a child?'

The king and queen wanted a baby so much they would have agreed to anything. So the goddess granted them their wish and vanished back among the trees.

Soon, as had been said, the queen gave birth to a lovely baby girl. Oh, what a beauty the little thing was, with her jet-black hair and thick eyelashes and long toes and fingers. They named her Beena. The kingdom rejoiced in their king's happiness and for a while there was complete joy everywhere.

Beena grew up a child loved by everyone. She became prettier by the day, and with her charming manners and ready laughter, she filled everyone's hearts with joy. But, as the goddess had said, she did have one flaw—she loved new clothes! She loved clothes so much she had to have a new outfit every day. She would refuse to wear the same clothes twice! Tailors from all over the kingdom and even outside created beautiful, extraordinary clothes for her. Silk, cotton, wool, you name it, and Beena had a dress or sari of that material. Blues, greens, reds, pinks, every colour in nature was present in her wardrobe.

For a while the king and queen were happy to let her have new clothes every day. But soon they realized they were spending all their money and time in finding new tailors and clothes for their daughter! This had to stop.

They coaxed and cajoled and pleaded and scolded, but Beena remained unmoved. Her parents understood this was the flaw the goddess had warned them about, and finally decided to send Beena to the goddess to find a solution.

Beena entered the dark, green forest and waited for the goddess to appear. She came in a flash of green light, which lit up everything around her. Folding her hands, Beena told the goddess why she had come.

'I know your problem, my child. I will send you a new outfit every day. It will be unique, its colours and design will delight you. But you should remember one thing: you cannot wear anything else, or exchange these clothes with anyone else. If you ever do that, your life will be miserable.'

Happily Beena agreed to this. After all, why would she be unhappy if she got a new dress every day?

From then on, Beena woke up each morning to find an extraordinary new sari or dress lying by her bed, ready to be worn. It was a dream come true for her! She enjoyed herself no end, choosing matching earrings and bangles and shoes, and everyone kept telling her how pretty she looked.

Yet after some months the excitement died down. No one remarked when Beena sashayed in wearing another fantastic dress. 'Oh, it's the goddess's gift,' they all said. 'It's not something you or I can ever have,' all her friends said and shrugged and went their way.

Beena grew sad. Then one festival day, while walking near the river, she noticed a girl wearing a simple cotton sari. There was something about the way the girl walked and how attractive she looked which made everyone turn and stare. Beena noticed how the people were admiring the girl. She became jealous because no one noticed her beautiful clothes any longer, yet they had such praise for this simply dressed girl. She forgot all about the goddess's warning and went up to the girl and said, 'Will you take my dress and give me your sari in return? It is so lovely that people can't take their eyes off it.'

The girl was astonished. The famous Princess Beena was offering to take her sari, and was giving her a marvellous outfit in exchange! She could not believe her luck and happily gave her sari to Beena. She then wore Beena's dress and went away. No sooner had Beena worn the girl's sari than there was a flash and a bang. Her surroundings changed, and she found herself transported deep inside the forest, in front of the goddess.

'Beena,' the goddess called. 'I had told you that you cannot give away or exchange the clothes I gave you. But you have done just that! I am afraid there is a punishment for not listening to me. I will have to take you away from the world of humans forever.'

Beena looked down in sadness. She thought of her parents' tear-stained faces, the grief of the people in her kingdom who had loved her dearly. Then she spoke aloud, 'I will go away, but do grant me one last wish. Turn me into something that will remind everyone about their beloved princess, something they may even find useful.'

The goddess smiled and turned Beena into a plant. Do you know what plant Beena became? An onion! Have you noticed how the onion has so many layers? Those are all the dresses that Beena once wore. And have you noticed your mother's eyes water while she cuts onions? That is because unknown to ourselves, like all the people in Beena's kingdom, we still shed tears for the beautiful, kind-hearted princess!

After listening to this story, Krishna wailed, 'Ajji, I don't want to be like Beena. I don't want to get turned into an onion! I promise not to fuss over my clothes from now on!'

The Story of Paan

Vishnu Kaka had invited the entire family for dinner. It was a lavish meal with many courses. Everyone ate their fill, enjoying each dish. After it was over, the children gathered around Kaka as he brought out his big box of paan. They loved watching Kaka choose and mix his ingredients to make delicious paans which the grown-ups then ate with blissful looks on their faces.

He explained to the children, 'A paan contains betel leaf, betel nut and lime. But we should use only so much of each ingredient. Only then will it taste good.' All seven children wanted to try this experiment on their own. Some of them chewed on only the leaf, some on the nut, and others on the nut and leaf, or the leaf and only lime. It was true, when the three were not put together, the paan tasted horrible! In fact, Sharan vomited when he added more lime than necessary! Everyone made a beeline for the mirror to check if their tongues were red or not.

Ajji was sitting and chatting with Sharan's mom and watching their antics. Then she called out to them and said, 'Children, by this time you must all know that the leaf, nut or lime on their own taste very bad. Even if you put just two together it is no good. Only when you add the three in a perfect combination can a paan be eaten. And that's when you get that red colour in the mouth!'

'Why is that, Ajji? Is there any special meaning?'

'Yes there is a special meaning and I'll tell you the story, which I first heard from my grandmother.'

⁓

Once upon a time, there were two brothers, Bhanu and Veer. Their parents died when they were young and Bhanu brought up his younger brother with a lot of love and care. When Bhanu was old enough, he married Bharati. She was a gentle, loving person and looked after Veer with as much love as her husband.

When Veer was about twenty years of age, he heard that their king was looking for soldiers to join his army, as there was going to be a war. Veer decided to join the army. Oh, how much his brother and sister-in-law cried and pleaded, telling him to remain at home with them. They could not bear the thought of the boy they had brought up with so much affection going so far away from them. But Veer insisted on becoming a soldier, so they let him go away, with a heavy heart and tears in their eyes.

For many days there was no news of Veer. The king went to war, vanquished his enemy and returned. The soldiers who went with him also came back home. But of Veer there was no sign. Day after day his brother and sister-in-law watched out for him, hoping to see him come walking down the road, back home. But there was no one. Then, one day, a group of soldiers passed through their village, returning home from the war. Bhanu called out to them and asked about his brother.

'Veeru, oh yes, so sad, he died, you know, in the battlefield,' said one, shaking his head.

'No no. He was injured, and he recovered. Did he not come home?' said another.

'He was on his way home when he fell ill,' informed a third.

On hearing these awful tidings, Bhanu was deeply saddened. He decided he could not live at home waiting for his dear little brother to return. He would go and look for him. When he told his wife, Bharati too decided to go with him. Together, they set off one day to look for the missing Veer and bring him home.

They decided to go to the site of the king's big battle, where Veer was last seen by his companions. This place was far away and they had to travel through forests and valleys and mountains and deserts. The two walked and walked, over many miles, but poor Bharati was not strong enough. One day, after travelling through a thick forest, they reached a little hamlet. Bharati sat down, exhausted. Then to Bhanu's great horror she died out of sheer exhaustion. Unable to bear his grief, Bhanu too died immediately.

Over many years at the place where the couple had died, two trees grew. One was a tall tree and the other a creeper that hugged the tree. It was as if Bharati and Bhanu were together even in death.

Meanwhile, Veer, the brother they had loved so deeply, was not really dead. He had got terribly wounded in the war and spent many years recovering from his injuries in a little village far away from home. When he finally recovered, he came back as fast as he could to his old house, knowing how anxious his family would be for him.

But imagine his surprise when he found the house locked and bolted, abandoned for many years. Slowly the neighbours gathered around and told him how Bhanu had decided to go looking for his lost brother.

That night Veer cried many bitter tears. How would he find his beloved brother and sister-in-law now? Where were they? By the time morning dawned he had made up his mind. He would try and go the way they had travelled and find them. Immediately he set off.

Veer was a soldier, but he had only lately recovered from many wounds and was not too strong. It took him many days to walk across the difficult land Bhanu and his wife had crossed. Then one day, near a forest, he came across a little shrine. The villagers told him the sad story of how the shrine came to be. Years ago a couple had arrived at the spot, tired from days of walking. Legend had it that they were on the way looking for a long-lost brother. When the two died without fulfilling this wish, two wonderful plants, unknown to anyone earlier, had grown at the spot. The leaves and nuts from the trees were so sweet and refreshing that the villagers decided to build a small temple for the man and the woman at the place.

Veer listened to the story with growing sorrow. He realized the couple they talked about was none other than his brother and his wife. Unable to bear the news, he turned into a statue of limestone.

Do you know how they have all been remembered ever since? The tall tree grew nuts called areca nuts, the creeper's leaves were paan or betel leaves and from the statue came the lime paste that is added to preparations of paan. And this is how this loving family came together even after death. Together they taught people the values of love, unity and loyalty, and when people chew paan they remember this story.

Sharan's mom was surprised to hear this story. 'Really, Ajji,' she said, 'even I was not aware why these three ingredients are always used to make a paan. I too will come to listen to your stories from now on!'

Ajji nodded, then she added with that glint in her eyes, 'Chewing paan is not good for your teeth. Everyone, off you go to brush your teeth!'

Payasam for a Bear

Ajja and Vishnu Kaka were planning something! They could be spotted grinning and nodding and whispering. The children were dying to know what it was. Then one evening, they finally broke the news. They were all going on a picnic! It would be a picnic at the nearby falls. These waterfalls were really beautiful, with the river meandering close by and the forest just across. The children got even more excited when the two grandpas revealed the rest of the plan. Tomorrow would be a rest day for Ajji and Sharan's mother, because all the cooking would be done by them and the children! And they would do it the traditional way, by gathering firewood and then cooking the meal from scratch.

The children were so excited they could hardly sleep that night. All they could talk about was the picnic and what they would cook. Before nodding off they had decided the menu—pulao and kheer! Payasam or kheer is so easy to make, and who doesn't love it?

The next day, even the usual late risers were up and about and ready to set out for the picnic by seven o'clock. Oh, what a beautiful spot it was! They all ran around exclaiming over everything and getting ready with their cricket bats and balls for a game. Ajji sat comfortably under a big tree. Then it was time to get lunch ready. Everyone started looking for twigs to use as firewood. Ajji spotted Divya straying towards the dense thicket of trees and called out, 'Divya, come back, don't go there. Who knows what animal is there, and on top of that you all are going to cook payasam . . .'

Minu's ears pricked up immediately. 'Why, Ajji, what does payasam have to do with animals?'

Ajji grinned, 'But bears love payasam! Don't you know?'

Everyone declared they had never known this piece of information. So cooking and games forgotten, young and old gathered around her to hear the story of a bear who wanted to eat payasam.

———

Did you know that you must never ever anger a bear? It is true; an angry bear can do some really awful things, so it is always safer to keep your word to him. Poor Mohan and Basanti did not know this, and tried to trick a bear, and see what happened to them!

Mohan had a banana plantation, where he grew delicious bananas. He also had a huge mango tree that provided him with baskets of juicy mangoes every summer. He would sell these fruits in the market and lived happily enough with his wife, Basanti.

Once, his trees yielded an exceptionally large crop of bananas and mangoes, and he decided to sell them in the market in the city, where he would get a higher price for them. So off he went with his sacks and baskets to the city. There he sat in the market, sold everything that he had brought, and made quite a bit of money. At the market, he ran into an old friend, Amar. Mohan and Amar were overjoyed to see each other after many years.

'Come to my house, dear friend,' insisted Amar. 'Let us enjoy a good meal and talk about our childhood days.'

Mohan thought this was a wonderful idea, and went with Amar to his house. There the two friends ate huge quantities of rice, dal, lovely vegetables and all kinds of sweets. Then, finally, out came the best part of the meal—the payasam!

Payasam is known by many names all over India. Some call it kheer, some payesh, and others, payasam. It is made with milk, rice and jaggery and many other ingredients, and it is always yummy! So was the payasam that Amar served his friend. It was made with fragrant rice, creamy milk, sweet-as-sugar jaggery, and strewn with nuts, cardamoms, saffron and all kinds of wonderful, mouth-watering things. Mohan ate and ate bowl after bowl of this dessert, till he was ready to burst.

Then the two friends chatted and rested, till it was time for Mohan to head back home. When he reached his house, he told his wife about the scrumptious meal, particularly the payasam he had eaten. Oh, how Basanti sighed and longed to have tasted this dish too! Seeing her face Mohan suggested, 'See, I have earned plenty of money by selling the fruits. Why don't I buy the things required to make payasam, which you can cook and both of us will enjoy it together?'

Basanti thought this was a wonderful idea. But first Mohan needed to go to the forest to collect some firewood. Then he could go to the shop and get all that was required to make the dessert. So off Mohan went, swinging his axe and whistling a tune. Now who would be sitting dozing under a tree in the forest but a big black bear. He had just had some nice berries for lunch and was enjoying his snooze, when Mohan walked by. First the bear opened one eye, then another, and watched as Mohan cut a few branches of a nearby tree and collected twigs for firewood. Just as Mohan was tying it all up in a neat bundle, the bear spoke up.

'Hi there, friend. Where are you off to in such a happy mood, and why are you collecting so much firewood? Tell me, are you cooking a feast tonight?'

Mohan was astonished and a little scared to be addressed like this by a bear. 'Y-yes, your honour, I mean, dear bear, ss-sir,' he mumbled and stammered.

The bear was happy after his meal, so he decided to chat some more with Mohan.

'So tell me, what are you going to cook tonight?' he asked, patting his tummy.

'P-p-payasam,' answered Mohan.

'Paya . . . what?' The bear was puzzled.

'Pa-ya-sam,' Mohan said slowly. 'It's a sweet dish.'

'Tell me more!' The bear was intrigued.

So Mohan described payasam and how it was made. As he talked about milk and rice and nuts and jaggery, the bear's eyes started gleaming, his stomach started rumbling, and he realized he absolutely, totally needed to taste this wonderful human food.

'Oh Mohan, my friend, do let me come and share your payasam tonight,' the bear begged.

Mohan was astonished. A bear as a guest for dinner! Who knows how much he would eat! But neither could he say no—that seemed so rude, and the bear was looking at him hopefully.

He sighed and replied, 'All right. You can come. But to cook so much payasam I will need much more firewood. Can you bring that with you?'

Cunning Mohan thought he would make the bear do his work for him, so he would not need to come to the forest for the next few days.

'Yes, yes!' The bear jumped up. 'Just tell me how much firewood you need. Ten? Twenty? Thirty bundles?'

'Umm, fifty would be enough,' decided Mohan. Then he slung his bundle of firewood over his shoulder and went back home. On the way he bought lots of milk, rice and everything else they would need to make the payasam.

When he reached home he told Basanti about the unusual guest who would come to share their dessert. So Basanti cooked a huge quantity of payasam. She added lovely nuts, aromatic saffron, sweet cardamoms and many wonderful things into it as she cooked. Oh, how marvellous the payasam smelt. Unable to wait any longer, the two started eating helping after helping of the dish, without waiting for their guest to turn up. They ate and ate and ate, till they realized they had eaten up everything! There was not a grain of rice, nor half a nut left for him!

They sat around wondering what to do. What would they say to the bear when he came expecting to eat payasam? Then, a devious plan entered Mohan's head. What if they made payasam with all kinds of other ingredients? After all, it was only a bear, and he had never tasted this dish earlier, so how would he know what it really tasted like?

The cunning man and his wife then took a little bit of milk, added lots of water to it, threw in a handful of rice, and instead of jaggery and nuts and spices they added pebbles and sand and cardamom husks and stirred and stirred the mixture till it looked somewhat like payasam. They placed the brass pot filled with this in front of the house and went and hid in the bushes somewhere at the back.

As soon as night fell, a huge dark figure appeared down the road. On its back it carried fifty bundles of firewood. It was the bear, come to dinner!

He reached Mohan's house and looked around. There was no one. Then, right in front of the house, he spotted the pot full of payasam. Unable to wait any longer, he flung down the bundles he had carried and fell upon the payasam. Only after he had eaten more than half the potful did he realize something was wrong. The milk was watery, the rice was half cooked and there was horrible grit and pebbles between his teeth! Ugh!

Oh, how angry he was now! Furious, he shouted out for Mohan. But Mohan was cowering behind the bushes and did not reply. Now angrier than

ever, the bear spotted the mango tree and rubbed his back against it. The mangoes came raining down, he shook the tree so hard. The bear continued to stamp and shake the tree, till it fell with a huge crash right on to the banana field and crushed the best banana plants. Seeing the firewood he had carried all the way from the forest lying around, the bear started throwing them around. One fell into the oven in the kitchen and set fire to the house. Soon Mohan and Basanti's house was in flames, his field in ruins and his prized mango tree destroyed.

Finally satisfied that he had taken his revenge the bear stormed back into the forest. When Mohan and his wife crawled out of their hiding place and came back home they saw everything was in ruins. How they wailed and wept and wished they hadn't been so greedy and left the bear his share of payasam.

But what was the use of lamenting now? The damage was done, and the greedy couple had learnt what I told you earlier—never anger a bear! And if you make a promise to one, keep it!

Fire on the Beard

What a grand picnic everyone had! They played and ate and splashed in the water till late evening. Ajja and Ajji had to drag them back home. That night the children tumbled into bed and were fast asleep even before Ajji switched off the lights. Quietly she tucked them in. The next morning there was no sign of anyone waking up. Ajja and Ajji went about their work, not waking the children. But when it was ten o'clock, Ajji decided they had to wake up now. So she came into the room and found all four were up and chatting in bed. She looked at them for a while with her hands on the hips. Then she said, 'So, I think you've had enough rest. Now up all of you. Wash up and get ready. I'll give you your lunch by noon.'

All the others jumped up except Anand. He grinned at Ajji and said, 'You know, I can live without food if I get to lie in bed all day.'

'Really?' Ajji said. 'So be it. Everyone else, lunch will be ready at twelve, so be there on time. Oh, and those who lie around in bed will also miss the afternoon story.' Then she walked off trying to hide a smile. Anand and miss a meal! He was the one who loved his food the most!

Anand was quiet. The rest sprang out of their beds and went to brush their teeth and have a bath. Soon the aroma of onion dosa wafted through the house. It was too delicious to resist. Everyone gathered in the kitchen to help grind the dosa batter.

By now Anand was bored and hungry, lying alone in bed. He quietly went and took his bath. He was worried—what if Ajji had taken him seriously and not kept a share of the dosa for him? And what if he had to miss that day's story? When Ajji saw him appear at the kitchen and join in, she laughed and said, 'You have become like Brij.'

'Who is Brij, Ajji?'

So Ajji started the story while the children ate the dosas.

———

Yaaawwnnn! Brij stretched out in the sun, yawned loud and long, and went back to sleep. Is Brij a rich man on a holiday; or has he worked hard all day and just resting for a while? Neither! Brij was the laziest, most good-for-nothing fellow you'll ever meet. He would spend entire days just lying around on his bed doing nothing. He was too lazy to even trim his beard and it had grown right down to his knees. All day he sat around combing it and admiring it, doing nothing else. His mother would call him, his wife would scold him, but Brij was not one to mend his ways.

This is how most conversations with his wife, Shanti, would go:

'Can you get some water from the well? There is no water in the house.'

'The well is dry. There's no water there.'

'Can you fetch water from the pond, at least?'

'The pond is too far. I can't walk so much for a pot of water.'

'Then pluck those coconuts from the tree.'

'Oh, those coconuts are still tender. Let's pluck them next month.'

'What about getting some areca nuts from the tree then?'

'Don't you know, areca nuts are not good for health?'

'Help me plough the field then.'

'It is too hot. The sun will burn my skin. It's better if you too did not go there.'

'Can you at least look after the house when I am in the field?'

'There is nothing to look after in the house.'

And so on and on Brij would make excuses for not doing any work that was asked of him. Of course he was never too tired to eat! As soon as his wife would lay out the meal, he would jump out of bed saying, 'Oh you have prepared food for me with such love, it is my duty to eat it.' And then he would gobble down all that was given.

When evening fell, Brij would roll out of bed, comb his hair and beard and set off to meet his gang of friends. Seeing how he managed to get out of doing any work, many others in the village had decided to do the same. All these people had formed a club, The Idlers'

Club. They would meet every evening and sit around and talk about all kinds of things. They claimed this way they were improving their general knowledge, but all they were really doing was gossip and boast.

Brij, as the leader of the club, would get to boast the loudest and longest. One day, the topic was who was the laziest of all.

'Bathing every day is such a waste of time and precious water. I take a bath once in two days. That way I even save water!' said Manoj, the environmentalist.

'I never make my bed,' boasted Suresh, the innkeeper. 'Why bother when you have to lie down in it once again at the end of the day?'

'I eat my food out of the vessel in which it is cooked,' claimed Raju, the cook. 'Putting the food in the plate only increases the work for you will need to wash it too.'

Now Brij thought he should say something that would beat all these other tall tales. So he said, 'I am always cool and calm. Why, even if my beard were to catch fire I would start digging a well at that time, and never store water close at hand!'

As these discussions were happening, a real fire broke out in the village! It burned down buildings and roofs and sheds, crackling and throwing up sparks, making villagers run helter-skelter looking for water to douse the flames.

The Idlers' Club heard all the commotion but no one bothered to step out to see what was happening. 'What is going on?' they only asked each other.

'Oh nothing,' Brij dismissed the topic. 'Must be some circus or the other. So, what were we talking about?'

By now the fire had spread to their road. It was fast making its way to the house where the idlers were sitting. It got hotter and hotter. Brij's friends started sweating and getting nervous now. Soon the roof of the house caught fire. Still Brij kept saying, 'Don't worry, don't worry. It will rain now and put this out.' Then 'The wind is blowing in the opposite direction and will blow it down. We are really cool people, we should not be afraid of a fire!'

Finally his friends could stand it no longer and rushed screaming out of the house. But Brij was too stubborn, and refused to move. Finally the fire caught up with him and his beard started getting singed. Now even Brij was scared. 'Heellp!' he shouted.

'Now you can start digging the well,' his friends suggested.

'Oh, get me some water from the pond,' Brij begged.

'That's too far away,' the others shouted from outside. 'Maybe it will rain,' they added.

By now the beard was burning away merrily, and all Brij could do was leap and dance away from the flames. Till suddenly there were splashes and splashes of water! Someone was emptying cool, cool water on the fire and putting it out!

Brij could not believe his luck. Who had saved him? Why, it was Shanti and many other women of the village who had worked hard and drawn water from wells and ponds to save their homes.

Finally Brij learnt his lesson. Being lazy and pretending to be cool had certainly not helped him in his hour of need. So he shaved off his half-burnt beard, woke up early each morning and did all that Shanti told him to do, and more!

The Way You Look at It

On a sleepy afternoon, while the sun continued to shine, the clouds opened up and it started to rain. Sharan had fallen asleep after eating at least fifteen pooris for lunch. When he woke up, he saw a rainbow in the sky. There was a mild drizzle and the bright sunshine of summer. In the sky was a bold, bright, clear rainbow. Sharan ran to Ajji's house and started calling out to his friends.

Suma and Krishna were playing in the garden. Raghu and Divya were reading. Anand was sleeping. Sharan was so excited he called out to each one, 'Ajja, Ajji, Suma, Krishna, Raghu, Anand, Divya, come and see this!' Everyone rushed out to see what was up. The children gazed in amazement at the rainbow. Living in the city, none of them ever got to see such a vast expanse of the sky, unhindered by tall buildings. Ajja and Ajji were used to it and went back to their work.

That evening, while having their milk, the children were talking about rainbows. 'The colours of the rainbow are known as VIBGYOR,' said Raghu.

'A rainbow is called Indra Dhanush in Sanskrit,' said Suma.

'It is known as Kamanabillu in Kannada—the bow of Lord Kamadeva,' said Sharan's mother.

'In the olden days if the sun and rain came together, we used to say it is the fox's wedding and all of us have to go on the rainbow to reach the wedding,' said Ajji.

'Ultimately it is the same thing, seven colours that appear in the sky when the sun's rays are reflected by the rainwater,' said Ajja. 'It depends upon the way you look at it.'

Ajji nodded. 'The same thing appears different, depending on the way you look at it, and today I can tell you a story about that.' Immediately everyone turned their attention from the sky to Ajji.

During one monsoon season, it rained and rained in Chitpur, a little village by a mighty river. It rained so hard that the river swelled up. Huge waves lashed against the riverbanks and carried away trees, houses and big chunks of earth. The villagers were really scared and prayed hard for the rains to stop.

When finally the skies cleared, one by one people emerged from their homes. One of them was Raju. He walked down to the riverside. There he saw something that made him rub his eyes in disbelief. Why, a huge black rock had appeared there out of nowhere! And what was more, the rock looked exactly like the head of Ganesha, the god with the elephant head. Raju immediately prostrated himself in front of the rock. 'Ganesha not only heard our prayers and made the rains go away, he has come himself to protect us!' Raju shouted to no one in particular. 'I must tell everyone about this!' he yelled and ran back to the village to shape the news.

Next came Chetan, the sculptor. He had spent so many days cooped up in his house waiting for the rains to stop. Now he was glad to be out in the open, and was thinking of his next piece of work. Suddenly he caught sight of the new rock by the river. It was just the right colour, worn smooth with age and river water. It was perfect for the scene he wanted to carve! Giving a whoop of joy, he ran home to gather his carving tools.

Just as he turned the corner, a merchant came by on his horse. The animal was thirsty and he stopped there for it to have a drink of water from the river. He too spotted the stone. 'What a big stone!' he remarked. 'And it is nice and smooth and flat. Let me sit for a while on it and rest.' After enjoying a nice rest on the rock, the merchant decided he would tell his friends about it. They were travelling together and all of them would be thrilled to be able to sit there for some time, by the river.

He went off to find his friends.

Just then, Ajit, a soldier, came on his horse. He got down and washed his face. While his horse was drinking water, he was looking around and the same stone caught his attention. He was surprised and said to himself, 'What a huge stone on the riverbed! Maybe I should get it removed so that in an emergency it should not become a hindrance on the road. Our army can march better if such obstacles are not there. I must inform my commander.' Thinking so, he rushed back to his camp to talk to his commander.

Later in the day Bholu, the village washerman, appeared by the river with his big bundle of clothes. To his astonishment, he found a crowd right around his favourite washing spot. They were all arguing over a rock! Pushing his way into the crowd, Bholu spoke in a loud voice, 'Hey! What do you think you all are doing?'

Raju now burst out, 'This rock is a sign from Lord Ganesha, I want to worship it.'

Chetan raised his voice even louder and said, 'No no, this rock is going to be used for my next sculpture.'

The merchant shouted, 'I have invited all my friends to rest on it! It is ours!'

Ajit was giving orders to his soldiers to remove the stone.

Bholu now grinned and said, 'But this rock has been here for years and years! Earlier half of it was submerged in the mud. Now with the rains the mud has got washed off, and you are seeing more of it. The washermen of Chitpur have been using this rock to do our washing for many, many years! There's nothing miraculous about it. Now off with all of you, I have work to do.'

So saying Bholu emptied his bundle of clothes and set to work. What could the others do? They had to go away grumbling quietly to themselves.

Roopa's Great Escape

Ajja's and Vishnu Kaka's houses were teeming with people! There was a village festival, and friends and relatives from near and far had come to Shiggaon. There were people the children had not seen or even heard about before. Some said, 'I am your father's fourth cousin.' Someone else said, 'I am your grandmother's second cousin.' The houses were full and there was a lot of fun and laughter everywhere. Nobody expected a separate bedroom or a special dish at the dining table. They all ate together and talked to everybody and slept on the floor on mattresses. The city children were surprised at the ease with which the guests made themselves at

313

home. The women helped out in the kitchen in the morning and in the evening they dressed in shining silk sarees and went to the fair. In fact everyone dressed in their best, put the two hundred rupees Ajja gave in their pockets and purses and made for the fair.

The fair itself was quite astonishing. The children from Mumbai said, 'It is just like Chowpati on Juhu beach.' The Delhi kids said, 'It is similar to Janpath.' Others said, 'It is like Karaga or Kallekai Parishe in Bangalore.' Vishnu Kaka explained, 'In every village there is a village god or goddess and once a year we worship them in a grand way. At the festival and fair it is not just about selling and buying, it is also about meeting people, exchanging gifts, having a feast and a good time.'

The group moved from shop to shop, peeping into the photo studios, examining bangles, waiting for a turn on the merry-go-round and clapping along to the dances, when someone noticed Suma was missing! Somewhere in the crowd she had got separated from the rest, and now there was no sign of her. Immediately her mother started wailing, and Ajji consoled her. Vishnu Kaka too looked really worried. The children were scared and thrilled too. This was just like *Home Alone*! As Vishnu Kaka was about to make his way to the police assistance booth, they heard Suma's voice on the mike! 'I am at the police station, Vishnu Ajja please come and fetch me.' When Suma had been traced, her mother started scolding her. But Suma was not bothered. 'I was not worried,' she said. 'In the crowd when I realized I was not with you people, I straightaway went to the police station and told them to make an announcement.'

Everyone declared she was a very brave and sensible girl, and for a change that day Vishnu Kaka said, 'Today I will tell a story about a young girl like Suma who had a lot of courage. I read this story in a book when I was young.'

Once, there lived a very clever young girl called Roopa. She was an orphan and had been taken care of all her life by the people of the village in which she lived. She was very hard-working and once she became old enough, she lived all by herself and looked after herself. But she always missed having a family of her own, even though her neighbours were such loving and caring people.

One day, when Roopa was about sixteen years old, she went down to the river along with some other women and girls to wash clothes and fetch water. Diwali was around the corner and everyone was excited. They were discussing what new clothes they would get. Some were expecting their husbands and fathers to return to the village with lovely gifts for them and were looking forward to all the merrymaking that would happen over the next few days.

Only Roopa was quiet. She did not have anyone to buy her new clothes or shoes or presents. The villagers were kind to her, but they had barely enough for their own needs so how could she expect them to get anything for her? Yet today, hearing all the happy chatter around her, she could not keep quiet any longer.

'Even I will get a new sari this year!' she told Rama, her best friend.

Rama and all the other girls were astonished. Who was going to get Roopa her new sari? 'I heard from a distant uncle the other day. He was working for many years in a faraway city and did not know that my parents had died. Now that he is back, he has promised to visit me on Diwali. I am sure he will bring some marvellous gift for me!' Roopa had started weaving a story, and now she kept adding, telling all kinds of tales about her imaginary uncle. Her friends listened open-mouthed. Then they went home, telling each other what luck Roopa was finally no longer all alone in the world.

As soon as the bunch of women had gone away, who emerged from behind a tree, but Bholu the trickster. He had been sitting under the tree, planning his next theft, when he had fallen asleep. Then he had woken up and seen the women at the river and had sat there still hoping to hear something about the villagers. Sure enough, he had heard Roopa's story, and was now ready with a plan!

Bholu decided to dress up as an old man and appear at Roopa's house a few days before Diwali pretending to be her uncle! Then he would take her away along with any valuables she may have got from her parents.

A week before Diwali, an old stranger appeared at Roopa's door. He was carrying new clothes, sweets and other gifts. Roopa was out doing some errands so her neighbours came around to find out who he was. Bholu acted perfectly like Roopa's long-lost uncle, eagerly waiting to meet her. When Roopa returned home, she found everyone sitting around an old man, who said he was the uncle she had made up a story about!

Roopa was astonished. How had this happened? She had only been pretending to have a relative just so her friends would not feel sorry for her, and now here he was, a real person! Then her neighbour, who had looked after her all these years, said, 'Roopa, this is your Uncle Bholu; he learnt he had a niece and came here looking for you. He wants to take you home with him and look after you like his own daughter. You are so lucky, Roopa, and we are so happy for you!'

Roopa looked around at everyone, beaming happily at her, and thought what harm would there be if she went away with this uncle. She happily packed whatever little things she owned and waving goodbye to her friends and neighbours, went off with Bholu.

No sooner had they reached his house than he took off his disguise and appeared before her as a young man. Roopa was horrified. Oh, what a fool she had been to believe his story and come away with him! He was nothing but a trickster.

In Bholu's house there was no one else but his mother, who was old and deaf and blind. After eating his lunch,

Bholu decided to walk about for a while, meeting his friends and telling them how he had kidnapped Roopa. She too ate her lunch, pretended she was very sleepy, yawned loudly and told his mother, 'Aunty, I am very tired after that long journey. I am going to bed for a little while. If your son comes round tell him not to wake me up.'

Bholu's mother nodded, though she had not heard much. Roopa quickly went to the other room, borrowed some of Bholu's clothes, wore them and ran off. She took with her a few coins and a thick stick to defend herself if need be. Before leaving, she arranged the pillows in such a way on the bed that in the evening darkness it looked like someone was sleeping on the bed. Then she covered the pillows with a dupatta and a sheet. If anyone only looked in from the door it would seem as if a woman was sleeping on the bed.

Bholu returned home when it was well past evening. His mother told him Roopa was in her room. He peeped in, saw someone sleeping and went away. Many hours passed, Bholu kept checking whether Roopa was awake or not, but each time he saw her sleeping without moving a muscle. Finally, he realized something was wrong.

He went up to the bed now and pulled back the dupatta and the sheet. Imagine his shock when he saw nothing but pillows on the bed! Roopa had disappeared! He ran out immediately and asked everyone around if they had seen a young, pretty girl walk out of his house. But no one had, because Roopa had cleverly disguised herself as a man!

Meanwhile, Roopa too had walked many miles till she reached a different town. There she looked around for work, and was taken in by an innkeeper to look after the guests and to show them their rooms. Roopa, who now called herself Rupesh, was happy doing this work. She could not return to her village till she did something about Bholu, otherwise he would be sure to land up there and bring her back with him, pretending to be her uncle.

After many days, Bholu turned up at the town. He walked from shop to inn to market, asking if anyone had seen someone like Roopa. Of course no one had. Roopa got to know and decided to teach him a lesson. When Bholu reached her inn, he did not recognize her in men's clothes. She agreed to give him a room for the night. She told him, 'Sir, I will give you a room in the attic. It is nice and warm and cosy there, and you will be away from this harsh winter cold.'

Bholu happily agreed and followed her to the room. A ladder was kept in the middle of the room which went up to a little trapdoor. If you climbed through the door, you entered the attic. Bholu quickly went up the ladder, found his bed, wrapped his blanket around himself and went off to sleep.

When it was the middle of the night, Roopa sneaked into the room and removed the ladder. Then she threw some marbles right under the trapdoor and stamped loudly around the room. Bholu woke with a start. Who was that walking around his room? He called down nervously, 'W-who is there?'

Roopa called out in her man's voice, 'Nothing to worry sir. The soldiers are looking for a thief they believe is hiding in this inn.'

Bholu was really scared. How did the soldiers know he was a thief and a trickster? He was sure they were looking for him, and decided to make a run for it. He opened the trapdoor and stepped down. But there was no ladder! Bholu fell with a loud thud on to the floor! When he tried to get up, his feet slipped on the many marbles strewn about the room and he went crashing and sliding all over the place! Finally he hit his head against a wall and passed out, unconscious.

Roopa had been watching this from the door with great delight. Her plan was working! As soon as Bholu fainted, she heaved him up and packed him up in a large box. She placed a nice silk cloth on top of him. Then she dragged the box outside the inn and stood there.

Soon a bullock cart passed by with two travellers heading for the inn. When they saw Roopa, or Rupesh, standing outside the inn, they asked, 'Are you the manager of this inn?'

Roopa nodded yes.

'Why are you standing here then?'

Roopa replied in a worried voice, 'I look after this inn. I was supposed to go to my own village earlier today to attend a wedding. But there was so much of work that I could not leave, and now here I am waiting for my cart with this heavy box.' Then she lowered her voice and whispered, 'This box is full of gifts I bought for the wedding, and if I don't reach in time, everyone will be really disappointed.'

The two travellers, who were up to no good themselves, looked at each other. The same thought had come to both! They said, 'Don't worry, brother. You can take a ride on our cart. Why don't you

put your box on the cart here? But before we start, would you mind getting us a drink of water?'

Rupesh, or Roopa, smiled to herself, and dragged the box on to the cart. Then she went inside to fetch the water. She took her time. As soon as her back was turned, the two travellers opened the box to see what it contained. They saw some lovely silk cloth on top. Now assured that they had got their hands on some valuables, they quickly urged their bullocks forward and made a dash for it. Once they were well and truly out of sight, Roopa grinned to herself. Her plan had worked! She ran to the nearest police station, and told them all about the theft.

The two men in the bullock cart were just celebrating their theft of the box, when they were horrified to see soldiers waiting for them down the road. What could they do, they wondered. They were crossing a bridge over a river at that time, and quickly tipped the box into the water. Then they heaved a sigh of relief and went their way.

So that was the end of Bholu, and Roopa too returned to her village, where she lived happily on her own. She was not going to trust any stranger any more!

'And that's what brave Suma did too! When she was in trouble she did not talk to any stranger, but went straight to the police for help. We must always remain cool like this when in trouble,' signed off Vishnu Kaka. Suma was delighted at this praise, and ate her bhajias with great happiness all the way home!

Five Spoons of Salt

One morning, Ajji told Ajja, 'Today is a Santhe (a village market day which happens once in a week). Why don't you take the children and show them the Santhe and buy vegetables and other things for the house?' Ajja, who normally would have said yes, was hesitant. 'How will I manage all the children, that too at the Santhe? Remember what happened at the jatre—the fair? At least there they had a temporary police assistance booth. There will be nothing of the sort at the Santhe.' Ajji agreed. This was a problem. Then she had an idea. 'Why don't we ask Vishnu if he can spare Damu for a few hours? Damu can accompany you and help see that the children are all right.'

Damu was Vishnu Kaka's right-hand man. Everyone called him 'Mr Dependable'. He drove the car, cooked, looked after the fields, the accounts and made sure Vishnu Kaka was well cared for. Without him, Vishnu Kaka could not run the house or do anything in the fields. Vishnu Kaka's son lived with his family in Delhi and came only for holidays, so Damu was his real companion.

So it was that all seven children and Damu and Ajja were now ready to visit the Santhe. Damu had a plan. 'The Santhe is only two kilometres away. Why don't we walk, and let your Ajja go in the auto?' The children were horrified. Walk for two kilometres in the heat! 'It would be so boring too!' added Raghu. But Damu had made up his mind. 'Walk with me. I will tell you such wonderful stories that you will forget everything, even the heat!'

The children agreed. Then Meenu had a condition. 'It has to be a true story, Damu Anna!'

Damu was unfazed. 'I'll tell you a story about my sister. Do you know how I came to be "Mr Dependable"? I saw what happened to her once because she was forgetful and decided never to let that happen to me.'

So he started his story.

—

'Gita, where are you? I need you to run down to the store and get these medicines for me!' Gita's grandfather called out for her. Where was Gita? She was lying in bed, reading a book! For a long time she pretended not to have heard what her grandfather was saying. The book was just too exciting, and it was so hot outside, she really did not feel like stirring out of bed.

'Gita!' This time her mother's voice also called out to her. With a sigh, the girl got out of bed and went to see what needed to be done. Her grandfather handed her some money and said, 'I have a really bad headache since morning. Will you get these medicines for me?'

Gita took the money and set off for the store. On the way she passed by a sweet shop. Oh, what lovely gulab jamoons and laddoos and jalebis were displayed! She had to have some. Forgetting all about her errand she entered the shop and started tucking

into sweets. Soon a friend came by and joined her. The two girls ate and chatted for a really long time. Gita had forgotten all about her poor grandfather with his headache! Afternoon turned to evening, the medicine store shut for the day, when Gita remembered why she had stepped out of her house. When she hurried back home, how upset her grandfather was. 'When will you grow up, Gita, and become responsible?' he sighed and asked.

Gita felt really bad, but did she mend her ways? No, she remained the same forgetful person. When her mother told her to collect the clothes from the washing line outside, she remembered to do so only the next morning! By then, the clothes were soaked through all over again because of the overnight rains. Another day, she had to take her sister's lunchbox to the school. On the way she saw a circus was in town. All morning Gita spent wandering around the circus tents, watching the animals eating and training for their acts. It was only when she felt hungry herself did she look down at the lunchbox in her hand and realized her sister must have gone home by then, after spending a day in school without her lunch.

Another time her father, while rushing to get ready for work, asked if she could quickly iron his shirt.

Gita picked up the shirt and placed it on the ironing table next to the window. Just then the fruit vendor passed by with big, fat, juicy mangoes in his basket! Of course Gita forgot all about the hot iron sitting on the shirt and got engrossed in choosing the best mangoes to buy. Only when smoke started billowing out and the shirt had burnt as crisp as a toast did she look around and see what had happened. Her father was very upset indeed that day.

Some days after this incident, Gita came home from school and announced that the whole class was being taken for a picnic the next day. The teacher had asked each student to bring one food item from home which would be shared by all the children. Gita had chosen to bring sambar. She was very proud of her mother's tasty, tangy sambar and was eager to share it with her friends so they could taste it too. Gita's mother agreed to make a big pot of sambar for her to take to the picnic the next day, and that night Gita went to bed feeling very happy, dreaming about the exciting day ahead.

The next morning, her mother woke up early and started making the sambar. She boiled the dal, added the vegetables, coconut and all the spices, and set the pot boiling on the stove. Soon a delicious aroma wafted out from the pot and tickled Gita's nose as she lay sleeping in bed. Seeing her stir, her mother told her, 'Gita wake up now, dear. See the sambar is nearly done. I am going to the temple, so after some time just add five teaspoons of salt to it. Don't forget now, and wake up and get ready quickly!'

So saying she bustled off. Gita's grandmother, who was in the kitchen, heard all this and muttered to herself, 'When will my daughter-in-law learn that Gita can never remember anything. I'm sure the girl will forget to add the salt. Then she will be teased by all her friends. Better be careful.' So saying she went and added the salt in the pot.

Gita's grandfather was sitting on the veranda reading his newspaper. He remembered only too well the day he had spent with a headache waiting for Gita to return with the medicines which never came. 'Gita and remember something? That'll be the day!' he muttered, and went into the kitchen and added the salt in the sambar himself.

Gita's sister was combing her hair, ready to go off to school. She too recalled the day she had spent feeling hungry in school waiting for Gita to turn up with her lunchbox. Sure that Gita would forget about the salt and be laughed at by her friends, she quickly went into the kitchen and added five spoons of salt.

Gita's brother was brushing his teeth and hearing his mother's words to his sister, guessed she would forget about the salt. He dropped in a few spoons of salt into the pot and went off.

Gita's father was carefully ironing his own shirt. Like the others he too slipped into the kitchen and added salt to the pot of sambar.

By now Gita had woken up and wonder of wonders, remembered she needed to add the salt! So she too went and added five teaspoons as her mother had told her to do. By now her mother had returned and quickly poured the sambar into a big container and sent her daughter off for her picnic.

At the picnic spot the children had a wonderful time, roaming around and playing. Soon they were too hungry to do anything else. Out came the plates and spoons and all the containers filled to the brim with food. Plates were piled up with rice, chutneys, vegetables, pooris and all kinds of goodies. Everyone took large helpings of the sambar as Gita served it out. But no sooner than they put the first spoonful in their mouths, 'Blaagh! Horrible! Water!' everybody started shouting. Astonished, Gita wondered what was wrong, then gingerly tasted the rice and sambar on her own plate. It was disgusting! It was as if her mother had dredged out all the salt in the sea and added it to the sambar! Then Gita remembered, her mother had not added the salt, she had! So what had gone wrong?

That day everyone in Gita's house waited eagerly for her to get back from school and tell them about her wonderful outing. But what was this? She came trudging back, her face sad and tear-stained. What had happened? Gita burst out at them, 'Did anyone else add salt in the sambar?'

'I did!' said her grandmother.

'I did too!' said Grandfather.

'So did I!' said Father.

'Me too!' said her brother.

'And I!' said her sister.

They all looked at each other in dismay. No wonder Gita looked so sad. Her friends would have made her feel miserable about the salty sambar!

'Why did you all do it? Amma had told only me to do so!' Gita wept.

'Oh dear, you forget everything you are told to do, so we thought . . . perhaps . . . you wouldn't remember this time too,' all of them said sadly.

Now her mother pulled her close, wiped away her tears and said, 'See, all this happened because no one could believe you could do anything without being reminded many times about it. Promise you will be a careful, responsible girl from now on, and we will all trust you to do your work.'

Gita sniffed and nodded her head. She did become much more careful with her chores after that. And it took a lot of convincing, but her friends did come to her house for lunch one day to taste her mother's delicious cooking, especially her tasty, tangy sambar, and everyone agreed it was the best sambar they had ever eaten!

When the story was over, the children realized they were already at the Santhe. There were heaps of vegetables, sweets, flowers all around. There were goats, cows, buffaloes, fish, chicken and eggs for sale. The smell of nuts, cardamom and other spices hung in the air. It was unlike the fair where people had come to have a good time. Here a lot of business was taking place and everyone was buying and selling busily. The fruits and vegetables were very fresh.

The flowers looked as if they had just been plucked. Everyone was friendly.

The fruit vendor saw Ajja and said, 'Namaste Masterji. Oh! You have come with your grandchildren. It is nice to see everyone like this.' Then he gave each one a mango. When Ajja offered money, he wouldn't take it. He said, 'After all you were my masterji, my teacher. Can't I give seven mangoes as gifts to your grandchildren? They are from my garden, not that I purchased them.' The children were delighted at his warmth and kindness and returned home very happy that day.

How the Seasons Got Their Share

It was an unusually hot afternoon, and there was a power cut. The children were sitting in the house, wiping their foreheads and complaining. 'How do you stay without electricity, Ajja?' asked Raghu. 'In Mumbai, in our apartment, if ever the electricity goes off, the generator comes on automatically. We never even know that the power has gone.' Ajja looked around at the hot, sweaty faces, and said, 'All right, I'll show you a place which is as cool as an AC room. And it stays that way without any electricity! Come on everyone, grab a mat each and follow me.'

The children were intrigued. Ajja walked out into the garden, crossed it, right till the old neem tree that stood in a corner. Ajja told them to spread their mats under the tree and lie down. It was deliciously cool and comfortable under the tree. Everyone lay down and looked up at the gently moving leaves on the great branches over their heads. This was so much more fun than lying in a closed room! Ajja too had pulled up a comfortable old easy chair and was nodding off. After some time he said, 'This is why I love summer! What seasons do you children prefer?'

Immediately Anand said, 'I too like summer, because there is no school, and we can eat ice cream and mangoes. We can also go swimming.'

'I don't like summer, I like winter. You can wear colourful sweaters and eat different kinds of fruits. It is nice and cosy to be at home. You can drink hot soup and hot chocolate,' said Krishna.

'I don't like winter, I get ear pain. I prefer the rainy season. It is so nice when it rains and all the trees look so fresh and happy,' said Meenu.

'What about you, Raghu? Why are you silent?' Ajja asked.

'I like all the seasons, provided someone like you or Ajji is there with us.'

Ajja smiled. 'Well, each season has its own beauty and use. We could not do without even one.'

'How is that?' asked the children.

'Okay, I will tell you a story about what happened once when the seasons starting fighting with one another.'

—

God stepped back and looked happily at the Earth he had just created. He had filled it with humans, animals, trees and seas and it looked a wonderful place to be in. But something was missing. After thinking for a while, he called out to six brothers: Day, Night, Summer, Winter, Monsoon and Wind. He commanded the six brothers to go down to Earth and help the creatures there live comfortably and prosper. 'You must help the creatures on Earth grow food and live comfortably. I have divided Time into two parts—twenty-four hours and 365 days. You must share this among yourselves so that people on Earth get all that they need.' The six brothers nodded obediently, but no sooner was God's back turned than they all started quarrelling!

Everyone wanted a big share of the time available to spend on Earth. Day and Night decided each would get twenty-four hours each. But the seasons

kept quarrelling. Summer was the eldest, so he said, 'I will be on Earth for 365 days first!'

Rain said, 'If I don't show up all the water on Earth will disappear, so I will come next.'

Winter said, 'After the rains I help trees to flower, so I will come in the third year.'

Poor Wind was the youngest and no one paid him any attention, so he got the last year.

So life started on Earth. For twenty-four hours at a time there was Day, then twenty-four hours of Night. Summer continued for one whole year. While in the beginning the heat helped the crops to grow, soon it became too hot for anyone to do anything. All the water dried up and there was great discomfort. The people of Earth pleaded with Summer to stop and he had to leave before his year was up.

Then it was the turn of Rain. When he started pouring down, how happy everyone was to get some respite from the year's summer. But soon the lakes, ponds, rivers, oceans all filled to the brim and started overflowing. The crops got spoilt in the rain and there was nothing for anyone to eat. When people prayed for him to stop, he had to step aside and make way for Winter.

With relief people greeted Winter. Now there was neither the scorching sun nor the pouring rain. But when day after day went by like this they started falling sick from the constant cold, the plants started dying because of less sunshine. At the people's request Winter too had to stop.

Now it was the turn of Wind. Within a few days of his constant huffing and puffing people were scared to step out anywhere. Trees were uprooted, the roofs of houses went flying and there was chaos all around.

The brothers realized what they had done would displease God mightily. So they decided to change their ways. Instead of each taking a year they decided to share one year among each other. But again, Wind being the youngest got left out and got no time for himself. He sat in a corner and sulked.

During summer time people sowed their crops and waited for the rains. Rain came with loads of water but there was no wind to distribute it equally. Some parts of Earth got buckets of rain and other parts none at all. Now everyone realized that Wind was as important. They called out to him and he finally agreed to do his work. But he did not get a separate time for himself. He was allowed to blow all through the year. So in Summer he blew and helped reduce the heat. During rains he blew the clouds from one place to another and took rainwater everywhere. In Winter he still blew and made it even colder!

Day and Night too learnt from the four brothers and decided to divide the twenty-four hours equally. So one half was Day and the other was Night.

Now everyone on Earth was happy, and the six brothers learnt to share their time.

―

By this time Ajji called from the house, 'The electricity is back. You can come inside now.' But the children were happy to remain outside and enjoy the breeze.

The Island of Statues

One day, early in the morning, the children heard a loud voice booming outside. 'Where are your grandchildren? I have come to take them to my place.' They went running out to see a very tall man with twinkling eyes and a grey beard sipping coffee with their grandparents. He wore a crisp white dhoti and shirt and a black cap. His smile was so charming that the children instantly warmed to him. Ajji was shaking her head and saying, 'Rehmat, there's no way Peerambhi can manage four children. Take them out for the day, why do you want to have them over for the night?' But the man called Rehmat shook his head. 'No no, I will take them for a night's stay.

My Usman is a great cook and will look after everything. Peerambhi will not be troubled at all.'

Ajji saw the questioning look on the children's faces and explained, 'This is Rehmat. A long time back when your Ajja was a schoolteacher, he was your Ajja's student. He lives a little far away now. He has a mango grove there, and a large house. All his children live abroad. In his house there's a large library of books and what can be called a mini zoo with goats, cows, peacocks, pigeons and parrots. He wants to have you all over for the night. I'm sure you'll have a good time, but do you want to go?'

'He also tells very beautiful stories,' added Ajja.

Rehmat grinned and said, 'Masterji, don't exaggerate. I started reading children's storybooks only after my grandchildren were born. Then I remembered the stories you used to tell us in school and passed off some of them as my own.' He turned to the children and said, 'So what do you think, kids, will you come with me? I will show you a different part of the village.'

Everyone was thinking, when Raghu spoke up, 'Can we bring our friends with us?'

'Oh, you mean Vishnu Kaka's grandchildren? Of course they can come. The more the merrier.

Peerambhi will love having so many children in the house.'

Raghu ran to Sharan's house to give the news.

Rehmat Chacha, as everyone called him, had brought a jeep and soon all seven had packed a change and their toothbrushes and piled into it. Rehmat Chacha's house was far, about thirty kilometres away, and on the way they had to go through a forest. The road cutting through the forest was narrow and winding. Tall trees stood on both sides. It was a dark, scary place. Suma looked around nervously and said, 'Will anyone ever cut down these trees and widen the road?'

Rehamt Chacha shook his head. 'Oh no, the villagers will never allow it. We love our trees and try to see as few are cut down as possible. Trees must never be cut unnecessarily. Do you want to listen to a story about a kingdom that cut down all its trees?'

Of course the children did, so Rehmat Chacha began his story.

Once there was a beautiful verdant green island. It had forests filled with huge trees, waterfalls gushing with clear blue water and mountains where there was a quarry of a unique kind of stone. This stone was valued for its attractive white colour. It was also easy to turn into sculptures.

The island had been ruled for years by a king who was now old. He looked after his people well and loved the natural beauty of his land above all. His closest friend was a sculptor called Amar. Amar too loved the land more than anything else. He had a school where students from far and wide came to learn the art of creating sculptures out of stone. But Amar had one odd condition for the students who studied in his school. He insisted they bring their own supply of stone! Only for their final sculpture were they allowed to use a piece of stone from the island's quarry. Many grumbled at this rule. After all, dragging tons of stone to an island in the middle of a sea was difficult, but Amar was adamant.

Once his king asked him the reason for this condition, and this is what wise old Amar had to say: 'This stone and indeed everything on this remarkable land of ours is a gift which we need to preserve. Unless we use it wisely how will we be able to save this quarry for our children? If we start using the stones and woods from trees without a thought they will soon finish and then we will be left with an empty, barren land. This is why I insist that students learning the craft of sculpting bring their own material, and only when they make their final piece of art can they use this unique stone from our land.'

The king applauded this thought in his mind and let Amar run his school the way he wanted. But then a day came when the king, now very old, died, and his son took over the throne. Rajdip, the new king, wanted to do everything differently from his father. He started changing many laws. One day he remembered the art school and went to visit it. There he saw the students working on their sculptures. But his ministers whispered to him the complaints that other students, who had not wanted to bring their own material, had made about Amar's rule.

Rajdip realized that if he lifted the rule then many more people would come to study in the school. Their fees would add to the prosperity of the island and in addition they would create lovely works of art that could be used to beautify the towns. He ordered Amar to step down as the teacher and brought someone else to run the school.

Soon the island was full of students chipping away on the stone. Their demands increased the mining at the quarry. They created large sculptures which now needed to get transported back to the town. Trees were cut down to make carts and to clear roads. Without trees to provide wood for their boats the fishermen of the island could not go out to sea. They started fishing near the land and got into fights frequently with one another. New houses were not strong as both wood and stone were scarce. It was difficult for farmers to make good ploughs and so farming suffered. All the mining created so much of pollution that plants started dying out, diseases spread, and the tinkling waterfalls fell silent as water became scarce. The climate changed, it became hotter and drier. Soon there were famines and the once beautiful green island was reduced to a wasteland of weeds and scrub.

Rajdip's wishes of lining his capital city and palace with giant sculptures was fulfilled. Each student in the art school made a beautiful huge statue and gifted it to him. Soon these statues filled up the entire kingdom. Where once there were deep forests and blue rivers and streams, the island was a barren land now. The forests were gone. The rivers had turned into dirty trickles of water. The climate had become hot and dusty as the rains no longer

came on time. People started leaving the island. The houses, schools and palaces slowly fell silent as they were abandoned. With time, everyone forgot about this island. Many, many years later when explorers landed here, they found hundreds of statues strewn all over a bare island: a land destroyed by the king's greed.

———

How everyone enjoyed the story. The rest of the journey was spent in each one acting out a part from the story, with Rehmat Chacha taking on the role of the wise old king. Cheerful and at the same time very hungry, they soon reached their new friend's house.

It was a huge rambling place. Peerambhi was waiting for them at the doorstep. She told Usman to make a sherbet of mango, and Shurukumbha (a kind of kheer) for lunch. There was also paratha, biriyani, and all kinds of mouth-watering dishes which Usman was more than happy to prepare. After lunch they roamed around the house, examined the books in the library and the many awards Rehmat Chacha had received for his innovative skills in agriculture.

The Kingdom of Fools

'Rehmat Chacha, you must be very intelligent. You know so much about farming, fishing, stories and so many other things,' Meenu remarked that night as they sat outside, watching the fireflies twinkling all around them.

But Rehmat Chacha did not agree. 'No, not really. There is plenty I still don't know. In fact, one can never stop learning. Knowledge is the only thing it's good to be greedy about.'

It was a beautiful, clear night. The moon and stars shone in the black, unpolluted sky. Peerambhi was feeling very happy. Her own grandchildren lived so far away, and came to visit her only once in two or three years. After so long the house was filled with laughter and young voices. She was too frail to do much, and was enjoying sitting among them and talking to them.

Soon they started yawning and rubbing their eyes. But no one was going to bed till Rehmat Chacha told another story!

———

There once lived a king who was very intelligent. He looked down upon anyone he thought was dull. He was also very proud about the fact that in his kingdom there were no stupid people.

Some distance away from the capital city lived an old teacher. He had taught the young prince, who was a sweet-natured boy once but had turned into a proud, rude king. Many people told him about the king's boastful nature, and the teacher decided to teach his old pupil a lesson he would never forget. He called his three best and brightest students, Harish, Mahesh and Umesh, and said, 'We need to bring that proud king down a peg or two. I want the three of you to teach him a lesson and make him realize the foolishness of his pride.'

The three students set off for the capital. Harish walked to the city market. There he met a man selling betel leaves.

'How much for these leaves?' he asked.

'Ten rupees for two hundred leaves,' the shopkeeper replied.

'Here are ten rupees. Give me only twenty-five leaves. My servant will come and collect the balance one hundred and seventy-five leaves.'

The betel-leaf seller agreed and gave Harish twenty-five leaves.

Harish now strolled into another shop where beautiful shawls were being sold.

'How much for this?' he asked, fingering the best shawl in the shop.

'Two hundred rupees,' answered the shopkeeper.

'Here are twenty-five rupees. You can collect the remaining hundred and seventy-five rupees from the paan shop there,' Harish said, handing the shopkeeper a note.

'Please give the person who brings this note the remaining one hundred and seventy-five,' the note read. The shawl shop owner sent his servant with the note to the paan shop to verify if indeed this was true. The other shopkeeper glanced at the note and said, 'Yes, it's true. I have to give him one hundred and seventy-five more. Come back in half an hour—I will count and keep them ready.'

The servant returned and whispered to his master: indeed, the betel-leaf seller was going to give them the remaining one hundred and seventy-five. Harish walked out with the shawl. After half an hour, when the servant went to collect the money, he found the shopkeeper busy counting out leaves. 'Hundred seventy-three, hundred seventy-four, hundred seventy-five . . . There you go, here are the rest of the leaves.'

The servant was amazed at being handed a sheaf of paan leaves instead of money. He called his master and the two shopkeepers started arguing loudly. Slowly they realized that someone had made fools of them. They rushed to complain to the king.

The king was surprised to hear how a stranger had tricked the clever shopkeepers of his kingdom. He decided to keep a lookout for this man.

The next day, Mahesh walked into the royal carpenter's shop. It was the middle of the afternoon and the carpenter was in his shop tinkering with some strange-looking instruments. Mahesh was well dressed, so the carpenter thought he was rich.

Enthusiastically he started showing off his various creations. He picked up a large wooden lock and said, 'See this? Will you believe that with this you can even lock a man? Place the person's head between the lock and a pillar and turn the key, and there, the man cannot escape.'

Mahesh pretended to be sceptical. 'Go on now. How can a simple wooden lock do such a thing? I don't believe you.' The carpenter got very agitated. 'But it's true, sir. I am the king's carpenter after all. I create many complicated instruments for the state. Here, let me show you.' Saying this, he put the lock around his neck and the nearest pillar and turned the key. 'Now, see? I cannot even move my neck! Are you convinced? Now just turn the key the other way to set me free.'

But Mahesh would not turn the key. He just stood there laughing. Then he coolly picked up the key and walked out of the shop. The carpenter could only shout at Mahesh's retreating back. 'You villain! Come back! Set me free!' But it was in vain. Mahesh had fooled him.

Later that evening the king came to know of this other stranger who had duped his clever carpenter. He was worried. Who were these men, making the brightest people of his kingdom look stupid? He decided to go around the city in disguise to try and catch them.

As he walked near the city gates, he found a man sitting there with a heap of mangoes, waiting for someone to buy them. The fruit seller had chosen the loneliest spot, so the king was suspicious.

'Why are you selling your fruits here?' he asked.

The fruit seller was actually Umesh. He pretended to look nervously around and answered in a whisper, 'Sir, I have heard there are some clever cheats roaming around the kingdom wanting to cheat us and our clever king. I have heard one will be walking by this way soon, so I am waiting here hoping to catch him and deliver him to the king.'

The king was surprised that this person knew all about the clever gang of cheats.

'Have you seen him before?'

'Yes, sir. I know the gang. The person who is coming today is the chief.'

'What does he look like?'

'He is tall, hefty and very cruel.'

'Is there any way I can see him?' the king asked excitedly.

'Sir, the best way is to hide. As soon as he comes, I will whistle, and you can see him.'

But at that spot there was neither a tree nor any rock behind which the king could hide. Then the fruit seller held out a sack. 'Hide in this, sir,' he suggested. 'I will keep you next to me, and anyone will think it is a sack of mangoes.'

The king agreed and hopped into the sack. Quickly Umesh tied it and walked away, laughing. The king soon realized he had been tricked. But he was tied in the sack and could do nothing. Many hours later, when his soldiers came looking for him, he managed to wriggle around in the sack and attract their attention. How embarrassed he was, to be set free by them! He also knew now that he and the people of his kingdom were not as clever as he loved to boast. He realized his mistake.

The king's old teacher came to the court and explained how his three students had tricked everyone. Harish, Mahesh and Umesh apologized for their actions. And the king promised to rule his kingdom with wisdom and humility.

The Story of Silk

No sooner had the children gotten over their excitement of the visit to Rehmat Chacha's house than Ajji sprung another surprise. There was a wedding in the village! Having attended some village weddings earlier, the children knew what to expect. Here, it was not like the city where you went at a certain time printed on the card, gave your present, ate and came back. In the village, everyone was invited, whether your name was on a card or not. And not only were you expected to come as early as possible, you were also expected to pitch in and help the host! So Damu was seen rushing off in the jeep to pick up guests from the railway station. Rehmat Chacha was in charge of providing fresh vegetables from his farm. Ajji was herding a group of women into the kitchen and telling them what to do. Ajja was supervising the cleanliness and had stocked up on big bottles of phenyl and other cleansers. And Vishnu Kaka was dressed in his best, most spotless dhoti and kurta and was looking after the guests.

Ajji told the children to wear their nicest clothes and come to the venue. Krishna, always careful of the way she looked, wore her pretty blue silk frock. Ajji noticed and said, 'Krishna, remember to be careful. There will be a lot of people and food there. Don't get your clothes dirty.'

Krishna promised to be careful. Soon Ajji disappeared into the kitchen which was lined with people chopping and stirring and cooking. Outside, guests were pouring in and Vishnu Kaka was making sure everyone was served breakfast. Ajja was seen hurrying about with a bottle of phenyl in his hand. Rehmat Chacha was taking care of the flower decorations while Peerambhi Chachi was stringing piles of garlands. Children were playing all over the place, film songs played on the mike and there was a happy chaos everywhere.

After the wedding, during lunch time, while eating sweet pancakes of chiroti with badam milk, someone jostled Krishna and a big puddle of milk fell on her dress. She was grief-striken. Ajji consoled her. 'Don't cry. Silk can be washed and made to look just like new. That is the wonderful thing about it.' Seeing Krishna's tear-stained face she said, 'Today when we go home I will tell you the story of how silk was made for the first time.' That made Krishna happy. That night, though Ajji was tired, she still told the children the story of silk.

———

Did you know that silk was discovered in China?

A long time ago, in a tiny village in China, there lived a poor girl belonging to a weaver's family. One day, the emperor was passing through the village and saw her working in the fields. He noticed her red cheeks and rosebud-like mouth, her proud bearing and her rough, work-worn hands, which meant she worked very hard through the year. He immediately fell in love with her and though he was much older, decided to marry her.

The girl married the ruler of the land and went to live in his palace as his beloved queen. But she was unhappy. She had grown up in the wide open spaces of the countryside, and now she was confined to a palace, magnificent though it was. She was used to working from dawn to night without a moment's rest, but now she had many servants to take care of her needs and did not know how to fill her time. In the village she had been surrounded by family and friends who exchanged news and gossip as they worked, but in the palace it was quiet and no one spoke out of turn. The emperor noticed his new wife was sad and tried his best to make her happy. He bought her grand clothes, jewels and artefacts, threw elaborate parties, hired the best musicians of the land to amuse her. Yet she was sad.

One afternoon, the empress sat under a mulberry bush in her garden, lost in her thoughts about her village. She slowly sipped hot water from a cup. Staring up at the blue sky, the girl remembered the birds that flew over her village. Then, sighing softly to herself, she picked up her cup to take another sip. But what was this! A cocoon from the mulberry bush had dropped into the hot water! Her first thought was to throw away the water and the cocoon. But then she took a closer look, and she saw some threads peeping out from the cocoon. Where

had they come from? She pulled the threads. They were thin, strong and shiny. She kept pulling and a long line of thread came out. Now the empress had a great idea. She would take the thread from many cocoons and weave soft, strong cloth from it!

She called her servants and everyone got to work. They took cocoons out of the mulberry tree, dropped them in hot water, and removed the thread. They gathered a fair amount of yarn. Then the queen ordered a special weaving machine and wove the first piece of cloth using this new thread. Thus silk, the best and brightest form of cloth, was weaved.

The manufacture of silk spread throughout China. It was the cloth that only royalty could wear, and was much in demand in lands as far away as Rome. The route through which silk was traded between China and Europe through Asia was called the Silk Route.

Now that the Chinese had learnt how to make silk cloth, they did not want to share this knowledge with anyone in the world. Generations of Chinese royalty were sworn never to reveal the secret to anyone. When princesses got married and went away to far-off lands, they were not allowed to tell anyone in their new home how silk was made.

Many, many years later, when a clever princess was leaving her house on getting married, as was the custom, her bags were searched carefully to check that she did not carry anything that would help her make silk. This princess had been weaving silk from a young age and wanted to continue to do so wherever she went. She had hidden the cocoons in her long, elaborate hairdo. No one thought of looking there! When she went to her husband's house, she took out these cocoons from her hair and started gathering silk thread! In this way, legend goes, the knowledge of how to make silk left China.

When Yama Called

One day, Ajji was sitting and stitching a tear in an old sari. The children came and sat around her. The holidays were finishing and they did not want to be away from her for even a minute. Meenu and Krishna affectionately put their arms around Ajji's neck and said, 'Ajji, why do you have so many wrinkles on your hand?'

'Because I am old,' said Ajji.

'Why do old people have wrinkles?' asked Meenu.

Ajji took off her glasses, which she wore only when sewing or reading, and said, 'Once upon a time I was also young like you. My skin was smooth and shiny. My hair was long and black. I had very sharp eyes and an excellent memory. But as I grew older, everything changed slowly.'

'We will all grow old like this one day, shan't we?' asked Divya.

'Yes, every living being gets old. It is a part of life. Come, I will tell you a story about old age.'

Many, many years ago, there lived, in a little town, a man named Arun. He was a merchant and though not very rich, he lived comfortably enough. He had a large family of brothers, sisters, wife and children. He looked after them well, and in whatever way he could, he also helped out the poor people in the town. He built rest houses for travellers, and in these there were dining halls where anyone could come and have a good, wholesome meal for very little money.

One day, while returning home from work, he happened to pass by one such rest house. It had a veranda where people stopped and rested. Sitting there, looking tired and hungry, was a stranger. He was a tall man. His clothes were travel-stained and showed that he had come from afar. With him was his horse, looking as tired and hungry as its master.

Seeing them, Arun's kind heart melted, and he went up to speak to the man.

'Where have you come from, my brother?' he asked. 'Why don't you step inside for a hot meal and some rest?'

The man looked up, gave a smile and said, 'The rest house is very popular. There is no room for me, and the dining hall is full too. I will wait here for a while, then be on my way. I'm sure I will find another place to serve me some food down the road.'

Arun would not hear of this. The thought that someone was going away without food and rest was too much for him. He insisted on the man coming back to his house with him. There he invited the traveller to share a meal with his family. The man was served lovingly and ate his fill.

While he sat eating, the man noticed that Arun was sometimes a bit absent-minded. It was as if something was on his mind, and he was worried. Once they had finished eating and had washed up, the traveller rose to leave. He thanked Arun for his kindness, then said, 'If you don't mind me asking, sir, I could not help but notice that you were a bit worried. I know I am a stranger to you, but perhaps it would help lighten your burden if you shared your worries with me.'

But Arun only smiled and shook his head. He did not want to share his thoughts with the stranger.

Then the man said, 'Perhaps if I show you who I really am you will confide in me.'

And in a trice the man changed. He was no longer a tired traveller, but a god, resplendent in shimmering clothes with a crown on his head. His horse changed into a buffalo, and the man introduced himself, 'I am Yama, the lord of death. Now will you tell me what's wrong?'

Seeing this Arun nearly fainted. The lord of death had just shared a meal with him! 'Wh-what are you doing on earth, my lord?' he gasped.

Yama smiled and said, 'Oh, I like coming here once in a while, and seeing what everyone is doing. So, what's bothering you?'

Arun replied, 'You see, I need to grow my business more, but today I was not feeling very well. If anything happened to me, who would look after my large family?'

Yama nodded seriously. 'Don't worry, child,' he comforted. 'I have seen what a hard-working, kind-hearted person you are. You invited me home and let me have a meal with you, knowing me only to be a tired and weary traveller. I will do one thing. when it is time for you to leave the earth and come with me, like all living things have to do one day, I will not come all of a sudden. I will let you know many days in advance, so you can prepare yourself and your affairs for the time you have to go away with me.'

Arun bowed to the lord in gratitude when he heard this and Yama vanished.

Years went by. Arun became an old man. His business had grown many times over, his children and brothers and sisters were all well looked after. He had few worries left.

One night, he went to bed and had a dream. He saw Yama standing in front of him. Yama was holding out a hand towards him and saying, 'Come, it is time for you to go away with me.'

Arun was terrified. 'But lord, you had promised you would tell me days in advance before I would die. How can I come away right now?'

A small smile appeared on Yama's lips. 'But child, I did give you a warning. I made your hair turn white, I made your back stoop with age, I made your

teeth fall out one by one. These were all indications that your time on earth is coming to an end.'

'But these things happen to every man and woman! How could these be a warning only for me!'

Yama nodded, 'Yes, they do happen to everyone. And when they do, men and women should start getting ready to meet me. Life has to come to an end, there is no escape.'

Arun now understood. He looked back on his days and realized that even without meaning to, he had been preparing for this. His children looked after his business, all his work was done. There was nothing stopping him from going away with his old friend Yama.

He climbed on the buffalo behind Yama. 'Let's go,' he said. And off Yama went away with him.

The Unending Story

Today Ajja, Ajji and Vishnu Kaka were all feeling sad. The children's holidays were nearly over, and it was nearing the time when they would go back to their homes. For three weeks the houses had echoed with their laughter, games and quarrels. Now all would be quiet once again, till they returned for the next holiday. The children too were feeling sad, and had gathered around their grandparents in a tight little group. Raghu the eldest said, 'We had more fun this holiday then we've ever had. Even more than when we visited Disneyland. And it was all because of the stories.'

Ajja said, 'When I was still working as a schoolteacher, I always found it was so much easier to get my students' attention when I told the lessons in the form of stories.'

Anand said, 'I find it really boring to read history from a book. But if you tell us the stories from history I'm sure we will remember everything!'

Everyone now turned their bright eyes on Ajji. 'How can you tell us only one story even on this last day, Ajji! We want more!' they clamoured.

But Ajji shook her head. 'If you eat only pickles and laddoos will you be healthy? Stories are like that. You can't spend all your time listening to stories. Then it will be boring. Like the unending story that a king once had to hear.'

'I want a story! And that's an order!' shouted King Pratap Singh of Mayanagar. King Pratap was only fifteen years old, and still a boy at heart. He didn't like being a king much, because he was supposed to be doing serious things like keeping the law, listening to his people's problems and all kinds of dreary things like that. The only part he liked about being a ruler was that everyone had to obey him! How he loved giving orders and making all kinds of demands. And what he loved the most was listening to stories! Every day, he insisted on listening to at least ten stories. All the storytellers in his kingdom lined up at his court. They told him funny stories, scary stories, magical stories and anything else that came to their mind. King Pratap listened to all with rapt attention.

He loved stories and storytellers so much that whenever he heard a good tale he would shower the teller with gold, silver and all kinds of wonderful presents. His ministers sighed and shook their heads and tried to explain, 'Your Majesty, stories are all very well, but you should be listening to them after your work is done! Your people need you to do so many things for them. If you spend all your time wrapped up in fantasies, how will the land prosper?'

But King Pratap paid no attention. It was stories he wanted, and stories he would get. But how long could the people provide him with stories? Soon the tales began to dry out. Some tried to cleverly tell him ones they had related long back, but Pratap was sharp as a needle. 'I've heard that one! Off with his head for repeating a story!'

Oh, how his ministers had to plead with him to pardon the culprits!

Finally, disgusted with all the storytellers in his land, the king announced, 'I want someone to tell me a story that will go on and on, till I ask him to stop. Anyone who can do this will get half my kingdom as a prize!'

His ministers were even more horrified at this. Half the kingdom to some woolly-headed writer and teller of stories! How horrible! They all tried to show the king the foolishness of his ways, but he was adamant. A story that lasted for days, even weeks, was what he wanted and that was that!

Soon a long line of men and women appeared at his court. Each one wanted to win the big prize. But none of their stories were good enough for King Pratap.

'Boring!' he shouted at some.

'Rubbish!' he yelled at others.

'Cock and bull!' he bellowed at yet others.

Meanwhile work on the kingdom's affairs had come to a stop. All the ministers were sitting wringing their hands and wondering how to bring back their king to solving all the important issues. Finally the chief minister, who was wise and clever, had an idea.

The next day, a scruffy, crazy-looking man turned up at the court. His hair was in a mess, his clothes were half torn and on his feet he wore torn shoes from which his toes stuck out. He marched up to the palace and demanded to be given an audience with the king. The guards sighed and let him in. They were used to having all kinds of characters turning up at the gates wanting to tell stories to the king.

The old man was admitted into the king's chamber. There he made himself comfortable, drank a huge jug of water, and without introducing himself, started his story:

'This story begins in a humble farmer's field. The farmer had toiled days and weeks and months and grown a bumper crop of sugar cane. He sold the sugar cane to the nearby sugar factory and they made sacks and sacks of sugar out of it. Everyone was so happy. All this sugar would be sold in the markets and make everyone very rich! That year their children would get nice new clothes, their stores would be full of food and their wives would be very happy with them!

'Now all that sugar had to be stored and kept carefully till the sacks could be taken to the market to sell. The factory people poured the sugar into many sacks and lugged them into a storeroom. In the storeroom who would you find, but a colony of ants. They had decided that building their house near such a ready supply of their favourite food was a very good idea, and were always on the lookout for new batches of sugar to be stored there.

'No sooner had the sacks been kept than the lines of ants marched up to them. They found little holes to make their way in and the first ant went into the first bag of sugar, took one sugar crystal and went back.

'The next ant went into the bag and took a crystal and returned home.

'Another went into the bag and took a crystal and returned home.

'Yet another went into the bag and took a crystal and returned home . . .'

So on and on the storyteller droned. King Pratap found he had nearly dozed off, the day had passed by and he was still listening to the same story.

'Stop! Stop!' he ordered. 'I will listen to the rest of the story tomorrow.'

The next morning the old man turned up as usual and started from where he had left off the previous day. 'Yesterday I was telling you how the ants came and picked up the sugar crystals. Now the next ant went towards the bag of sugar and took a crystal and went back home. Another went and took a sugar crystal and returned home. Another ant . . .'

The story went on and on like this. Lunch and dinner passed by but nothing new happened. By now King Pratap was bursting with rage. How dare anyone tell him such a boring story? 'What kind of a story is this?' he complained. 'What will happen next? What happened to the farmer?'

But the old man only smiled and said, 'Have patience, Your Majesty. That year the yield was very good and there were thousands of bags of sugar. I have to tell you how the ants collected all the sugar.'

'Oh stop! Stop!' Pratap shouted. 'Stop this boring story at once!'

The man now stood up and said, 'Fine, if you are ordering me to stop, I have won the prize. Give me half your kingdom!'

The king was in a dilemma now. He had announced a competition and prize no doubt, but could he honestly give away half the kingdom to this crazy-looking storyteller with his boring tales?

As he sat pondering, the man grinned even wider, and took off his dirty robe, rubbed off the dirt from his face and shook back his shaggy white hair. Everyone was astonished. Why, this was the chief minister himself!

'Don't worry, Your Majesty,' the minister told his overjoyed king. 'I did not want half your kingdom. I only wanted to show you how you were wrong to neglect your work and listen to stories night and day. Your people deserve a good king, someone who will work hard to look after them; someone who will think of his own happiness only once his people are happy. That's what good kings do, you know. Not just giving orders and enjoying yourself.'

Poor Pratap looked ashamed at this. Yes, he had been an extremely selfish king. From now on, story time was only at night, after all his work was done.

⁓

So that was how the summer holidays ended. Everyone packed their bags and reached the station. Their mothers had come to take them back home. Ajja, Ajji, Vishnu Kaka, Damu, Rehmat Chacha—everyone had come to see them off. No one felt like leaving Ajji's side and Meenu kept hugging her till she had to board the train.

Soon the train puffed out of the station. The children leaned out to wave their goodbyes. Slowly Shiggaon got left behind. But the children would continue to remember their Ajja and Ajji and everyone else, and all the stories, which would remain with them forever. And they would be back, during the next summer holidays, when they would hear so many more . . .

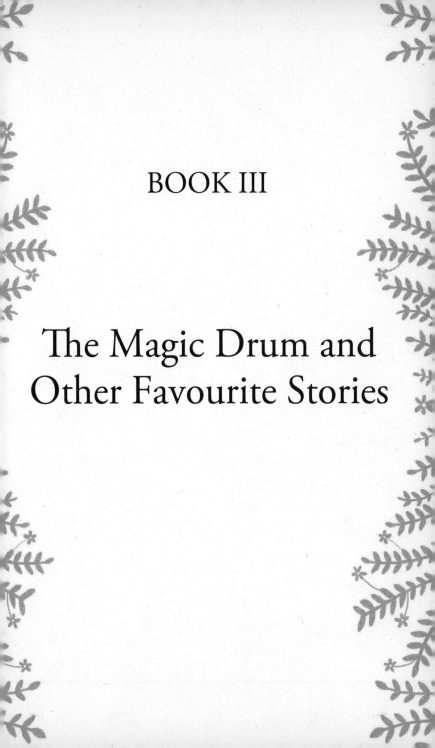

BOOK III

The Magic Drum and Other Favourite Stories

The Supermen

The men of Suvarnanagari were very lazy. They only liked to gossip and tell each other tall tales. As soon as the sun rose, the men would tuck into a hearty breakfast and start gathering in groups. Then they would spend the rest of the day telling each other impossible stories. They came back home only at lunch and dinner time.

Suvarnanagari had fertile land all around it, and if the men had spent even a little time in the fields, they would have reaped wonderful crops. But as they did nothing, all responsibilities ended up on the shoulders of the women, who had to slave the whole day. They cooked, cleaned, sent the children to school, worked in the fields, took the crops to the market—in short, they did everything. One day, the tired women got together and decided the men needed to be taught a lesson. Someone suggested writing to the king, who was known to be just and kind, about their problem. So a letter was written and sent off. The women went back to their work, but kept a sharp lookout to see if the king would send any help. But many days passed, and slowly the women began to lose hope. After all, why would the king of such a vast empire be concerned about the plight of a few women in a tiny village like theirs?

A month passed by and soon it was a full-moon night. The men ate their dinners and, because it was so beautiful and well-lit outside, they gathered again to chat and boast. That night, they were trying to prove to one another that they were capable of performing the most impossible tasks. As they sat talking, and the stories flew around, a tall and handsome stranger joined them. Seeing his noble features and intelligent eyes, each man wanted to prove himself better than the others and impress him.

One said, 'I knew the map of our kingdom even before I left my mother's womb. As soon as I was born, I ran to the capital and met the king. My mother had such trouble bringing me back home!'

Everyone was impressed with this story. But not to be outdone, a second man said, 'So what is so great about that? When I was just a day old, I could ride a horse. I sat on a big horse and rode all the way to the king's palace. He received me with a lot of love and we had the most delicious breakfast together.' At the thought of food, everyone got dreamy-eyed and the story was greeted with a round of applause.

Now a third man said, 'Huh! That's nothing. I sat on an elephant when I was a week old and had lunch with the king in his palace.'

Before the admiring murmurs could die down, a fourth one said, 'I was a month old when I flew like a bird and landed in the king's garden. He picked me up lovingly and even let me sit with him on his throne.'

While everyone seemed to be awed by these stories, the stranger spoke up. 'Do you four men know the king very well?'

'Of course we do!' they replied together. 'Our king knows and loves us. In fact, he is proud to have supernatural beings like us in his kingdom.'

The stranger looked thoughtful. 'That makes my task so much easier . . . You see, I work in the king's court. Some time back, the king had called four supermen to the city in order to repair a large hole in the city walls. As you know, we use the largest, toughest stones for building these walls, and they could be lifted and put in place only by these supermen. The four asked to be paid in gold bars and the king gave them the money. But that night itself they disappeared from the palace. I have been wandering the kingdom ever since, looking for them. The king has ordered me to find the four men and bring them back to the capital to finish the work. They will also have to return the gold they ran away with. It looks like my search has finally ended. I will take you four to the king, along with the gold you stole from him . . . And I shall be the rich one now.'

By the time the stranger finished telling this amazing story, the men's faces had turned ashen. What trouble had their lies landed them in? Together they dived at the stranger's feet.

'Save us!' they wailed. 'Those were all lies. We are just a bunch of lazy men. If you forget our stories, we promise to stop telling lies and do some honest work.'

The stranger smiled. 'So be it. I will tell the king there are no supermen in this village. Only hard-working, ordinary men and women.'

That night itself he left the village, and the women were sure they saw a happy twinkle in his eyes as he rode away on a handsome, white horse, fit to belong to the king's stables!

A Fair Deal

Himakar and Seetapati were two young men living in neighbouring villages. Once, a fair was being held nearby, and they set off from their homes hoping to do some business there. Himakar filled his sack with some cheap cotton, overlaid it with a layer of fine wool and, slinging the sack over his shoulder, set off for the fair. Seetapati collected wild leaves from some bushes, put a layer of fine betel leaves on top and made his way too to the fair.

On the way, both stopped to rest under a big tree and got talking. 'I have the finest wool in these parts in my sack. They come from the most special sheep,' boasted Himakar.

'I have the best betel leaves in my sack. They are so soft they melt in your mouth. Usually I don't sell them, but this time I need the money, so I am going to the fair to sell them without telling anyone,' said Seetapati.

Quickly the two crooks struck a deal. They would exchange their goods and, since wool was more expensive, Seetapati would pay Himakar an extra rupee. But Seetapati had no money on him. So after agreeing to pay Himakar the rupee later, the two made their way home, secretly laughing at the other's folly.

However, it did not take long for them to discover that they had been duped.

The very next day, Himakar landed up at Seetapati's door and yelled, 'You cheat! Give me my rupee at least.'

Seetapati was drawing muddy water from his well and was unperturbed by Himakar's words. 'Of course I will pay,' he said. 'But first help me find the treasure lying at the bottom of this well. If we find it, we can divide it.' Both were soon hard at work and there was no more talk of wool or betel leaves. Himakar went inside the well where he would fill with muddy water the bucket Seetapati lowered to him. Seetapati would

then pull it up. With each bucket Seetapati pulled up he exclaimed, 'Oh, no treasure here. Try again.'

This went on for a few hours. It started getting dark and Himakar realized that Seetapati was using him as free labour to clean his well. There was no treasure. He was sure that if he stayed much longer, Seetapati would abandon him in the well for good. So he gave a loud shout, 'Here is the treasure! Watch out, it is heavy.' Seetapati was amazed that there really was treasure hidden in the well. He pulled hard, and as soon as he pulled up the bucket, he threw away the rope so that Himakar could not come up. But what, or rather, who did he find in the bucket but Himakar, covered in mud.

They started fighting again.

'You tried to cheat me!'

'You were going to leave me in the well!'

Soon it got too dark to argue and they left for their homes. But Himakar was not one to give up. He arrived at Seetapati's house after a few days, demanding his one rupee. Seetapati saw him coming and told his wife, 'I will pretend to be dead. You start crying loudly. Himakar will then have to give up trying to get the money from me.'

But Himakar was clever. As soon as he heard Seetapati's wife wailing, he understood the trick being played on him and rushed out to gather the villagers. 'My friend has died,' he shouted. 'Let's take his body for cremation.'

Seetapati's wife got scared. 'No, no, go away. I will arrange for the cremation myself,' she said.

But the villagers thought she was too grief-stricken to know what she was saying and carried Seetapati to the cremation ground. There Himakar told the villagers, 'It is getting dark. We cannot burn the body now. You go home and come in the morning. I will watch over him in the night.'

As soon as the villagers had gone, Himakar said to Seetapati, 'Stop pretending now. Get up and give me my money . . .'

As they were fighting, a gang of thieves came to divide their loot in leisure at the cremation ground. They saw one person sitting on a pyre and another standing next to him. Both were arguing loudly. Thinking them to be ghosts, the thieves dropped their bag of stolen goods and fled at top speed. The two heard the commotion and saw the bag full of gold and silver ornaments lying on the ground. Quickly they divided it up between themselves. Himakar made sure he got an extra gold coin for the rupee that was due to him and the two men made their way back to their homes, the account settled at last!

The Seed of Truth

Long ago, the country of Gandhara was ruled by the just and good king Vidyadhara. His subjects were very happy, but as the king grew older, everyone got more and more worried. The king did not have any children who could take over the reins of the kingdom after him.

The king was an avid gardener. He spent a lot of time tending his garden, planting the finest flowers, fruit trees and vegetables. One day, after he finished working in the garden, he proclaimed, 'I will distribute some seeds to all the children in the kingdom. The one who grows the biggest, healthiest plant within three months will become the prince or the princess.'

The next day there was a long line of anxious parents and children outside the palace. Everyone was eager to get a seed and grow the best plant.

Pingala, a poor farmer's son, was among these children. Like the king, he too was fond of gardening and grew beautiful plants in his backyard. He took the seed from the king and planted it in a pot with great care. Some weeks passed and he plied it with water and manure, but the plant did not appear. Pingala tried changing the soil and transferred the seed to another pot, but even by the end of three months, nothing appeared.

At last the day came when all the children had to go to the king to show the plant they had grown. They started walking to the palace, dressed in their best, holding beautiful plants in their hands. Only Pingala stood sadly, watching them go by. Pingala's father had watched his son working hard with the seed and felt sorry for him. 'Why don't you go to the king with the empty pot?' he suggested. 'At least he will know you tried your best.'

So Pingala too wore his best dress and joined the others outside the palace, holding his empty pot in his hand and ignoring the laughter around him. Soon the king arrived and began his inspection. The

pots held flowers of different shades, beautiful and healthy, but the king did not look happy. At the end of the line stood Pingala, and when the king reached him, he stopped in surprise.

'Child, why have you come with an empty pot? Could you not grow anything?'

Pingala looked down and said, 'Forgive me, Your Highness. I tried my best, I gave it the best soil and manure I had, but the plant would not grow.'

Now the king's face broke into a smile. He enveloped Pingala in his arms and announced, 'Here is the crown prince! I had given everyone roasted seeds, which would never grow, just to see which child was the most honest one and would admit he or she had not been able to grow anything. Only this boy told the truth. I am sure he will rule this kingdom one day with truth and honesty.'

And indeed that was what happened. When the king grew old and died, Pingala, who had learnt everything from him, came to the throne and ruled Gandhara justly for many years.

Haripant the Wise

During the reign of one of the Vijayanagar emperors, there lived a wise magistrate named Haripant. His verdicts were always fair and people came to him from all over the vast kingdom so he could settle their disputes.

In the city, there lived a greedy ghee merchant named Shiriyala Shetty. His shop always had twenty barrels of ghee, but of these, fifteen would be good and the remaining five adulterated. He would mix the adulterated ghee with the good one and sell it to the people. This went on for a long time, till finally the people got tired of being cheated and complained to Haripant.

Haripant got the ghee examined and found it to be adulterated indeed. He gave Shiriyala a choice of punishment. He could either drink the five barrels of adulterated ghee from his shop, or he could get hundred lashings, or pay a thousand gold coins to the treasury.

Shiriyala started thinking. Losing a thousand gold coins was too much and a hundred lashings too painful. So he decided to drink up the five barrels of ghee.

Though Shiriyala sold adulterated stuff in his shop, he had always made sure his own food was of the best quality. So after drinking one barrel of the bad ghee he started feeling sick. By the third barrel, he was vomiting. At this point he decided to opt for the lashings instead. But his was a pampered body, unused to any hard work. After ten lashes, he started trembling, by twenty he was giddy, and by forty he was half dead. 'Stop!' he screamed. 'I will pay the thousand gold coins! Just let me go.'

Finally Shiriyala had to pay the money, and he ended up suffering all three punishments, something he would not forget in a hurry. The people of the city got to use only the best-quality ghee in their food from then on!

Another time, Gunakara, a poor coolie, was walking by Vibhandaka's clothes store. Vibhandaka

was a rich merchant who owned a huge clothes store right in the centre of the town. It was a winter morning and Gunakara was carrying a large sack of waste from a nearby eatery to the rubbish dump. As he was passing by Vibhandaka's store, he slipped and fell. His sack opened up and the stinking waste lay all over Vibhandaka's shop floor. The merchant immediately started screaming, 'Look at this mess. Clean it right away before my customers come.'

Trembling, Gunakara took a broom and bucket of water and started cleaning. He cleaned and polished till not a speck of dirt remained on the floor. But Vibhandaka would not give in so easily. 'The floor is wet,' he shouted. 'Get a cloth and wipe it.' Gunakara scratched his head. 'I don't have any cloth on me,' he said. 'Anyway, by the time your customers come the sun will be out and it will dry up. Or you give me a cloth and I will wipe the floor.' Now the merchant was even angrier. 'Is this a warehouse of old clothes? Where will I get a spare cloth from? You take off your coat and wipe the floor with it.'

This was too much. Gunakara was wearing an old, worn woollen coat, the only warm clothing he possessed.

'I am a poor man,' he tried to explain. 'Some rich person like you gave me this used coat for the winter. If I use this coat to clean the floor, what will I wear? Please let me go.'

But Vibhandaka was adamant. 'No. If the dirty smell persists after you go no customer will come to the shop. I will suffer big losses. My reputation will be ruined and I will become a pauper. So quick, take off your coat and clean up.'

By now, word of the argument had spread and a crowd had gathered. Haripant, on his way to court, heard the angry exchanges and pushed his way through the crowd. Everyone fell back. Justice would now be done, they were sure. When he had heard the entire story, Haripant turned to Gunakara. 'He is right. If you don't clean up well, Vibhandaka will suffer huge losses. Take off your coat and clean the floor.' A hush fell on the crowd. How could Haripant deliver such an unjust verdict? As the murmurs grew, Haripant held up his hand. 'I am not done yet,' he announced. 'There is a second part to my verdict.' Turning to the merchant he said, 'And you will compensate Gunakara's family for his untimely death.'

'What death?' howled an enraged Vibhandaka. Haripant was calm. 'Your complaint was based on an "if". "If" customers smelt the dirty smell, they would abandon your shop and you would be ruined. Similarly, "if" Gunakara loses his coat today, he may catch a cold and fever and die in a few days. His whole family depends on his earnings, so they may starve. Some of them might also die due to starvation. So you have to compensate his family.'

Haripant smiled as Vibhandaka stood looking worried. 'Gunakara, clean up,' he said. 'And, Vibhandaka, let him go inside the store and choose the best and warmest coat for the winter.'

The people who had gathered around applauded the clever verdict.

The Last Laddoo

Once upon a time, there lived a miserly old couple, Devaiah and Devamma. They did not have any children and never spent a paisa on themselves. They never repaired their house or cooked good food. They wore old patched clothes and lived in a rundown little hut.

One day, a family moved into the village, close to Devaiah and Devamma's home. It was their little boy's birthday and they sent two delicious besan laddoos to the old couple. The two ate a laddoo each with great relish. For many days after that they could talk of nothing else. 'How soft they were! How the ghee dripped from them!' they exclaimed to each other. Finally, the old man, Devaiah, could take it no more. He told his wife, 'Let's buy the ingredients to make just two laddoos.' Devamma was delighted. Then she warned her husband, 'If I make the laddoos at home, the neighbours will get to know and want a share. Let's go to a secluded spot in the woods and cook there. That way no one will ever know.'

So the next day Devaiah got the ingredients from the market and they set off to the woods to make the laddoos. They indeed turned out delicious, but since they had never cooked anything like this before, and had not known the correct measurements, they ended up with three laddoos instead of two.

The old couple returned home with the bowl of sweets, dying to bite into them. But when they sat down to eat, a problem arose. How would they divide the three laddoos? 'It was my idea and I went to the market, so I must get two and you will get one,' said Devaiah. But Devamma was not one to give in so easily. 'I prepared the sweets. I must have two and you can have one.'

They started fighting. Day wore into night, but still they fought. At last Devaiah found a way out. 'Let us not talk to each other. Whoever breaks the silence first will get one laddoo and the other person two.'

Devamma agreed and the two sat quietly, waiting for the other to talk first. Hours passed, but no one spoke. After some time they lay down, bored, with the bowl of sweets between them. Two days passed thus and the neighbours got suspicious. They came and banged on the door but the old couple would not answer in the fear of losing the bet. Then one neighbour climbed to the roof and, after removing a tile, peeped in. He saw the couple lying on the floor, a bowl between them. 'They are dead! The food is still lying there untouched,' he screamed.

Soon the door was broken open and the house was swarming with villagers. They discussed the funeral and wondered where the misers had hidden their wealth. Devaiah and Devamma heard everything but did not get up, in the fear of losing out on a laddoo. Finally the villagers carried them to the cremation ground and placed them on two pyres, though someone did suggest using only one for the two of them, as they were such misers. As the flames started licking their feet, Devamma jumped up, screaming, 'You win! You win! I don't want to die.'

Devaiah too jumped up, happily. 'I have won! I will now eat two laddoos!' And the two rushed home, leaving a flock of bewildered, terrified villagers behind.

But alas, in the excitement of the funeral, the villagers had left the door of the hut open. The old man and woman rushed in to find a stray dog licking the last crumbs of the sweets from the bowl.

The Tastiest of All

King Shantivardhana ruled over the kingdom of Vaishali. He was a king who took his job very seriously. Every now and then he would leave the palace in the evening, dressed in the clothes of an ordinary man, to listen to what his people had to say about him and his ministers.

Once, he set out on a full-moon night. He walked into a little garden just in time to hear four girls debating an interesting issue: what is the tastiest thing of all? One said, 'Meat is the tastiest food of all.' Another said, 'No, it is liquor.' The third said, 'I think it is love, even though it is a feeling, not a food.' And the fourth said, 'It is hunger.'

413

The four friends argued amongst themselves, not knowing that the king was listening in the bushes behind them. The king had to go away after a while and he never got to hear the end of the argument. The next day, he woke up wondering who won the debate and what were the reasons the winner gave. He summoned the four girls to court. They came, trembling in fear, and were even more fearful when the king said that he had heard their conversation the night before. Now he said, 'Each one of you claimed a different thing as the tastiest of all. What were your reasons? If they are good, I will reward each of you.'

So the first girl said, 'I think meat is the tastiest thing in the world, even though I am a priest's daughter and have never tasted it.'

'Then how can you say so?' asked the king in surprise.

'Our house is opposite a butcher's shop. Every evening, the butcher throws the leftover bones and meat outside the shop. A big pack of dogs gathers there and fights over these few pieces of meat. And after they are done, swarms of flies sit on the bones. So I think meat must be very tasty.'

The king liked her reasoning and gave her a reward. Then he turned to the second girl. 'Why did you say liquor is tasty? Have you ever had any?' The girl shook her head. 'My father is a schoolteacher and no one in my family has had a drop of liquor ever. But I too stay opposite a shop—a liquor shop. There I see many people every day, spending so much money on their drinks. Often their families come and plead with them to come back home. Old parents and mothers with little children beg their sons, brothers and husbands to come home, but these people don't listen. They are only interested in their next glass. That is why I think liquor must be very tasty.'

The king liked her argument too and gave her a reward. Now the third girl said, 'I think love must be very tasty because I have seen how it transformed my sister. She used to be shy and obedient. But when she fell in love with a man my father did not like, she thought nothing of running away with him in the middle of a dark, stormy night.' The king smiled and rewarded her too.

Then the last girl said, 'I agree with them. But there is one thing that is tastier than all this. It is hunger. If your stomach is full, the grandest of feasts will be tasteless, but on an empty stomach the most ordinary, even stale food will taste like nectar.

Hunger makes our food tasty, whether we are young or old, rich or poor.'

The king now knew who was the winner of the argument. He gave the last girl a big reward for her clever words.

The Cunning Fruit

Udanka was a rich merchant with a vast business in north India. He had travelled all over the country and had seen many amazing sights during his travels. One day, his son Bhanuverma said to him, 'Father, you have seen so many new places. I have seen nothing. I am very keen to see the sea you described to me. Please let me go to the seaside.'

Udanka thought it was a good idea too and made arrangements for his son to travel to a south Indian town by the seashore, where he could stay with one of Udanka's friends. Thus Bhanuverma landed up in a town by the sea. His father's friend greeted him warmly and gave him a nice room in their house.

The next day, Bhanuverma set off to see the town. As he walked in the bazaar, he saw a man selling jackfruit. Now Bhanuverma had seen apples, oranges, mangoes, even jamuns, but jackfruit was something he had never set eyes upon. What a strange shape it had, and what a sweet smell! 'How do you eat this?' he asked the man selling it. 'Cut it, eat the fruit, and throw away the seed,' replied the man. When Bhanuverma heard that one big fruit cost only two annas, he was delighted and bought one. He carried it up to his room and proceeded to cut it open.

He ate and ate the sweet fruit. It was like honey. Finally when he was done, he realized that the gum from the fruit had made his hands all sticky. To get rid of the sticky gum, he wiped his hands on his dress, but that only made his dress sticky. He then tried washing his hands with water, but the gum remained. He slapped his head in despair and now his face too became sticky. Then he remembered there was a sack of cotton kept outside his door. He crept out quietly and tried to wipe his hands and face with the cotton. But he only managed to cover himself with cotton which now stuck fast on to his hands and face. The more cotton he used, the more it stuck to him.

Feeling ashamed, he went to the backyard, where he knew a pot of hot water was kept. By then it was evening and his host was calling him in for dinner. Not wanting to appear before him in that state, Bhanuverma hid behind a tree. The people of the house called out for him for some time, then thinking he must still be out somewhere, they took the vessel of hot water inside and shut the door. Bhanuverma looked this way and that. There was only the sheep-shed now for him to sleep in. He went there and lay down among the sheep.

That night, some thieves came to steal the sheep. When they saw Bhanuverma covered in cotton, they thought he was the biggest sheep of all and carried him away. Poor Bhanuverma dared not open his mouth to shout. At last, when they reached the outskirts of the town, they put him down. One close look at him and they fled, taking him to be a ghost.

Bhanuverma stood by the roadside, wondering what to do. A milkmaid who was walking by saw the young man covered in cotton and asked him what had happened. When he told her, she laughed for a long time. Then she said, 'You must always rub oil on your hands before you eat jackfruit. Otherwise the gum will stick to your hands and neither water nor cotton will take it off.'

She was very kind and took him to her house, where she gently removed all the cotton and the gum. Then Bhanuverma set off back to town.

After some weeks, when he came home, Udanka asked him, 'So what did you see? And what did you learn?'

Bhanuverma sighed and said, 'Father, I saw many strange sights, learnt many new things, but the biggest lesson I learnt was, whatever you do, never eat a jackfruit. It is the most cunning fruit of all!'

Nine Questions for a Princess

Princess Suryaprabha, who was very beautiful and intelligent, wanted to marry a man who was even more intelligent and learned than her. She was not too concerned about wealth or looks. So she said to her father, 'I have decided. Let any man ask me nine questions. If I am unable to answer even one of them, I will marry him.'

The king knew well how bright she was and was worried. 'And what if you answer all the questions?' he asked.

'Then he will be rejected and will not get a second chance.'

The king had no choice but to agree to her condition and so he made the announcement in the kingdom. Many people arrived to try their luck. But the princess was too clever for them, and she answered each one's questions in no time. The king became more and more worried. He decided to talk to his most trusted friend, Ganapati Maharaj, who was a teacher, about this. Ganapati heard him out, then said he would send his brightest student, Shashishekhar, to question the princess.

The next day, a handsome young man appeared in court. He was dressed simply but his eyes shone bright with the light of knowledge. He announced that he had nine questions for the princess and, in no time, was sitting before her.

'How many stars are there in the sky?' was his first question.

Suryaprabha replied, 'There are as many stars as there are hairs on a goat.'

'Which is the most beautiful child on earth?'

'For every mother, her child is the most beautiful.'

'What is the difference between truth and lies?'

'It is the difference between our eyes and ears. Our eyes will always see the truth but our ears can hear both truth and lies.'

'Which person has hands, yet is considered handless?'

'A rich man who does not share his wealth.'

'Who has eyes but is still blind?'

'A man without compassion, who does not see the suffering that exists in this world.'

Then Shashishekhar showed her a picture of a crumbling palace and asked what it meant. By now the princess was sure this was no ordinary man. But it did not take her long to give her answer.

'A house without a proper foundation, even if it is a palace, will collapse.'

He showed another picture—of an old lady collecting firewood, while carrying a heavy load on her back.

The princess smiled and replied, 'This picture depicts human greed. The woman has collected so much wood, yet she does not want to give up and go home.'

Now, the princess had answered seven questions accurately. There were only two left. Shashishekhar then asked a very clever question: 'Princess, which is the question you can't answer?'

Suryaprabha was stumped. If she told him, Shashishekhar would ask that question as the last one, and if she did not, she would lose anyway. She smiled and bowed her head. 'I accept defeat.'

Thus it came to be that the two wisest people in the kingdom got married and lived happily.

Dead Man's Painting

Raghupati was a rich landlord who had a son called Sahadeva. The boy's mother had died when he was very young, so Sahadeva was brought up by his father. He became a spoilt and mean child. When Sahadeva was about ten years old, his father married a second time. His new wife, Arundhati, was a sweet, good-natured woman.

Sahadeva was furious when his father got a new wife home and refused to behave well with his stepmother. After some time, when Arundhati gave birth to a boy, Sahadeva started hating her even more. He wanted nothing to do with his stepbrother. Raghupati tried his best to make him see reason, but he refused to listen. Then came a day when Raghupati fell very sick. Though he was treated by the best doctors in the kingdom, he soon realized his end was near. He decided to make a will and write down how his vast property should be divided after his death.

When he finished writing his will, he called his wife and told her, 'When you first read this, it may seem to you that I have done you a great injustice. But have faith. I only want to protect you and our son Janardan from Sahadeva's wrath.' Then he gave her a beautifully framed painting of his own face, done by one of the best artists of the kingdom, and told her, 'When our son Janardan is eighteen years old, take this to the king's minister, Krishnakant. He will see that justice is done to you.'

Arundhati was puzzled. 'Do you know Krishnakant?' she asked.

'No,' replied her husband. 'But I have heard a lot about his wisdom. He will know how to help you.'

A few days after this conversation, Raghupati died. Sahadeva could not wait for the rituals to be over so he could read the will. The day came when the will was finally opened and read out. In it Raghupati had left his large mansion and the surrounding fertile fields to Sahadeva. To Arundhati and Janardan he had left only a ramshackle outhouse and some dry scrubland surrounding it. Sahadeva was thrilled when he heard this. At least his father had seen sense on his deathbed! Happily he moved into the big house and poor Arundhati and her young son went to live in the broken-down little hut. But she remembered what her husband had told her and kept the painting safe with her, waiting for the day Janardan would turn eighteen.

Thus years passed, and on the day of Janardan's eighteenth birthday, Arundhati made her way to Krishnakant's house, the painting tucked under her arm. When she met him, she told him her entire story. Krishnakant was surprised. How was he to help her? After all, he had never seen, let alone known, Raghupati. But Arundhati was insistent. 'You must help,' she pleaded. 'My husband had great faith in your wisdom.' She left the painting with him and went back home.

After she had gone, Krishnakant laid the painting on the floor and looked at it carefully. He wondered what secret was hidden in it. Then he noticed the painting was crooked and pulled at a corner. To his surprise, the painting came out. And hidden behind it was a sheet of paper. A letter! 'Sir,' said the letter. 'You must be reading this many years after my death. In my life I heard many stories about you and how you helped people who were in trouble. I am sure my wife and son are in misery now. You have to help them somehow. The painting you are holding is my portrait. I can also tell you that the house where my wife now lives has ten golden bricks. It is up to you to extract those bricks and see she gets them without being harassed by my first son Sahadeva.' It was signed: Raghupati.

Krishnakant stood quietly for a while after reading this, deep in thought. Then he smiled. He had a plan!

The next day, Krishnakant called Sahadeva and a few wise men to Arundhati's house. He got chairs laid out for everyone in the open field outside. To their surprise, he kept one chair separate and would not let anyone sit on it. When everyone was seated, he turned to the unoccupied chair and spoke to it. 'I will see that things are carried out according to your will. The wisest men of this village are my witnesses You will at last go to heaven in peace.'

Then he turned around to the astonished group of people and said, 'I was visited yesterday by the ghost of Raghupati. Was he not a fair, tall man with a long nose and a mark on his forehead?' The people nodded in fear. Krishnakant had never met Raghupati when he was alive, so how did he know what he looked like? Surely, his ghost could not be around still?

Krishnakant now nodded and sighed sadly. 'So it was his ghost that came to me yesterday and said his wishes according to his will had not been carried out. And I promised to look into the matter.' He asked Sahadeva, 'Did your father leave you the big house and all the fields?' Sahadeva nodded. 'And he left the small outhouse and the land around it to your stepmother and stepbrother?' Sahadeva nodded again. 'And you are sure you have no claim to whatever there is in that house and on that land?' Sahadeva nodded again, vigorously.

Krishnakant now turned to Arundhati and said, 'Your husband's ghost wanted me to tell you that he wishes the house to be destroyed. Now that Sahadeva has said he has no interest in the house and whatever lies in it, I am ordering your house to be demolished right now.'

Arundhati, almost in tears, did not know what to say. She could only look in horror as Krishnakant's men went up to her little hut with hammers and

crowbars and started breaking it down. Sahadeva looked on happily till, imagine his dismay, the men came back to the group, holding ten golden bricks in their hands!

Krishnakant turned to Arundhati. 'Your husband left these bricks in the house. Since everything there belongs to you, and Sahadeva has said in front of everyone he has no claim on anything from there, you are now their rightful owner.' Taking a quick look at the empty chair he said, 'Raghupati is happy now. He will go to heaven at last, his soul in peace.'

With a twirl of his moustache, Krishnakant marched off, leaving behind an amazed Arundhati, now rich beyond her dreams, and a furious Sahadeva, who had been outwitted at last—all thanks to the painting of a dead man.

The White Crow

Umasundari was a very talkative woman. She loved to sit and gossip the whole day. What the neighbours did, what they ate, what the village carpenter said to his mother-in-law—she enjoyed talking about all this. Her husband, Shivasundara, was a mild-mannered man and often told her to stop discussing other people's affairs. But she would never listen to him.

One day, Shivasundara was sitting outside his house, when he suddenly looked up and said, 'Umasundari! Look, what a beautiful crow is sitting on the white roof of our outhouse . . . but don't tell anyone about it.' Umasundari looked up and saw an

434

ordinary black crow sitting on the roof. Why then had Shivasundara been so excited, and why had he asked her not to tell anyone about the crow?

Umasundari felt as though her stomach would burst with this news, so she went to her neighbour and said, 'Did you see our house today? Early in the morning a huge black crow was sitting on the white roof of our outhouse. I have never seen such a huge crow. My husband saw it too and he behaved like it was a big secret. He told me not to tell anyone. But I had to tell you. You will not tell anyone else, will you?' Saying this much, Umasundari ran back home.

Her neighbour, whose name was Satyabhama, was having lunch. She got up midway and ran to her friend Vimalavati's house.

Vimalavati had finished her lunch and was cleaning her gold bangles. Satyabhama told her in a low voice, 'Have you heard the latest news? A massive crow was sitting on the roof of Umasundari's outhouse today. It was as big as an eagle and would not budge even though they tried to shoo it away. Maybe they have some hidden treasure and the crow knows about it . . . But don't tell anyone about this.' So saying she ran back home.

Vimalavati was very jealous. Her grandmother had told her long ago that unusual things always pointed to hidden treasure in a place. The presence of a huge crow must mean Umasundari had some treasure in her house. She was angry now. Here she was with a pair of worn-out old bangles, and Umasundari had discovered treasure! She ran to her husband, Kamlesh.

Kamlesh was a writer and was trying to think of an idea for a story. Vimalavati told him, 'Stop writing imaginary stories. Look at Umasundari! They will soon have sacks of gold and diamonds without lifting a finger.'

Kamlesh too was upset to hear this. How could his neighbours get rich so quickly? He asked his wife how she had found out about the treasure. 'It seems there was a white crow sitting on the roof of Umasundari's outhouse. And that means there is a lot of treasure beneath it.'

Kamlesh had never liked Shivasundara; here was a good way to get back at him. He got up from his writing desk and went straight to the village headman. 'I have just got to know there is hidden treasure under Shivasundara's house,' he reported.

In their kingdom, the rule was that any treasure found below the earth belonged to the king, and not to the owner of the land. The headman rushed to Shivasundara's house with a few soldiers. 'We have to break down your outhouse,' they said. 'It is the king's order.'

Shivasundara tried to say something but no one listened. They started breaking down the house and digging away right then. After a lot of searching, they found nothing.

The angry headman now summoned Kamlesh and asked, 'Who told you about the treasure?' Kamlesh pointed to his wife, Vimalavati, who in turn pointed to Satyabhama, who pointed out Umasundari. She had to appear before the headman and confess that she had exaggerated in the first place.

After that day, no one believed a word of what she said and nobody would sit down to chat with her. And Shivasundara would smile secretly to himself and say, 'I used Umasundari's loud mouth to break down the old outhouse. How much it would have cost me to do it myself! Now I will make a nice garden there, and the two of us will sit there and talk only to each other in peace!'

The Horse in the Burrow

Niranjan was a very clever man. One day, as he was walking down the road, he met his friend Jayadev, who was returning from somewhere. He looked very sad, and in his hand he held the tail of a horse. 'What is the matter?' asked Niranjan.

'My horse died in an accident. By the time I heard about it and reached the place, a fox had taken away the body and only the tail was left.'

Jayadev was a poor farmer, and the horse had been his one expensive possession. Niranjan felt sorry for him. 'Give me the tail,' he told his friend. 'I will get a new horse for you.'

Jayadev had no idea how Niranjan would produce a new horse using only a tail, but he knew how clever Niranjan was, so he gave the tail to him and went back to his farm.

Niranjan walked down a forest path and saw a rabbit's burrow. He placed the tail at the mouth of the burrow and sat down next to it, holding on to the tail. Soon a rich merchant passed by, riding a beautiful horse. He looked in amazement at Niranjan sitting there holding the tail in his hands. 'What are you doing?' he asked.

'I was walking with my magic horse down this path when it ran into this burrow. You see, it can sense treasure and follow it anywhere. It has gone down the burrow to get the treasure and I am holding on to its tail. I will be rich when it comes up.'

The silly merchant believed this story. Then Niranjan said, 'I don't have a bag to keep the treasure. Can you give me one?'

Quickly the merchant replied, 'This bag has a hole in it. Why don't you go back to your village and get a bag? I will hold on to the tail till you come back. Here, take my horse, that will be quicker.'

Niranjan left riding the horse after feigning great reluctance. An hour passed by, but there was no sign

of Niranjan, nor of the horse emerging from the burrow. The merchant pulled the tail and fell back! When he peeped into the hole, he saw nothing of course—no horse, no treasure, not even a rabbit!

Niranjan often used his wit to teach people a lesson. Once he met Dayananda, the milkman. Dayananda cheated his customers by adding water in their milk. That day he was carrying a large mud pot on his head, filled with milk. As soon as he saw Niranjan he said, 'You think you are so clever! But you won't be able to cheat me.'

Niranjan smiled and said, 'Dayananda, why should I cheat you? Particularly today, when there are so many clouds in the sky! It will rain any moment and I don't want to get drenched in the rain.'

'Oh, I have a long way to go! Is it going to rain?' Dayananda said, and forgetting the pot on his head, looked up. The pitcher fell and broke, and the milk spilt all over the road. That day Dayananda could not sell his milk-mixed-with-water to anyone!

The Very Expensive Coconut

Chandrakant was a miser. He hated spending money on anything and his wife was tired of his stingy ways. One day, Chandrakant went to a wedding. There he was served coconut burfi. Chandrakant felt he had never tasted anything so good and decided he wanted another one.

He went back home and asked his wife to make him one. His wife looked at him and said, 'You hardly give me enough money to cook dal and rice. How will I make burfis? Go and buy a coconut at least and then I will make burfi for you.' So Chandrakant set off for the market. He saw a man sitting by the roadside with a heap of coconuts. He selected one and asked, 'How much is this for?' The man—who knew Chandrakant and his miserliness well, like everyone else in the bazaar—said, 'Five rupees.' Chandrakant nearly fainted when he heard this. Five rupees for a coconut! Seeing his face, the shopkeeper said, 'Walk ahead. You will come to a coconut grove ten kilometres from here. There you will get coconuts for three rupees.'

Chandrakant thought this was a wonderful idea. What if he had to walk ten kilometres, he would save two full rupees! So he walked, and after an hour reached the grove. When he saw the coconuts, he felt that even three rupees was a very high price for them and asked the gardener, 'Will you give it to me for one rupee?'

The gardener was busy. Without looking around he said, 'Ten kilometres from here, there is another coconut grove. There you can get it for one rupee.'

He would save two rupees more! Chandrakant set off at once. Tired, he reached the next coconut grove. But when he saw the coconuts, he felt like haggling again and asked the gardener, 'Will you give me a coconut for fifty paise?'

The gardener was upset. 'Walk ten kilometres further and you will reach the seashore where there are many coconut trees. Just pluck one, you will get it for free.'

Free! Chandrakant would walk to the end of the earth to get anything for free. He walked and walked and finally reached the seashore. Sure enough, there were rows of trees, with coconuts hanging from them. Anybody could just climb up and take one.

Chandrakant started climbing. Up and up he went. On the highest treetop he grabbed a delicious-looking coconut. Just then a gust of wind shook the tree and he lost his hold. He held on to the coconut for dear life. 'Help!' he shouted. A man came by on an elephant. When he saw Chandrakant hanging on to the coconut, he went up to the tree. Chandrakant begged him, 'Sir, will you stand on the elephant and hold my legs so that I can get down?'

The mahout said, 'I am in a hurry. But if you give me a hundred rupees, I will do it.'

A hundred rupees! But Chandrakant would break his bones if he remained there. He would have to pay up. He agreed sadly. The man stood on his elephant and grabbed his legs, but just then the elephant moved away and both of them were left hanging there.

Chandrakant was even more worried. Then, they saw a horseman and both of them begged, 'Will you

stand on the horse and hold our feet so that we can get down?'

The horseman said, 'Only if you give me a thousand rupees.'

There was no other way out, so Chandrakant agreed.

But when the man grabbed their feet, the horse got scared and galloped away. Everyone fell in a heap and a bunch of coconuts fell on them. They broke their bones, and Chandrakant had to pay a thousand rupees for their treatment. And all because he would not pay five rupees for a coconut!

The Wise King

In the city of Manmathapura, which stood by the sea, there lived a young boy named Veeravara. He was brave and intelligent. He also longed for adventure, and when he became eighteen years of age, he took up a job on a ship so that he could travel and see other countries.

He travelled to many places on the ship and had many adventures. One day, when the ship was out at sea, a fierce storm began. The ship was tossed about and everyone was thrown overboard, including Veeravara. He managed to clutch on to a piece of wood and save himself. As he was floating in the sea, he lost consciousness. When at last he woke up, he found himself lying on the sandy shore of an unknown island, under the piercing rays of the sun.

Glad to be alive, he got up. He was on a large island, and some miles inland, he could make out a city. Veeravara started walking in that direction. When he reached the city, to his surprise, he was greeted by a great crowd which was cheering him. Somebody came and garlanded him. He did not know what was happening. An elephant was brought forward and he was made to climb on to its back and sit on the howdah. A sad-looking old man was also sitting there silently. The elephant marched towards a palatial building. Veeravara asked the old man, 'Why did the people welcome a stranger like me in this grand fashion? What are they celebrating, and where are they taking me?'

The old man now looked sadder. 'This is an unusual island,' he explained. 'The people here are very intelligent but they have some funny rules. They are prosperous but they don't have a king. They feel if they choose a king from someone within themselves, he will be partial. So they wait for an unknown person to come to this island. When someone like you, a shipwrecked traveller, gets washed up at the

shore, they make him their king. They are taking us to the palace. You are our new king now.'

'What happens to the previous king? And who are you?' Veeravara asked.

'I was the king till you came along. The old king is given a day to teach the new one the ropes. Then he is sent off to the next deserted island, where he has to look after himself. That's the rule.' Saying this, the old man pointed to an island. Veeravara could see it was covered with dense forest.

Now he knew why the old man was sad.

Veeravara was crowned king with great pomp. He quickly learnt his new job and became a good and fair king. But deep inside, a little part of him remained unhappy. When would the next shipwrecked person show up and he be sent off to the other island to live till the end of his days with wild animals and other retired kings?

As he thought about this, he came up with an idea. As long as he was the king, he had absolute power. He ordered his men to go to the island and to clear a part of the forest. There he ordered roads and houses to be built.

Soon there were roads, shops and pretty little houses on the island. People would go to the forest and see the wild animals; they gathered honey and fruits from the trees there, and in a few years, the island was no longer deserted but a cheerful little town.

Now Veeravara was not worried at all. When the next king appeared, he would not have to fend for himself in a forest. Instead, he would live in a little cottage and grow vegetables. Years passed and he got older. The people loved him and were sad whenever they thought he would no longer be their king. Then one day Veeravara called his people and said, 'It is good when you make a person from outside your king. He is fresh and unbiased. But this may not always be a good idea. What if the next person who comes here is a crook? You will make him king without knowing anything about him. Instead, let us have a system where the cleverest people of this island are chosen and rule the place together. Then no one person will have absolute power, and if anyone turns dishonest, you can always remove him from the council.'

The islanders liked the idea, and in a few days, chose their new rulers. Veeravara handed over charge of the kingdom to them and retired happily to his cottage, where he stayed till the end of his days.

A Bottle of Dew

Ramanatha was the son of a rich landlord. His father left him large tracts of land when he died. But Ramanatha did not spend even one day looking after his land. This was because he had a funny idea—he believed there was a magic potion that could turn any object into gold. He spent all his time trying to learn more about this potion. People cheated him often, promising to tell him about it, but he did not give up. His wife, Madhumati, was tired of this and also worried because she saw how much money Ramanatha was spending. She was sure that soon they would be left paupers.

One day, a famous sage called Mahipati came to their town. Ramanatha became his follower and asked him about the potion. To his surprise, the sage answered, 'Yes, in my travels in the Himalayas, I heard how you could make such a potion. But it is a difficult process.'

'Tell me!' insisted Ramanatha, not believing his luck.

'You have to plant a banana tree and water it regularly with your own hands. In winter, the morning dew will settle on its leaves. You have to collect the dew and store it in a bottle. When you have five litres of dew, bring it to me. I will chant a secret mantra, which will turn it into the magic potion. A drop of this potion will transform any object into gold.'

Ramanatha was worried. 'But winter is only for a few months. It will take me years to collect five litres of dew.'

'You can plant as many trees as you want. But remember, you must look after them yourself and collect the dew with your own hands.'

Ramanatha went home and, after talking to his wife, started clearing his large fields which had been lying empty all these years. There he planted rows

and rows of banana trees. He tended them carefully and during the winter months collected the dew that formed on them with great care. His wife helped him too. Madhumati gathered the banana crop, took it to the market and got a good price for it. Over the years, Ramanatha planted more and more trees and they had a huge banana plantation. At the end of six years, he finally had his five litres of dew.

Carefully, he took the bottle to the sage. The sage smiled and muttered a mantra over the water. Then he returned the bottle and said, 'Try it out.' Ramanatha sprinkled a few drops on a copper vessel and waited for it to turn to gold. To his dismay, nothing happened!

'This is cheating,' he told the sage. 'I have wasted six precious years of my life.'

But Sage Mahipati only smiled and called Madhumati to come forward. She came with a big box. When she opened it, inside glinted stacks of gold coins!

Now the sage turned to the astonished Ramanatha and said, 'There is no magic potion that can turn things into gold. You worked hard on your land and created this plantation. While you looked after the trees, your wife sold the fruits in the market. That's how you got this money. It was your hard work that created this wealth, not magic. If I had told you about this earlier, you would not have listened to me, so I played a trick on you.'

Ramanatha understood the wisdom behind these words and worked even harder on his plantation from that day on.

Two Thieves

Saranga was a clever minister in the court of King Devaprasanna. Saranga was such a good adviser that none of the neighbouring kings could ever succeed in attacking the kingdom. Naturally, they were very jealous of Devaprasanna and his brilliant minister.

Saranga was also a great patron of the arts. Many artists, writers and thinkers gathered in his house. He gave them shelter and the means to work on their art. One day, two strangers appeared at his doorstep. 'We have been wandering in many places. We heard you are kind to talented people, so we have come to ask you for shelter,' they said.

'What are your talents?' asked Saranga.

'I can bark like a dog,' said one. 'My imitation is so good that even real dogs get confused. And my friend here can crow better than a cock.'

'What have you been doing all this while with these talents?' asked Saranga, amazed.

Now the two friends looked embarrassed. Finally they said, 'We will be honest. We were thieves and used these talents to confuse the owners of the houses we robbed. Now we have decided to mend our ways and do some honest work. That is why we have come to you.'

Saranga decided to let the two stay in his house, even though his other guests protested. He felt they were truly repentant and should be given a chance. So the two stayed with him and became a part of his group.

Now, Himabindu was a wicked old king of a neighbouring kingdom. Several times he had wanted to invade Devaprasanna's kingdom but had failed miserably because Saranga would always foil his plans. He wanted Saranga to become *his* minister, so he could easily conquer Devaprasanna's kingdom.

One day, he sent a letter to Devaprasanna: 'I want to honour your minister Saranga. I want him to come to my kingdom and give my ministers some lessons in statecraft. Please send Saranga to my kingdom and allow him to stay here for a few days.' Saranga was suspicious when the king informed him about the letter. But Devaprasanna wanted to be on good terms with his neighbours, so he said, 'Why don't you go? If you suspect something is wrong, just come back.'

Saranga now had no choice but to go to Himabindu's court. He took his group of artists and writers with him, as well as the two ex-thieves.

Himabindu welcomed Saranga with great respect. Saranga too had come with many gifts for the king, among them a beautiful, rare shawl. Finally, the king sat down to talk to him. 'Saranga, I know you are the brain behind Devaprasanna's success as a king. You have served him for many years. Why don't you work for me now? I will make you richer than ever. You will be my chief minister.'

Saranga, who had suspected all along that something like this would happen, had his answer ready. 'My family has served King Devaprasanna for many generations. I cannot leave his service. I am sorry.' As soon as the words had left his mouth, Himabindu flew into a rage and ordered that Saranga be thrown into prison.

When his friends, who were waiting in another room, heard about this, they were shocked. How could they save their beloved Saranga now? They came up with many plans, none of which could be carried out by a bunch of artists. Finally, one said, 'Queen Sanmohini is the king's favourite queen. She is beautiful and intelligent. She loves rare art objects, especially shawls.'

'But we came with only one shawl, and Saranga presented it to the king. If only we could get it back . . .'

The two former thieves listened to the discussion in silence. After some time, they walked out quietly. They went to the royal chamber where the gifts were piled up. A ferocious-looking guard stood at the door and frowned at them. Quickly, they slipped behind a tree, and one of them began barking like a dog. The guard was startled. How could a dog enter the royal palace? Surely, if the king heard the noise it was making, the guard would be out of a job!

He rushed off to find the dog while the other friend went inside and found the shawl. Then they quickly made their way back to the group of friends, who were still deep in discussion. 'Here is the shawl,' they said, giving it to the oldest and wisest person in the group. 'Now you can present it to the queen.'

The man took the shawl to the queen, who was delighted with it. 'What a beautiful design! Such soft wool! How much do you want for this?'

Saranga's friend bowed low and said, 'Your Highness, I don't want any money for this. But please request the king to free our dear friend Saranga.'

The queen agreed. That night, when Himabindu came to have dinner with his favourite queen, she served him the most delicious dishes. He was delighted, and after tucking into a huge dinner, leaned back happily and asked, 'What is it, my dear? You look worried. Is there anything you desire?'

Quickly the queen said, 'I have heard that a clever minister called Saranga has been imprisoned by you. He is said to be a wise man. Should we treat him like this? Why don't you free him? Just for me . . .'

The king, already sleepy after his enormous dinner, said, 'Yes, yes,' and ordered Saranga's release.

Saranga was greeted by his friends with great delight. Then someone said, 'We should leave the kingdom before the king discovers we stole his shawl and gave it to the queen.'

Everyone agreed and, quietly, the group packed their bags and left the palace. But there was a problem when they reached the city walls. The huge gates were locked! The soldier guarding them said, 'That is the law. I cannot open them till it is dawn.'

Saranga and his friends sat down to wait. As the hours passed, they grew more and more nervous. What if the king got to know about the theft before they could escape? Finally, one of the two former thieves got up. He climbed a tree near the soldiers guarding the gates and crowed loudly like a cock. The soldiers jumped up and, thinking it was morning already, rushed to open the gates. Saranga and his group were ready. They left as quickly as they could and reached their own kingdom by early morning.

In the meantime, King Himabindu woke up after a long, refreshing sleep and saw his queen dressed in a beautiful sari with an even more exquisite shawl around her shoulders. But why did the shawl look familiar? When he quizzed her, she told him the story of the man who gave it to her as a present and asked for Saranga's release in return.

The king now ordered his men to bring him the shawl presented by Saranga, but it was nowhere to be found! Finally he understood what had happened. He could only smile at the cleverness of Saranga and his friends. It was better to have such clever people as friends than enemies, he decided, and from that day the two kingdoms became friendly neighbours.

The Best Friend

Keshava was a lonely washerman. His only friend was his donkey. They worked together the whole day, and often Keshava would talk to the donkey and pour out his heart to it.

One day, Keshava had many clothes to wash. He was walking home with the donkey when suddenly he felt very tired. He tied the donkey to a tree and sat down to rest for a while. Nearby, there was a school. The window of a classroom was open, and through it, the noise the children were making could be heard. Then came the voice of the teacher. He was scolding the students. 'Here I am, trying to turn you donkeys into human beings, but you just won't study.'

As soon as Keshava heard these words, his ears pricked up. What! Here was a man who could actually turn donkeys into humans! This was the answer to his prayers. Impatiently, he waited for school to be over for the day. Then, when all the children had gone home, and only the teacher remained behind to check some papers, Keshava entered the classroom.

'What do you want, Keshava?' asked the teacher, who knew him well.

Keshava scratched his head and said, 'I heard what you said to the children. Please take my donkey and turn him into a human being. I am very lonely, and this donkey is my only friend. If it became a human, we could have such good times together.'

The teacher realized Keshava was a simpleton and decided to fool him. He pretended to think for a while, then he said, 'It will take some time. Give me six months. Oh yes, and it is an expensive request. It will cost you a thousand rupees.' The foolish washerman agreed and rushed home to get the money. He left the donkey with the teacher and settled down to wait.

Exactly six months later, Keshava appeared at the teacher's door. Now, the teacher had been using the donkey for his own work and had found it most useful. Not wanting to give it up, he said, 'Oh, your donkey became so clever that it ran away.'

'Where is he now?' asked Keshava.

'He is the headman of the next village,' said the cunning teacher and slammed his door shut.

Keshava trotted off to the next village. There the village elders were sitting under a tree, discussing some serious problems. How surprised they were when Keshava marched up to the headman, huffing and puffing, grabbed his hand and said, 'How dare you? You think you are so clever that you can run away? I spent a thousand rupees to make you a human from a donkey. Come home at once!'

The headman understood someone had played a trick on Keshava. 'I am not your donkey!' he said. 'Go to the sage sitting in the forest. He will explain everything to you.'

Sadly, Keshava went to find the sage. He found him sitting under a tree, deep in meditation. He crept up and quickly grabbed the sage's beard. 'Come back now!' he shouted. 'Enough of this!'

The startled sage stood up and somehow calmed Keshava. When he finally heard what had happened,

he had a good laugh. Then he told the washerman, 'The teacher made a fool of you. Your donkey must be still with him. Go and take it back from him. And then try to make some real friends, who will talk with you and share your troubles. A donkey will never be able to do that!'

Good Luck, Gopal

Gopal was a good-natured but very dull boy. His father was a learned man and despaired for his son. 'You must study hard, Gopal,' he would tell his son. 'Without learning, you will remain a frog in the well.'

Poor Gopal tried very hard, but he was rather stupid and could not progress much with his studies. Some years later, his father died. By then Gopal was married and had a family to look after. But no one would give him a job; he was just so silly. One day, there was no food in the house and Gopal's wife said to him, 'I have heard that our king is very fond of good literature. Why don't you write him a nice poem? Perhaps he will like it and give you a reward.'

Gopal had no choice but to agree, and he set off to have a bath in the pond before sitting down to write his verse. At the pond he saw a pig, covered in mud, rubbing its back against a tree trunk. The pig was rubbing so hard that Gopal was afraid its skin would come off. So he said, 'Don't rub so hard. It is not good for you. It will put your life in danger.' Then, unable to think of anything else to write, he put down these words on a palm leaf and made his way to the palace.

By the time he reached there, it was evening and the palace gates were shut. The guard refused to let him in. 'Please,' Gopal pleaded. 'I have an important document for the king.' One of the guards took pity on him and agreed to leave the palm leaf where the king would see it in the morning.

Gopal handed over the palm leaf and went to rest in a dormitory. The royal guard placed the palm leaf on the king's table for him to see when he woke up.

The next morning, the royal barber came to trim the king's hair and was sharpening his knife against a stone, while the king waited for his haircut. Just then, the king's eyes fell on the palm leaf and he read

aloud what was written on it: 'Don't rub so hard. It is not good for you. It will put your life in danger.'

The barber had been sharpening his knife because he planned to use it to kill the king. An evil minister had made him agree to take on the job. When he heard the king's words, he was scared out of his wits. The king knew his plan! He fell at the king's feet and begged for forgiveness. He also told the king about the minister and how he had made the barber agree to carry out the killing.

The king got the minister arrested and threw him into prison. Then he realized the words on the palm leaf had saved his life and he wanted to know who had written them. An astonished Gopal was dragged out of bed and presented before the king, who showered him with rewards and appointed him as the court astrologer.

A few days later, the queen could not find her favourite necklace. The whole palace was in a turmoil. Even the king was worried. If the queen did not get the necklace soon, he would have to face the consequences. So he summoned Gopal. 'You saved my life with your divine powers. Now help us find this necklace,' he commanded.

Poor Gopal, he did not know what to do. Trembling, he said, 'I can look at the past and predict the future only when I am alone. Please let me go to my room. I will come to you shortly with the whereabouts of the necklace.' Then he rushed to his room, bolted the door and lamented to himself loudly, cursing his wife for the situation, 'O lady, your desires have doomed your husband. Because of you your husband is in trouble, and you may be a widow soon. Your husband escaped once, but this time there is no escape for him.' On the other side of the door, a maidservant heard these words and started trembling. She had stolen an earring once with the help of her husband, who was the palace gardener, and this time, the two had got greedy and stolen the queen's precious necklace. Hearing Gopal's words, she thought he was talking to her and knocked on his door. As soon as he opened it, she fell at his feet and begged forgiveness. Then she told him where the necklace and the earring were kept. Gopal happily went and told this to the king and once again everyone marvelled at Gopal's divine powers.

A few weeks went by peacefully. Then one day, a messenger arrived from the neighbouring king. In his hand he held a wooden box, its lid shut tight. The message from the king said: 'We have heard much about the new astrologer in your court and his powers. Here is a test. Can he tell what is in this box?'

The court now turned towards Gopal. The kingdom's reputation was hanging on his words. Gopal, who of course had no idea what was in the box, muttered his father's words to himself, 'Oh frog, your life is indeed becoming very difficult.'

No one understood what he meant, but the messenger looked amazed. He opened the lid and out hopped a frog!

By now the king was very impressed with Gopal and showered him with gold coins. But Gopal had had enough. 'I was told I would be able to predict only three things correctly,' he told the king. 'I have finished making all three prophecies. Now please let me return to my wife.' Sadly, the king agreed and sent Gopal home, but not before plying him with many more gifts. Gopal and his wife lived the rest of their lives in happiness and comfort.

Nakul's First Lesson

Bhaskar was a wealthy, worldly-wise merchant. He had one son, Nakul. One day, Bhaskar fell ill and realized he was going to die. So he called Nakul to him and gave him some advice. 'When you do business and travel to foreign lands, make sure you know the local culture well. Try to gain as much information as you can before you go there, as only your knowledge and presence of mind will come to your help in an unknown land.'

Nakul listened to his father's words carefully. Bhaskar died soon after and Nakul began to look after the business. Once, he had to sail to a faraway country on work. There, he stayed in an inn. He got talking to its owner and, without realizing, ended up telling the man all about his life, the business and his father.

Next day, he went to the market, and was amazed when a one-armed man rushed up to him and said, 'Your father took one of my arms as a loan. You must return it to me.' Not knowing what to do, Nakul asked for a day to think about this. Then, a woman came up to him and said, 'Your father married me. He used to send me money every month. Now that he is dead, you must give me money.' Again Nakul asked for a day's respite and walked on. He stopped at another inn and ate some breakfast. When he went to make his payment, the owner said, 'I only want you to make me happy.' Though he had to pay only two coins, Nakul gave the man five, but still he said he was unhappy. Puzzled, Nakul walked on.

A man invited him to a game of dice. Poor Nakul did not know that they were playing with a trick dice. He lost all the games. But the man who won set an unusual condition. 'You must drink all the water in the sea, or else give me all the goods in your ship.' Poor Nakul again said he would be back the next day with his answer.

That night, as he lay in his bed, he remembered his father's words, 'In a foreign land only your wits will come to your aid.'

The next morning, as soon as he went to the market, the one-armed man appeared before him. Nakul greeted him with a big smile and said, 'You were right. My father took many hands like yours and our house is full of hands. Give me your other hand. I will find the matching one and send it to you.' The man ran away in fright.

Then he found the woman who claimed to have been married to his father. 'Mother!' he shouted. 'My father was wrong not to have told us about you. Now you are like a second mother to me. Come home with me and help my mother in the fields.' The woman too made a quick getaway when she heard this.

Next he went to the hotel. The owner was standing outside. Nakul shouted to him, 'Hail the king! Your king is the best in the world!' The man had no choice but to answer, 'You are right. I am happy you think so.'

'If you are happy, I have paid for my meal,' said Nakul and went to find the man with the dice. When he found him, he said, 'I have thought over the challenge. I will drink all the water in the sea. But you have to bring me the water in jugs.' That man too ran away when he heard this.

Nakul went on to do a lot of business in that country and returned home richer—in wisdom too!

Golden Silence

Somesh was a boy of ten. He was a chatterbox and loved to talk to anyone who had the time to listen to him. Sometimes he would talk so much that his parents would have to tell him to stop and rest his tongue awhile!

Every night, he would lie down to sleep with his father, who would tell him a story. At that time Somesh was all ears. He would listen to his father's story attentively and then drift off to sleep. One day, he listened to his father's story as usual. The next morning when he woke up, his parents were shocked. There was pin-drop silence in the house. Somesh had stopped talking! At first they were relieved, thinking he was playing a game. But when he did not talk even after many days, they got worried. They took him to the best medicine men in the country, to all the sages and holy men they could find, but no one found anything wrong with him. Neither did any of their treatments have any effect on the boy.

Years passed and Somesh grew into a young man. His parents and everyone who knew him now thought him to be dumb. One day, he was travelling with his father's friend Lokesh to another village. They sat down to rest under a huge banyan tree. A crow was cawing loudly on one of the branches. Lokesh was telling Somesh a very funny story involving a milkman, his cow and the village goonda, and was mighty irritated to have the crow cawing loudly overhead as he spoke. Finally he could take it no longer. The crow was spoiling a perfect story! He first tried to shoo it away, but it paid him no heed. Then he picked up a stone and threw it at the crow, thinking that would make it fly away. Instead, the stone hit the crow and it fell dead.

Lokesh was horrified. He had not meant to kill the bird at all. As he stood staring at the dead form lying under the tree, he did not realize when Somesh had come up behind him. He was stunned when he

heard a voice behind him say, 'Foolish crow, if only you had kept your mouth shut and been silent, you would not have met this end.'

Lokesh forgot all about the crow and turned to stare at Somesh. The boy had spoken! 'Say it again, Somesh!' he begged. But Somesh just smiled mysteriously and refused to utter one more word. Lokesh hurried back to the village and told Somesh's father the story. Now Somesh's parents begged him again and again, 'Speak once more, son. For the sake of your dear old parents.' But it seemed as if Somesh did not know how to talk, and everyone put the incident down to Lokesh's imagination.

After that day, Somesh's father and Lokesh, who had been business partners and friends for many years, stopped speaking to each other. They took on other partners in business and suffered losses. They were miserable as they had no one to share their deepest sorrows and joys with. Somesh saw all this, and one day, as he sat down to eat with his father, he noticed his father was just toying with his food. His mind was clearly elsewhere. Suddenly Somesh spoke again, 'If Lokesh Uncle had remained silent, he would have been your friend still. You were right, Father, silence is golden and speech is silver.'

His father nearly fainted when he heard this. Suddenly he remembered the bedtime story he had told his ten-year-old son. It was about a king who lost his kingdom because he was too busy talking to prepare for war. And his final words before his son had drifted off to sleep were: 'Silence is golden, speech is silver.'

He hugged his son and explained, 'That was just a saying. How I have longed to hear you talk again. Please do not do this again. I will never complain about your chattering again.'

From that day on, Somesh spoke again, but he remembered to think carefully before he opened his mouth!

Emperor of Alakavati

Sumant was a bright young man who lived in Vidishanagara in ancient India. He had been orphaned when he was very young and had had to fend for himself from a young age. As a result, he was smart and cunning.

One day, he felt very hungry. He went to a sweetshop just in time to hear the shopkeeper tell his son, 'Child, I am very sleepy. Look after the shop while I take a nap. Call me only if something important comes up.' Sumant immediately smelt an opportunity. He hung around outside the shop for some time. Then he went in and announced loudly, 'I am your father's best friend's son. Give me the best sweets in the shop.' The boy, who had never seen Sumant earlier, was suspicious. 'What is your name?' he asked. 'My name is Fly,' said Sumant, helping himself to some delicious jalebis. As he sat eating, the boy ran to his father. 'Father! Fly is eating the sweets. What should I do?'

The sweetshop owner was in deep sleep. He mumbled, 'How much can a fly eat? Let him be. Now go away.' So saying, he turned over and started snoring loudly. Sumant, meanwhile, had finished the jalebis and had pulled a pile of gulab jamuns towards him. The poor boy could do nothing but watch him demolish them all. Finally Sumant took two boxes of the best sweets in the shop and left without paying a single paisa.

He walked straight to Kanaka Chandra's shop. Kanaka Chandra was the biggest miser of Vidishanagara. Sumant presented the boxes to him and said, 'Here is a present for one of Vidishanagara's greatest men. I am only a poor man. I have nothing more to give you.'

Kanaka Chandra peeped into the boxes and was delighted to see them chock-full of delicious mouth-watering sweets. 'Sir,' said Sumant humbly, 'I have only one request. Can I have these two boxes back,

please?' Kanaka was only interested in the sweets, so he said graciously, 'Of course, of course. Please go inside the house and tell my wife to give you two vessels to put these sweets in. Then you can take the empty boxes.'

Sumant walked into the kitchen, where the wife was cooking lunch. 'Your husband has asked you to give me two gold coins,' he announced to the astonished woman. 'What! Are you out of your mind? My husband would never say such a thing!' said the woman. So Sumant called out at the top of his voice, 'Your wife is refusing to give me what you had asked for.'

Kanaka was in the middle of negotiating a handsome deal with a merchant. Irritated by this disturbance, he called out to his wife, 'Just give him what he wants.' So Sumant walked out, whistling loudly, with the two coins in his pocket. Of course he had left the boxes and the sweets for Kanaka and his wife.

Now he walked to the outskirts of the city and buried one coin under a bush. Then he sat down next to it, a stick in hand.

As soon as he heard the sound of a horse approaching, he started waving his stick around and pretending to examine the nearby bushes. The soldier sitting on the horse watched Sumant behaving in this odd fashion. When he could no longer hold back his curiosity he asked, 'What are you doing?' Sumant, pretending to be very busy, answered, 'My magic cane leads me every day to a hidden treasure buried under a shrub. Today it led me here and I am looking for the treasure.' Saying this, he started digging under the shrub where he had just hidden the coin and pretended to find it with a triumphant yell. The soldier could not believe his eyes and got down from his horse. He examined the coin closely. Then he said, 'Give me your magic stick. You can take my horse in return. It's the best you can get in this kingdom. And that is a fair deal.' Sumant pretended to hesitate. 'No, no. This stick is my life. I cannot part with it.' After much cajoling and threatening, the soldier managed to take the stick from Sumant, who in turn rode off with the magnificent horse.

He rode all day, till he reached a rich farmer's farm. He knocked on the door and said, 'I am a weary traveller. Can you give me and my horse shelter for the night?' The farmer saw the beautiful horse and agreed to shelter them for the night. The horse was given a place in the stables and Sumant a room to sleep in.

The next morning, Sumant woke up early and asked the farmer, 'Can you give me a sieve?' The farmer, though astonished at this strange request, gave him one. Then he told his servant to follow Sumant. Sumant first went to the stable, where he collected some fresh dung from his horse, then he went to his room, and pretending great secrecy, started sieving the dung. He knew all the time that the servant was watching him, and making sure the man could see what he was doing, Sumant produced the other gold coin from the dung.

The servant excitedly reported everything to his master. The farmer immediately made his way to Sumant, who was grooming his horse, as if readying to leave.

'Tell me about this horse,' he demanded. 'Tell me only the truth, mind you.' Sumant, pretending to be scared, stammered, 'T-this h-horse has m-magical powers. Once a d-day it produces a g-gold c-coin in its d-dung.' The farmer, who was very greedy, said, 'Give me the horse. I will give you a hundred gold coins in return.' Sumant pretended to hesitate for a while and then, making a show of great reluctance, handed over the reins of the horse to the farmer and trotted off on foot, a bag full of coins jingling in his pocket.

It was evening by the time he reached the next village, and he took shelter in the house of an old couple. When he went out into the nearby forest in the morning, he spotted an old woman sitting outside a small hut. Her young granddaughter was washing some clothes nearby. He told the old woman, 'Do as I say, and you'll be rich.' So saying, he went back to the couple with a bottle full of a green liquid in his hand. 'What is this?' asked the old man, when he saw Sumant. 'It is a medicine to make you young. I discovered it during my wanderings in the Himalayas,' answered Sumant. The man asked, 'Do you have any proof of its effects?'

'I'll show the effects to you only if you pay me in gold,' said the wily Sumant, and having struck the deal, led them to the old woman's hut in the forest.

The old woman was sweeping her courtyard. Sumant pointed her out to the couple and said, 'I'll give her my medicine. Just wait and see what happens.' Then he marched up to her and, slipping some money into her hand along with the medicine, said, 'Drink this.' The woman had the medicine and disappeared into the house. Immediately her granddaughter emerged wearing identical clothes and started sweeping the courtyard, as if nothing had happened.

The couple was impressed. 'Give us the medicine,' they clamoured. Sumant took a hundred coins from the man and gave him some herbs to make him unconscious. Then he told the wife, 'He is sleeping. He is so old, it will be some time before the medicine takes effect. He will be a young man when he wakes up. I will give you your dose tomorrow.' But the old woman would not agree. 'Give me my dose now. If my husband wakes up and sees his wife is an old woman, he will start looking for someone younger.' Sumant, pretending to be very reluctant, gave her a spoonful of the herbs which made her unconscious— only after she had paid him another hundred coins, of course.

Thus many days passed and Sumant made a living by cheating ordinary folk with his smooth talk and tall promises.

The king of Vidishanagara heard about him and ordered his arrest. Sumant walked into the king's trap one day and was produced before him. 'You are a cheat,' said the king. He ordered his soldiers, 'Put him in a bag and when the sun sets, throw him down the mountain cliff.' The soldiers stuffed Sumant into a bag and left him under a tree, waiting for the sun to set. Inside the bag, Sumant's clever brain was ticking away. Suddenly he heard what sounded like the footsteps of an elephant nearby. He started shouting, 'Help! I don't want to be king. Help, someone, please!'

The man riding the elephant heard these strange words coming out of the bag and opened it. Sumant jumped out and said, 'Thank you, sir. Our king has no heir. But this morning, his elephant touched me with its trunk and he decided I should be the king after him. When I said I was just an ordinary man, he tied me in this sack and left me here till I agreed.'

The stranger was tempted. 'I will take your place. You take my elephant,' he said. Sumant happily agreed and rode off on elephant back just before the soldiers arrived. They picked up the bag and threw it down the cliff.

The next day, Sumant came back into the city, seated on the elephant. He marched up to the king's court and in answer to everyone's surprised questions said, 'When I was thrown off the cliff I landed in a beautiful kingdom called Alakavati in the valley. Its streets are paved with gold and everyone has masses of gold and silver scattered all over their houses. But they have no king, and when I landed among them, after being thrown from the mountain, they decided to make me the king. Today is my coronation. Please come with me to Alakavati.'

The king heard the story in silence. Then he said, 'Sumant, you have told many stories in your life. But this one I will not believe. I know that valley well. There is no Alakavati there. Since you are so clever, why don't you use your wits for the betterment of this kingdom and not just for yourself?'

Sumant was silent. No one had praised him or offered him a better life ever before. He accepted the king's offer. He went on to study under the best pundits of the kingdom and one day was known all over the country as the wisest of the king's ministers.

The Case of the Missing Necklace

Princess Chandravati was very beautiful. She loved all kinds of jewellery and always wanted to wear the most precious, most lovely jewels. Once, a jeweller came to the palace and gifted the king a wonderful diamond necklace. It glittered with small and big diamonds. It was certainly a very expensive necklace. The princess fell in love with it as soon as she saw it, so the king presented it to her.

After that, the princess always wore the necklace, wherever she went. One day, she was walking in the palace garden when she felt like taking a dip in the pond. She took off the necklace and put it in the hands of her oldest and most trusted servant.

'Hold this,' she said, 'and be careful. This is the most precious necklace in the whole world.'

The servant, an old woman, settled down under a tree, holding on to the ornament tightly. But it was a hot summer afternoon and they had been walking for a while . . . Slowly the woman's eyes started closing and soon she was snoring gently. Just as she was drifting off into a wonderful dream, she felt someone tugging the necklace from her hands. She woke up with a start and looked around. There was no one, and the necklace was gone! Scared out of her wits, she started screaming. The royal guards rushed up and she pointed in the direction she thought the thief may have taken. The guards ran off that way.

Now who should be walking on that road, but a poor and slightly stupid farmer. As soon as he saw a platoon of the king's palace guards rushing down the road, thundering towards him, he thought they wanted to catch him and started running. But he was not a very strong man and could not outrun the hefty guards. They caught him in no time.

'Where is it?' they demanded, shaking him.

'Where is what?' he stammered back.

'The necklace you stole!' the guards shouted, giving him a few more shakes.

The farmer had no idea what they were talking about. He only understood something was lost and he was supposed to have it. 'I don't know where it is now,' he said quickly. 'I gave it to my landlord.'

The guards now ran to the landlord's house. 'Give us the necklace!' they demanded of the fat landlord as he sat balancing his account books.

'Necklace!' The landlord was startled. 'I don't have any.'

'Then tell us quickly who does!'

The landlord saw the priest walking by the house. He pointed a chubby finger at him. 'He does! That man has it.' The guards now caught hold of the priest who was walking to the temple, thinking about the creamy payasam his wife had made for lunch. He was stunned when a pack of burly guards jumped on him and demanded a necklace. He remembered the minister Bhupati, who was at the temple now, praying to the goddess. He took the guards to the temple and pointed at the praying minister. 'I gave it to him.'

Bhupati too was caught and all four men were thrown into jail. Now, the chief minister of the kingdom knew Bhupati well. He was a good and honest man who had served the king faithfully for many years, so the chief minister was puzzled. Why had Bhupati suddenly stolen the princess's favourite ornament?

He decided to find out and asked one of his spies to listen to the men as they sat talking in the jail.

First Bhupati asked the priest, 'Why did you say you gave me a necklace? I was praying quietly in the temple, and you have landed me in jail.'

The priest scratched his head and pointed to the landlord. 'I didn't know what else to do. But he set the guards on me. I was only walking by his house.'

The landlord looked sheepish. Then he turned to the farmer, his eyes blazing. 'You lazy good-for-nothing! Why did you say I had the necklace?'

The farmer, trembling under the angry gaze of the three men, said, 'The guards jumped on me so suddenly, I did not know what to say . . .'

When the spy reported this conversation to the chief minister, he understood that none of these men was the thief. So who was it? He ordered a thorough search of the palace garden, especially where the servant had sat dozing. The soldiers searched high and low, till they saw something glinting in the tree. There sat a huge monkey. And around its neck was the most beautiful, most precious necklace in the whole world!

Of course, it took a lot of coaxing and a huge bunch of bananas, before the monkey agreed to have the necklace removed from around its neck. And the princess decided the world's most expensive diamond necklace was best worn indoors!

A Question of Maths

Srimukha was a clever but poor farmer. One day, he learnt that the king was passing through his village and would be stopping there for a night. He decided to give the king a gift and perhaps earn a small reward. He took his best cock to the king and presented it to him.

The king was very pleased to get such a fine bird. Then he saw the intelligent look on Srimukha's face and decided to test him. 'In my family, I have a wife, two sons and two daughters, and you are my guest today. Tell me, how can I divide this one cock among seven people?'

Srimukha thought for a while and said, 'It is easy. You are the head of the family, so you should get the head. Your wife will get the cock's back as she is the backbone of the family. Your daughters will one day get married and go away, so they should get the two wings, and your sons will follow the path you show them, so they should get the legs.'

'And what about you?'

'I am the guest, so I should get whatever is left over.'

The king was pleased by this clever answer and presented Srimukha with a gold coin. Now Srimukha had a foolish neighbour, Sripati, who became very jealous when he heard about the reward. He decided to present the king with five cocks and earn five pieces of gold.

When he appeared before the king with the five cocks, the king asked him the same question. 'How can five cocks be divided between seven people?'

Sripati was dumbstruck. Who knew the king would ask such a difficult question? As he stood trying to calculate, the king sent for Srimukha. The farmer heard the question and quickly worked out the answer. 'We will divide everyone into groups of three,' he said. 'Your Majesty and the queen and one cock will be one group. So the king and queen will get one cock. The two princesses and one cock will

be another group. The two princes and one cock will form the third group. I will form the last group with the remaining two cocks, so I will get two cocks.'

The king smiled delightedly at this answer. He presented Srimukha with some more gold coins and turned to Sripati who stood there open-mouthed, still counting on his fingers. 'The coins are rewards for Srimukha's intelligence, not the cocks,' he explained gently.

The Clever Brothers

Once upon a time, there were three brothers. They were all very clever and one day decided to make their fortune using their powers of reasoning and logic.

As they walked to the nearest big city to look for work, they saw some footprints on the dirt road. As they stood looking at the marks, a merchant came rushing up to them. 'Did you see anything go by on this road?' he asked in a panic. The first brother looked closely at the prints and said, 'Yes, a large camel.' The second said, 'It was a one-eyed camel.' The third, who had been looking further down the road, said, 'It was carrying a woman and a child on its back.'

Now the merchant was furious and shouted, 'You have kidnapped my wife and child. Come with me to the king.'

The three brothers could not get him to see reason and the four men ended up in the king's court. 'Hmm,' the king said, after he had heard the entire story. 'If you three claim to be so clever, let me set a task for you. I will place before you a wooden box which will be locked. You will have to tell me what contains it without looking inside.'

The three brothers agreed, and soon the king's men placed before them a stout wooden box, firmly shut. The first brother said immediately, 'It has something round inside.'

The second said, 'It is a pomegranate.'

'An unripe pomegranate,' added the third.

The box was opened and indeed, inside there was an unripe pomegranate.

The king now asked them for an explanation. The first man said, 'When your servant was bringing the box, I heard something rolling inside. That meant there was a round object in it.' The second man said, 'I saw your servant coming from the pomegranate orchard, so I knew he had placed a pomegranate in the box.'

'And this is not the season for pomegranates, so it had to be an unripe one,' piped up the last brother.

The king now had proof of the brothers' powers of observation and asked them how they knew about the merchant's wife and child being on camel back.

'The footprints we saw were large ones, so I deduced it was a big camel that had gone that way,' said the first brother.

'The camel had grazed on only one side of the road,' said the second, 'so I knew it was one-eyed.'

'And I saw the footprints of a woman and a child where the camel had sat down to rest,' said the third. 'Which meant they were on the camel's back.'

The king, now convinced of their cleverness, appointed the three brothers as ministers in his court.

The Lucky Purse

Mallika was the daughter of a rich widow. She was very beautiful and kind. When she got engaged to be married to the son of a rich landlord, her mother started making all sorts of preparations. She bought beautiful saris, lovely jewellery and all kinds of gifts for Mallika and her in-laws. Mallika wanted to put some of these gifts in a silk bag to take with her. So her faithful old servant, Veda, was sent to the market to buy one.

Veda returned with a bag, but Mallika did not like the design. So she sent Veda back to the shop to change it. Now, there was only one bag left, and even though it had a peculiar design and a very odd shape, Veda brought it back home. Of course Mallika did not like it one bit. However, she had no choice but to use it.

Soon Mallika got married and it was time for her to leave for her new house. It was in the next village, and her mother packed lots of food for the journey. She put it all in the odd-shaped silk bag. As Mallika was saying her goodbyes, her mother whispered in her ear, 'I have put lots of fruits, coconuts, flowers and some other gifts in the silk bag. Keep it carefully.' She also said something else, but Mallika's friends set up such a wailing then over their departing friend that she could not hear her mother's last few words.

There was a terrible thunderstorm that night and Mallika and the people accompanying her had to stop to take shelter in an old abandoned temple. There, as Mallika stood gazing out at the rain, she heard the sound of someone crying. She looked around and saw a girl, about her age, also dressed like a newly married bride, sitting and crying on the temple floor. Kind-hearted Mallika went up to her and asked what the matter was. Sobbing, the girl told her that she was an orphan. She had just been married off by her uncle who had looked after her all these years. But he was too poor and had not been able to give her any

gifts to give to her new family. Now she was worried about what her in-laws would have to say. Mallika felt sad when she heard the story. Then her eyes fell on the peculiar silk bag her mother had given her. It was full of fruits and flowers. Mallika picked it up and gave it to the girl. By then, the storm had died down, and the two brides went their different ways.

Mallika soon got accustomed in her new house. She had a son and was happy with her husband who loved her dearly. Ten years went by, till one day, disaster struck. There was a severe earthquake. Mallika was outside, inspecting the field, so she was unhurt. But her husband and son could not be found anywhere. Almost mad with grief, Mallika started wandering in search of them. Her beautiful house was nothing but a pile of bricks now. Her wealth was gone. Her whole life had been destroyed all of a sudden.

She went from village to village. There were many people like her, homeless and hungry, walking about. Then she heard that in the next town there was a wealthy couple who had built some rooms to shelter people like her and also gave them food. She decided to go there.

When she reached the place, she saw there was a long queue of people waiting for food. Not having eaten a morsel for many days, she joined them. Many more people joined the queue behind her. But as soon as the man distributing the food gave her her portion, he announced that the food was finished for the day. The people behind her had to go away empty-handed. Just as Mallika was about to start eating, she noticed a tired old woman sitting by the roadside, watching her. The woman had obviously not eaten in many days. Without thinking twice, Mallika gave her portion to the woman.

The man distributing the food saw this. That night, when he was telling the woman who had donated the food about the events of the day, he mentioned Mallika and her generosity. The woman, Soudamani, was touched. 'Bring her to me,' she said. 'My little son needs someone to look after him, and I want someone who is honest and kind-hearted.'

So Mallika started living with the couple. She loved the boy like her own. Indeed, he was exactly her son's age and she would often think of her past life and lost family and shed tears. Soudamani would console her and soon the two women became friends.

Mallika was allowed to take the child to any part of the house except for the prayer room. That was always kept locked and only Soudamani and her husband went in there to offer their prayers. When Mallika asked Soudamani, she said, 'Don't bring the child there. We have kept something very precious to us in the room and we don't want him spoiling it.'

One day, when Mallika and the boy were playing ball, the child threw the ball hard and it sailed through a window and landed in the prayer room. The boy started crying; he wanted the ball right then. Mallika tried her best to make him understand but he would not listen. Unable to bear his crying, Mallika decided to get the ball, even if it meant disobeying her mistress.

She entered the room and was surprised to see that instead of a deity, the only thing in the room was a peculiar silk bag! She recognized it immediately as the one she had given to the orphan girl the night she had left for her new home. Old memories rushed up and she started crying. Just then, Soudamani entered the room and was furious to see Mallika there.

'Why did you touch that purse? I told you never to come in here,' shouted Soudamini.

'This is my purse,' Mallika answered in tears. 'I had given it to an orphan girl one night, when I was on my way to my in-laws' house for the first time.'

'When did you get married?' Soudamini asked, her anger dying down.

'Ten years ago, in the month of Shravan.'

Hearing this, Soudamini too burst into tears. She came and hugged Mallika. 'I was that girl. Perhaps you did not know it when you gave the purse to me, but along with the fruits, it also contained several diamonds and coins. I opened the bag only after I reached home. We tried to find you so we could tell you, but we did not even know your name. We became rich with your gift but never forgot how you helped a poor orphan girl in her time of need. We kept the bag in the prayer room and used it to remind us every day of your generosity and kindness. That is why we decided to help others when we were no longer poor. Whatever we have today is also yours.'

Mallika and Soudamani became even better friends after this. They sent out people to look for Mallika's family and one day, to her great joy, she was reunited with her lost son and husband.

Two Unforgettable Lessons

Amrutananda and Kapiladeva were landlords in neighbouring villages. Both were cunning and extremely sly. They had made a lot of money by cheating and ill-treating their labourers who worked in the fields.

One day, a young man named Manikya came to Amrutananda, asking for work. Amrutananda was pleasantly surprised. No one ever wanted to work for him because of his reputation, and here was someone walking right into his house! Manikya's next few words got him even more excited. Manikya said, 'I will work for you for free. You need not pay me a salary. Only give me a place to sleep, two sets of clothes and two meals a day.' Amrutananda was beside himself with joy when he heard this and was about to agree, when Manikya added, 'I have only one condition: I will tell you the truth always, but one day in the year, I will tell lies.'

Amrutananda, who lied happily every day of the year, agreed to this odd condition. So Manikya joined him. He was a wonderful worker—hard-working and trustworthy. He was very honest and soon became Amrutananda's right-hand man.

A year went by. Because of Manikya's hard work, Amrutananda had an excellent harvest. He and his wife, Mandakini, decided to have a big feast to celebrate. They invited all their relatives and friends, who gathered from all over the village and outside too. Everyone was looking forward to the delicious feast being planned. On the morning of the feast, Amrutananda decided he would also give away some gifts to his relatives, just to show off. So he set off for the market in his cart. As soon as he was out of sight, Manikya went running to his mistress, Mandakini. He wept loudly and beat his chest. Then he fell on the floor, sobbing, and announced, 'The master is dead! The cart overturned on the road. Our master has been flattened like a chapatti!' As

soon as Amrutananda's wife and relatives heard this, they started wailing. Manikya rushed out, saying he would bring back the body, while everyone started preparing for the last rites.

Manikya now went running to his master and said, 'Master! Your wife is dead. My kind, loving mistress is dead. A cobra bit her and she fell to the ground, as blue as the spring sky.' Amrutananda was stunned. What! His beloved Mandakini, his partner in all his schemes, was dead! He rushed back home shouting her name.

Mandakini too was weeping loudly, sitting in the courtyard. When she saw her husband run in, she stopped mid-wail, and Amrutananda too stood open-mouthed. Then they fell into each other's arms, unable to believe their eyes.

As one, they turned to Manikya. 'What is the meaning of this, Manikya?' his master demanded sternly.

Manikya smiled. 'Remember my condition, that I would lie only one day in the year? Well, I chose today. You see what lies can do? They nearly destroyed your life. Now think what happens to the people to whom you lie every day of the year!'

Saying this, he walked out, leaving behind a stunned and ashamed landlord.

Manikya walked to the next village now, to Kapiladeva's house. Kapiladeva had heard all about him and was ready with his own conditions.

'You will not lie, ever,' he said. 'And you cannot leave the farm. If you do, you will have to pay me ten gold coins. If I want to get rid of you, I will give you five coins. In return you will be given clothes, shelter and one leaf-plate filled with food every day.'

Manikya thought for a while, then agreed. He began his work, and at the end of the day, stood waiting for his leaf full of food. The cook came and handed him a tiny leaf on which there were a few grains of rice. Quickly Manikya produced a large banana leaf. 'The master did not say what kind of leaf. I want this leaf to be piled up with food. That was the agreement.' The cook had no choice but to fill Manikya's banana leaf-plate with rice, dal and three types of vegetables. Manikya took it and had a hearty meal, which he did not forget to share with the other labourers, his new friends.

This went on for a few days. Manikya was not at all interested in working. All day he would sit around with the other workers, telling them also to while away time chatting, and at the end of the day he would tuck into a big meal. Word soon reached Kapiladeva and he decided to teach Manikya a lesson.

'Manikya, I want you to change the direction of the river so that it passes through my garden,' he ordered. Then he left, happy that Manikya would never be able to do this and would have to leave, after paying him ten gold coins.

When he came home in the evening, he was horrified to see the front wall and the front door of his house lying in pieces. 'Manikya!' he shouted angrily. 'What is the meaning of this?'

Manikya appeared, wiping his brow. 'Why, I am making way for the river to enter the garden. Now I will go to the river and ask it to come this way.'

Kapiladeva sat clutching his head. Manikya had got the better of him again!

The next day, he summoned Manikya and, just to keep him out of mischief, ordered, 'Bring me the wood from twenty trees.' That would keep him busy for the day, going to the forest and doing all the chopping, he thought.

Manikya picked up the axe and, whistling happily, proceeded to chop down the prized mango trees in Kapiladeva's orchard! When he returned, Kapiladeva had to admit that Manikya was too expensive to keep and happily paid him ten gold coins so that he would leave, and never come back again!

That was how Manikya taught the two meanest landlords in the land lessons they would never forget!

United We Stand

Maruti and Mahadeva lived in the same village. While Mahadeva was a rich businessman and owned the largest shop in the village, Maruti was a poor farmer. Both had large families, with many sons, daughters-in-law and grandchildren.

One day, Maruti, tired of not being able to make ends meet, decided to leave the village and move to the city with his family. There they were sure to earn enough to feed everyone. They said their goodbyes, packed their few clothes and set off.

When night fell, they stopped and rest under a large tree. There was a stream running nearby, where they could get a drink and refresh themselves. Maruti looked around and started giving instructions to everyone. He called his sons and told them to clean the area below the tree. He told his wife to fetch water. He instructed his daughters-in-law to make the fire and himself started cutting wood from the tree. Now, on the top of that tree sat a thief, resting with his booty. He watched as Maruti's family worked together to prepare dinner. He also noticed they had nothing to cook—no grains or vegetables.

Maruti's wife too must have thought the same thing, for she came to her husband as he sat resting under the tree and said, 'Everything is ready. Now what shall we cook?' Maruti raised his hands upwards and said, 'Don't worry. He is watching all this from above. He will help us.'

'But how will he help us?'

'We are many. We are united. He will come down for us.'

The thief got worried. He had seen that the family was a large one and they worked well together. They listened to each other and were obedient to the old man. Surely they did not know he was hiding in the branches? Were they waiting for him to come down? He decided to make a quick getaway. He climbed down swiftly when they were not looking and ran for his life. Unfortunately, he forgot his bundle of stolen jewels and money, which dropped down into Maruti's lap. He opened it and jumped with joy when he saw what it contained. 'Come here, quick!' he called out. 'See, I was right. I knew God above would look after us, and He has thrown down this bundle for us. Now our days of want are over. Let us go back to the village.'

So the family gathered its belongings and returned to the village. There was great excitement when they told everyone the story of how they got rich.

Fat old Mahadeva got greedy. This was a nice quick way to earn some money! So he commanded his family to pack some clothes and they set off as if on a journey. They stopped under the same tree and Mahadeva started commanding everyone just like Maruti had done. But the difference was that no one in his family was willing to listen to anyone or obey orders. They were used to having a bunch of servants wait on them. So the one who went to the river to fetch water had a nice bath and came back. The person who went to gather wood for the fire went off to sleep beneath the tree. And Mahadeva only ordered everyone about, not bothering to do anything himself.

The thief had returned to his treetop. He sat there sadly, thinking of his lost bundle and watching the family underneath. He noticed that the family members were greedy and selfish. They would never be able to put up a fight together, he was sure.

Then, Mahadeva and his wife started the conversation which they had rehearsed many times carefully.

Mahadeva's wife said, 'Everything is ready. Now what shall we cook?' Mahadeva raised his hands upwards and said, 'Don't worry. He is watching all this from above. He will help us.'

'But how will he help us?'

'We are many. We are united. He will come down for us.'

At this the thief jumped down from the top of the tree, a knife in his hand. Seeing him, everyone was scared and started running in different directions to save themselves. They started screaming and no one would help the other.

The thief stole everything—Mahadeva's wife's necklace and earrings, the greedy old man's pouch full of money, hidden under his fat tummy.

Mahadeva and his family returned to the village empty-handed, having lost all that they had taken with them.

Where Did It Go?

Once upon a time, there was a shrewd shopkeeper called Makarand. He had a friend called Mihir, who had saved a lot of money. Mihir was keen to go on a pilgrimage, but he did not know where to leave his precious savings. So he came to Makarand's shop and said, 'Friend, I trust you more than anyone. Please look after my life's savings till I return from my pilgrimage.'

Makarand pretended to think seriously, then said, 'No. Money spoils relationships. What if something happens to it when you are not here? You will no longer be my friend.'

As Mihir stood there thinking about this, an old woman entered the shop and bought some things.

One of the boys helping Makarand gave her less change than he should have. Makarand saw this and pretended to scold the boy, then ordered him to return the remaining money to the woman.

Mihir, not knowing this was an act put up by Makarand to make him believe in his honesty, was convinced. 'I have decided. I will leave the money only with you.'

Makarand smiled. 'Then let us do something. Let's take the bag of coins and bury it in a place about which only you and I will know. That way, even if something happens to me when you are gone, you will know where your money is.'

Simple Mihir thought this was a good idea and the two went and hid the bag in a secret place. Mihir left the next day on his pilgrimage, happy his savings were in safe hands. Six months later, Mihir returned. He dumped his luggage at home and went to dig out his bag. But even though he searched and searched, there was no sign of the bag anywhere.

In panic, he ran to Makarand, who was busy in his shop. When Mihir asked him about the bag, Makarand pretended to be surprised. 'But I did not even go that way in all these months. Why don't you search for it again?' he said, putting on his most

innocent look. Mihir had no choice but to believe him. Sadly, he made his way home.

On the way, who should he meet but the old woman he had seen in Makarand's shop. Seeing his sad face, she asked him what the matter was. Mihir told her the whole story. Then she smiled and whispered a plan to him.

Not long after, the woman came to Makarand's shop, carrying a big box. 'Brother, I heard you are a good and honest man. My son went on pilgrimage many months ago and has still not returned. I am worried and have decided to go look for him. Will you look after my box of two hundred gold coins while I am away?'

Makarand could not believe his luck. He was about to launch into his idea about hiding the box, when an angry Mihir entered the shop. 'Where is . . .' But before he could complete his sentence, Makarand, afraid of being accused in front of the old woman, said quickly, 'I forgot. I had seen some pigs digging around there, so I removed the bag just to keep it safe. Here it is.' And he handed Mihir the bag he had stolen many months back.

Now the old woman pretended she was seeing Mihir for the first time. 'Son, did you also go on a pilgrimage? Tell me, did you meet my son anywhere?'

Mihir, clutching his precious bag, said, 'Yes, Auntie. I met him on the road a few villages away. He was on his way home. He should be here in a week.'

The old woman leaned over and took her box away from Makarand. 'Thank you, son, you have saved me an unnecessary trip. Now I will need some money to prepare for my son's welcome,' she added to Mihir.

And the two left the shop, holding their boxes. Makarand could only stare at them open-mouthed.

The Princess Who Was a Bird

Long ago, there lived a beautiful princess. When she grew into a lovely young woman, her father wanted her to get married. In fact, there was a long queue of princes eager to marry her. But the princess would not even look at them. She would not have anything to do with a man apart from her father, she declared.

The poor king was puzzled and wondered what had happened for her to hate men so much. He tried pleading and begging and commanding, but the princess was firm. In the meantime, the entire kingdom had come to know about the princess's refusal to get married, and the people could talk of nothing else.

One day, a handsome prince from a neighbouring kingdom heard about the princess and was curious. He wanted to see this princess famous for her beauty and perhaps convince her to marry him. So he disguised himself as an ordinary young man and came to her kingdom. He stopped at an inn for the night, where he hoped to meet someone who could tell him the story of the princess who hated men. Then he got lucky. He happened to meet a woman who took flowers to the palace every day for the princess's garlands.

He chatted with the old woman for a long time and found out the entire story. The princess had lost her mother when she was a little girl. She had been brought up by a nurse. This nurse would tell her a story every day. The story was about a pair of myna birds that lived in a nest in a thick forest. They had many beautiful chicks and were proud of their neat little nest. They were also deeply in love with each other. But one day, a fierce fire started in the forest and the flames started climbing towards their nest. 'Let us take our chicks and flee,' the female myna told her husband, but he would not hear of it. 'There's nothing to worry,' he said. 'I will look after you all.' The flames came closer and closer and the female myna kept begging her husband to save their chicks, but he told her to relax and did nothing. When finally the fire reached the tree and started licking at the nest and the wife was getting burnt with her babies, she saw her husband fly away, leaving them to die.

The princess would ask her nurse to tell her this story every day, and after a while began to believe she had been the female myna in her previous life. So, in this life, she did not want to trust any man or get married.

The prince thought hard all night and decided what he would do next. As soon as it was morning, he arrived at the king's palace. There he demanded an audience with the king. He introduced himself as a storyteller. 'I have travelled many lands and know many stories,' he said loudly. 'I can tell you wonderful tales from all over the world. My only condition is, I will not talk to a woman.' The king was surprised. 'Why do you say such a thing?' he asked. By then the prince saw that the princess too had arrived in the court and was listening to him from behind a screen.

He cleared his throat and said, 'That is the oddest tale in my collection. During my wanderings, I met a sage. I served him for many days and he became very pleased with me. One day, happy with my devotion, he told me the story of my previous life. I was a male myna then. I used to live in a thick green forest with my myna wife and our little chicks. One day, there was a fire and the flames started creeping up towards our tree. I told my wife, "Let us go from here," but she would not listen. "There is enough time," she said to me. When finally the fire reached the nest and began to burn me and the chicks, I saw my wife fly away and save herself, leaving us to die. Ever since I heard that story I have hated women and have decided not to talk with, let alone marry, one.'

When she heard this, the princess pushed aside the screen and appeared before the prince, her eyes blazing with anger. 'How dare you!' she shouted. '*I* was the one who wanted to save everyone and *you* were the one who left us to die. I was that female myna in my previous life.' But the prince argued back, 'It was not you but I who died in that fire.'

The argument carried on for a while. Finally the king managed to get a word in. 'Stop, stop!' he commanded. 'No fighting in court! Perhaps you two were married to each other in your previous lives. And perhaps something did happen which made

one of you leave in a time of need. Now you must understand that friends and partners always stay together. When something goes wrong, they help each other. Why don't you two get married in this life too, and see if you can help one another, in good times and bad, like the best of friends, and make up for the mistakes of your past lives?'

The prince and princess stopped shouting long enough to take a good look at each other and think over these words. The princess saw the prince's intelligent and kind eyes. She decided to heed her father's advice and the two got married soon after. And yes, they lived happily for many, many years, through good times and bad, like best friends.

The Price Is Right

Somendra was a cunning merchant. He was ready to do anything to earn some money. No one knew what trick he would be up to next. Nandish was a simple village boy. He was poor and had nothing in the world but one beautiful white horse. He loved it more than anything else. Everyone in the village knew about him and the horse. Somendra had had his eye on the horse for a long time and was always trying to think of a way to get it for himself.

One day, Nandish rode his horse to the village fair. On his way back, he met Somendra. The crafty merchant thought, 'Nandish is a simpleton. Let me see if I can trick him out of his horse.'

So he said to Nandish, 'You live all alone. How do you manage? You must be in great need of money always. I have an idea. What does a young boy like you need with a horse? Sell it to me and I'll make you rich in return.'

Nandish replied, 'No. I don't want to sell the horse.'

But Somendra was not one to give up so easily. He followed Nandish, offering him more and more money. Finally, when the offer reached five hundred gold coins, Nandish paused and seemed to give it a thought. Then he said, 'Five hundred gold coins seems like a good price. But I have a condition. If you agree to that, I will give you my horse.'

By now Somendra would have agreed to anything. 'What is it? Tell me,' he said impatiently. Nandish said, 'You must give me the money right now, and I will give you the horse only when I have given you ten lashes.'

'That's all!' exclaimed Somendra. Ten lashes was nothing. He would resell the horse for over a thousand coins in the market. Why, he was ready to take twenty lashes to make such a profit. He agreed instantly. Then he ran home and got the money for Nandish. He also brought a whip for Nandish to lash him with. Nandish counted the coins carefully. Then he took the whip.

One, two, three . . . the lashes fell on Somendra's back in quick succession. By the eighth lash he was ready to cry, but he told himself, only two more and the horse would be his. He had dreamt of buying it for so long. Nine . . . Somendra waited, holding his breath for the last and final lash. But what was this! Nandish had mounted his horse and was riding off, merrily throwing the whip on the ground!

'Wait!' shouted Somendra in anger. 'What about the tenth lash? And where are you taking the horse? We had a deal.'

Nandish stopped and said, 'I agreed to give you the horse only after I have given you ten lashes. Now I don't feel like giving you the last one. It upsets my dear horse. I'll give it to you only when I am in the mood. Till then, goodbye!'

'Come back, you cheat!' screamed Somendra. But the crowd that had gathered around him agreed. A deal was a deal. Nandish could give the tenth and final lash whenever he wanted, and till then the horse could not belong to Somendra.

Nandish rode away, richer by five hundred gold coins. Somendra waited for many, many days for the whip to fall on his back finally. Of course, it never came!

A Lesson for the Uncles

Rajendra was a young boy who had lost both his parents when he was still quite young. He lived all by himself. He had one goat with which he stayed in a tiny hut. He also had three uncles, who were always trying to cheat him out of his goat and house. They made his life miserable.

One day, the uncles stole his goat and tied it alongside some other goats that belonged to the village butcher. Poor Rajendra looked everywhere for it. The butcher, meanwhile, took all the goats and killed them for their meat. Now, Rajendra's goat wore a special bell around its neck. When the butcher cut that goat, he threw away the bell.

Rajendra found it soon after and was griefstricken. He knocked on the butcher's door for justice. By then the butcher had realized that he had killed Rajendra's goat. Scared that the boy would tell everyone he had killed a stolen goat, he gave Rajendra some money and sent him away.

When the uncles saw their nephew coming home with the coins jingling in his pocket, they were astonished. How had Rajendra made money from a lost goat? When they asked him he said, 'Everyone wanted goat's meat today in the market. My poor goat somehow ended up at the butcher's and he sold its meat and made a lot of money. This is my share.'

The uncles thought this was a good way to make money. They owned twenty goats and they slaughtered them all and went to the market to sell the meat. But now there was so much meat in the market that the prices had come down and they got only a few rupees for their goats.

Angry at being fooled, they decided to burn down Rajendra's hut. So one day, when Rajendra had gone out, they set fire to his little hut. The young boy was shocked to come home and find a pile of smouldering ash where his hut used to be. At once he knew who was behind it. Sadly he gathered the ash in a bag and decided to leave the village forever. With the bag slung over his shoulder, he set off. After walking for many miles, he at last reached a village. He sat down under a tree to rest and think what to do next.

Soon a crowd of curious villagers gathered around him. Who was this stranger? Why was he carrying a bag of ashes, they wondered. Finally one man asked him, 'What is the matter? Why are you sitting quietly like this? Why are you carrying so much ash?'

Rajendra's hut had been his dearest, most sacred possession, so he said, 'It is the ash from a sacred place.'

Now the villagers were excited. 'Will you sell it to us?' they asked.

'No.'

But they would not give up. 'Give us a pinch at least,' they begged. Rajendra agreed and gave them a pinch of ash each. Soon, word spread in the village that a holy man had come from the Himalayas, who looked like he was twenty but was really eighty years old. He was carrying a bag of ashes with him that could cure all misfortunes and disease. He was giving away a pinch of it only to each person, and though he wanted no money, it was only right that you paid a coin at least for such happiness.

Thus a long queue formed in front of Rajendra. Each villager took a pinch of ash and left a coin in return. At the end of the day, Rajendra discovered the ash was all gone and in its place he had a pile of coins.

Happily, he decided to go back to his village and start life afresh. When he came back, his uncles could not believe their eyes. How had Rajendra done this? They asked Rajendra his secret. Rajendra said, 'There is a great demand for ashes in that village. I sold the ashes that I gathered from my burnt hut and got all this money.' The uncles were amazed. If Rajendra could get so much money by selling the ashes from his little hut, how much would they get if they burnt their sprawling houses? That night itself, they burnt down their houses, gathered the ashes in huge sacks and set off for the village. But as soon as they reached and uttered the word 'ash', why, all the villagers fell on them and beat them black and blue! By then the villagers knew there was no magic in the ashes. And here were three more people trying to fool them!

The uncles somehow saved their own skins and ran home. They were even angrier with Rajendra now for having tricked them a second time. They decided to kill him. One day, they invited him for a walk with them by the river. As they stood on the bridge, where the river was at its deepest, one of them pointed at the water and exclaimed, 'See! A beautiful mermaid!'

As soon as Rajendra leaned over to look in, they pushed him from behind and ran home. Poor Rajendra nearly drowned. Just in time, a girl washing clothes nearby heard his screams for help and dived in. She was a good swimmer and saved his life.

A grateful Rajendra told her the story of his life. She thought for a while and then whispered a plan in his ear.

The next day Rajendra arrived at his uncles' house. With him was the girl, dressed in beautiful clothes and jewellery. Rajendra also held a bag in his hands. His uncles were astonished to see him alive. How had he survived? Rajendra said, 'When I fell into the river, this beautiful girl saved me. She has a palace at the bottom of the river. She fell in love with me and married me. She also gave me half her riches. Now we will live in the river. Do come and visit us some time.' Saying this, they left in the direction of the river. The uncles had a quick discussion and decided they would follow Rajendra to his palace in the river and perhaps cheat him of his newfound wealth. So they ran to the river and dived into its deep waters.

They were never heard of again.

A Bag of Words

Keerti Kumara was a handsome young shepherd. He could play the flute wonderfully. Whenever he played on his simple bamboo flute, which he had made with his own hands, his sheep would listen to it, spellbound, and do whatever he wanted them to.

The princess of that kingdom was very beautiful. Her father, the king, wanted her to choose a prince and marry him, but she found fault with all the suitors he brought to her. They were so dull, they bored her to tears. Finally, she set an unusual condition. 'I will marry only that man who will be able to look after our hundred rabbits for a month, without losing a single one.'

Soon word of this strange condition spread in the kingdom. Keerti too heard it and decided to give it a try. He landed up at the king's palace, clutching his flute. The king and queen were shocked that a scruffy shepherd wanted to marry their daughter, but they had to keep their word, and Keerti was shown the cage with the hundred rabbits.

The next morning, Keerti went to the cage and, blowing softly into his flute, led the rabbits to a beautiful meadow where they played, grazed and listened to the music. Not one rabbit tried to escape, and predators like eagles and foxes too kept away.

The princess heard about this strange and exciting suitor and decided to see him for herself. She went to the meadow and instantly fell in love with the handsome boy who played such divine music. She started meeting him every day. When the king and queen heard about this, they were furious. Not only was the boy fulfilling the condition, but he was being supported by the princess! How could their beautiful daughter marry a poor shepherd!

One day, as Keerti lay on the soft grass with the rabbits hopping about him, a stranger approached him. 'Give me a rabbit and I will give you a gold bar,'

said the man. Keerti of course understood that this was no one but the king in disguise. He jumped up and said, 'Of course you can have a rabbit, but first you must wash my dirty clothes, massage my feet and polish my shoes. Then I will give you a rabbit.'

The king had no choice but to do all this. He was only happy no one saw him. Then he took a rabbit, popped it into a sack and walked back to the palace quickly. Keerti gathered the rest of the rabbits and took them home, softly playing his flute. As soon as the king reached the palace, the queen came out to greet him. Joyfully, he opened the sack to show her the rabbit. In a flash, the rabbit leapt out of the bag and hopped off to join its friends, who had followed the king to the palace with Keerti.

Furious, the queen now decided *she* would get a rabbit. A few days later, again Keerti was lying on the grass when an old woman came up to him and asked for a rabbit. She promised him two bars of gold for it. Keerti knew it was the queen and said, 'Of course you can have the rabbit. But first you must cook food for me, stitch my torn clothes and cut my hair, then you can have one of my rabbits.'

The queen reluctantly agreed to do all this and soon left with a rabbit in her bag. When she reached the palace, she first went into her room, carefully closed all the doors and windows, and then showed the rabbit to the king. Delighted that they had at last fooled the shepherd, the king flung open a window and yelled to the cook to make a delicious dinner to celebrate. Instantly the rabbit leapt out and hopped off to Keerti, who was standing outside the window, playing his flute.

One month passed and Keerti came to the palace to claim the princess's hand. But the queen spoke up this time. 'You may have carried out my daughter's wish, but in order to marry her, you need to fulfil my wish too.'

Keerti had to agree. The queen commanded three sacks to be brought in. Then she said, 'Now fill these sacks with your words.'

Keerti thought for a while, then he picked up a sack and, holding it near his mouth, said, 'This is a true story. Once upon a time there was a mighty king. The whole kingdom trembled at his words. But one day he met a poor shepherd boy who made him wash his clothes, massage his dirty feet and polish his shoes . . .'

Immediately the king shouted, 'Enough, stop! The bag is full.'

'But my story is not over yet,' Keerti protested.

'Yes, it is. The bag is full,' said the king.

So Keerti picked up the second bag. He held it to his mouth and said, 'Once upon a time there was a beautiful queen. The king listened to every word she said. But one day she went to a poor shepherd boy and stitched his torn clothes, cut his hair . . .'

'Stop! Stop!' the queen shouted and tied the second bag.

Keerti Kumara opened the third bag. 'Once there was a lovely princess who fell in love with a poor shepherd boy. She would come up to the hills to meet him and . . .'

Now the king and the queen together tied the third bag. They knew who the princess was and realized she had made a good choice in deciding to marry this clever, musical shepherd boy.

Magic in the Air

Sheelavati and Jayasheel were a poor old couple. Their only precious possession was one cow. Once, Jayasheel fell very sick. Soon all their money was used up in buying medicines and they realized they would have to sell the cow. Sheelavati would have to go to the market. She was a very simple woman, so her husband warned her, 'Don't talk to anyone. Just walk to the market, sell the cow and come back with the money.'

Sheelavati set off, leading the cow by a rope. On the way, she met four young men. They were local thugs, who enjoyed bullying and tormenting old people. When they saw Sheelavati with her cow, they decided to play a trick on her. One of them sneaked up behind her, untied the cow and tied a goat in its place. Sheelavati had been walking immersed in thought, worried about Jayasheel. She was surprised when she heard a goat bleating behind her. It was true: her cow had vanished and she was holding on to a goat!

The four came up to her and said, 'There is some magic in the air these days. It turned your cow into a goat.'

Poor Sheelavati walked on with the goat. After a while, the crooks untied the goat and tied a cock in its place. 'Cock-a-doodle-do,' crowed the cock and Sheelavati was surprised again. Now the goat had become a cock!

The thugs again shouted, 'Magic in the air, Grandma.'

Sheelavati now walked on with the cock. The boys crept up again and tied a log of wood in place of the cock. Sheelavati was surprised to hear the sound of wood dragging on the road behind her. 'Magic in the air, Grandma,' shouted the thugs again.

Then, as she dragged the wood, the thugs untied that too and ran away. When Sheelavati reached the market, she found she was holding only a rope in

her hand. Feeling sad, she came back home. She had lost the cow and not got any money either. When she told Jayasheel the story of the magic, he knew what had happened. He told his wife, 'Tomorrow, make chapatti, vegetable and kheer for lunch. Make sure you cook for four people. I will come home with some guests. As soon as they come, you must say, "I cooked what the rabbit told me. Come, eat your lunch." Leave everything else to me.'

The next morning, Jayasheel went and borrowed two identical rabbits from a friend. He left one at home and tied the other with a string and started walking towards the market with it. On the way, he too met the four thugs. 'Hey, Grandfather!' they yelled. 'Your wife's cow vanished yesterday. Where are you taking this rabbit now?'

Jayasheel sighed sadly and said, 'This rabbit is like my son. It obeys my every word. But now I am sick and we need money, so I am having to sell it in the market.'

The four were surprised when they heard this. 'Does it really understand what you say, Grandfather?' they asked.

'Of course it does. Here, watch me.' Jayasheel turned to the rabbit and said, 'Hop home, little one, and tell your mother to make chapatti, vegetable and kheer for four people.' Then he untied the string and let the rabbit hop away. He said to the boys, 'Come home and have lunch with me.'

When they reached Jayasheel's house, his wife welcomed them and said, 'I cooked what the rabbit told me. Come, eat your lunch.' And she laid out chapatti, vegetable and kheer for each of them. What was more, they saw the rabbit sitting in a corner of the room, tucking into a green leaf!

They were amazed and told Jayasheel, 'We will buy your rabbit.'

Jayasheel pretended to think, then said, 'It is very precious to me. How can I sell it?' When the four begged him and offered more and more money, he reluctantly agreed. They dropped a heap of coins in his hand and rushed away with the rabbit.

Now, the thugs had been blackmailing the landlord for some money. They said to the rabbit, 'Go tell the landlord to come and give us our money in ten minutes.'

The rabbit hopped off and they waited for the landlord. An hour went by, but there was no sign of him. They marched to his house, knocked loudly on the door and demanded, 'Give us our money and the rabbit.'

The furious landlord ordered his largest bodyguard to give them the thrashing of their lives.

Bleeding and bruised, the four went back to Jayasheel. 'You fooled us!' they shouted. 'Give us back our money at once.'

'There is magic in the air,' sighed Jayasheel. 'The money has disappeared!'

The Selfish Groom

Dhanagupta, a famous and rich merchant, had only one son, Yashodhana. The child was born when his father was already quite old, and being the only child, was brought up with great care. When he became a young man, his father started thinking about his marriage. But Yashodhana told him, 'I will choose my own bride. I want someone who is intelligent. She should also be careful with money, and not a spendthrift. After all, she will become the wife of a merchant with a vast business one day. Please give me a chariot, a servant and four horses. I will travel around the country and find such a wife for myself.'

His father agreed and gave him the chariot, servant and horses. Thus, Yashodhana set off to look for a bride. He travelled all over the country, met many women and their hopeful fathers. But whenever a beautiful woman appeared before him, he would say, 'I will marry you, but first take this bag of paddy. I want you to cook me a meal of rice, dal, vegetables and curd with this. Only if you do this will I marry you.'

Whoever heard this strange condition went away without trying. A few tried, but could not succeed. In this way many months went by and a weary Yashodhana arrived with his equally tired servant and horses at a small village. There he saw a small but neat hut, and sitting in front of it, an old man and his daughter. The girl was beautiful, with dark, intelligent eyes. Yashodhana was suddenly hopeful. He went up to them and told them about his condition. The girl smiled when she heard him and said, 'Of course I can do it. It is not difficult. Why don't you rest awhile and I will get your meal ready.'

An astonished Yashodhana settled down to wait. Soon he nodded off to sleep. After some time, he felt someone shaking him awake. It was the girl, inviting him to lunch. He washed his hands and sat down.

To his amazement, the girl served him fluffy white rice, two types of vegetables, a bowl of steaming-hot, delicious dal and soft, refreshing curd. He ate the meal and then could not hold back his curiosity any longer. 'How did you do it?' he asked.

The girl smiled. 'First I pounded the paddy and got a lot of rice. Then I took the husk to the village jeweller who needs it for his work. He gave me money in return, with which I bought the vegetables and the oil. Then, since there was more rice than could be eaten by one person, I sold the rest and got the curd and some ghee. It took me little time to cook it all and then your meal was ready.'

Yashodhana was amazed. Quickly he revealed who he was—the son of the country's richest man. But the girl was not impressed. She stood back, folded her arms, looked him in the eye and said, 'You may want to marry me, but I don't want to marry you. Look at the state of your horses and your poor servant. Did you think about them and feed them properly when you were travelling? I think not. You asked me to cook only for you. What about them? You need to learn some manners and kindness before you can even think of marrying me.'

An ashamed Yashodhana went back home empty-handed. Over the next few months he mended his ways, and one day arrived at the girl's hut, on foot. There, he humbly asked her father for her hand. The girl looked at his face, now shorn of arrogance. She also noticed the love in his gaze, and agreed.

Yashodhana and his wife looked after their large business with intelligence, compassion and honesty for many, many years.

The Tired Horse

Purushottam was a poor farmer. He lived in a village with his young son and a horse. They had never gone anywhere outside the village and were very simple people. One day, they decided to go to the grand fair that was on in the nearest town.

They set off early one morning. Purushottam thought his son was young and would not be able to walk the distance, so he made the lad sit on the horse and started walking beside it. When they had gone some distance, they passed a group of villagers. 'Look!' the villagers shouted. 'The young boy is sitting on the horse while his old father is walking. Hey, don't you have any brains? Let your father sit on the horse.'

Purushottam and his son thought this was right. So Purushottam sat on the horse and his son walked alongside. After a while they met another group of villagers. 'Look!' the villagers shouted. 'The man is sitting on the horse while the little boy is walking. Hey, don't you have any brains? Let your son sit on the horse.'

So Purushottam got off the horse, and not knowing what to do, the two walked beside the horse. Soon they met another group of villagers. 'Look!' the villagers shouted. 'There is a strong and healthy horse but they are walking on foot. Hey, don't you have any brains? Why don't you sit on the horse?'

Now they decided to both sit on the horse. A while later, they passed some more people. 'Look!' they shouted. 'Those two cruel people are sitting on that one poor animal. The horse looks tired. Hey! Why don't you both get off and carry the horse on your shoulders instead?'

Purushottam and his son got off. They used a rope to tie the horse's legs and, lifting it over their shoulders, started walking. They came to a stream. By then the horse was furious at being carried like this. As soon as the man and the boy set it down, it struggled out of the rope and ran away, never to be seen again.

A Minister's Test

Long ago, there was a king who ruled his kingdom with great wisdom. He made sure each person got a good education and as a result, the people of the kingdom too were clever and wise. The king of one of the neighbouring kingdoms once decided he would appoint one of these intelligent people as his chief minister.

So he set a test to see who was the wisest. He sent his messenger to the neighbouring king's court with a strange message, 'I want a person who can bring me fresh vegetables grown in the soil of your kingdom. He should also bring with him a pot full of intelligence.' Now, to get to the neighbouring kingdom, it was a good two months' chariot ride. So even if someone started off with fresh vegetables, they would be rotten by the time he reached there.

Even the wise king was perplexed. One young man from his court, however, knew the solution. He asked the king to give him a cart full of soil, manure and lots of vegetable seeds and saplings. He sowed these in the soil and set off with the cart tied to the rear of his chariot. He also planted a pumpkin plant, and when the vegetable appeared, tied a pot over it, so when the pumpkin grew, it would fill the entire pot.

By the time he reached his destination, he had a good crop of vegetables grown in the soil of his kingdom and freshly plucked. The pumpkin too had grown and now filled the entire pot. He took a big basket of the vegetables and the pumpkin in the pot and appeared before the king.

The king was delighted to see the vegetables but puzzled by the pot. What did it mean? 'I have got intelligence in this pot,' said the young man. 'Now you have to see how you can extract it without breaking the pot.'

The king was pleased. This was a very clever answer to his strange message. But he wanted to test the man some more. So he set before him three

wooden dolls, all identical. He said, 'These three are identical, but one is better than the others. Which one would that be?'

The young man asked for a piece of wire. Then he inserted it through the ears of one doll. The wire appeared from the other ear. Next he inserted it through the ears of the second doll. The wire came out of the doll's mouth. But when he inserted the wire from the ear of the third doll, it remained stuck inside. He held up the last doll and said, 'This is the best. In a court, if you told a secret to the first doll it would not understand its importance and would take out from one ear what it heard from the other. The second type will hear you, but immediately talk about it to others. The third kind will keep the secret safe in its head.'

The king was even more pleased now. But he wanted to set a final test. 'Here are three rings, with green, red and blue stones respectively. Let us assume they are magical stones. The red ring will give the person wearing it good ideas. The green ring will help the person carry out these ideas in normal circumstances. The blue one will help the person carry out the idea in any circumstance. In a court, who should wear which ring?'

The man thought and said, 'The king should wear the red ring, as he needs to get good ideas. The chief minister should wear the green one, as he needs to carry out these ideas in times of peace. The commander of the army should wear the blue ring, as he needs to carry out the ideas in difficult times.'

The king now knew he had before him a brilliant young man. He was made the chief minister and served the king for many years.

A Cure for Laziness

Basheer had promised himself that he would marry a girl who was as intelligent and hard-working as he was. Once, he went to a country far from his own to do some trade. He stayed in a little inn there. The innkeeper had a daughter called Ayesha. The minute Basheer saw her, he was struck by her beauty, and most of all, her big, bright eyes.

Basheer had to stay in that village for a while, and he got to know the villagers quite well. Among them was an old man, perhaps the oldest man in the village. In the evenings, the villagers would gather around him and he would ask them witty questions, to which the youngsters had to give quick answers. One day, as

Basheer was walking around in the evening, he heard the old man say, 'I have one sheep. How can I use it to earn some money without killing or selling it?'

There was silence. Then Ayesha spoke up. 'I know, Great Uncle. If I had a sheep, I would look after it very well. When it became fat and healthy, I would sell its wool, milk and dung and make a lot of money. Perhaps I would buy two more sheep and soon have a flock!'

That was a clever answer, thought Basheer, and he stopped to hear a few more questions and answers. Next, the old man asked, 'How would you capture fire in paper and hold the air in your hand?'

Again it was Ayesha who answered, 'I would use a paper lamp and a hand fan.'

The old man had one more question: 'My sister's husband's brother-in-law's wife's friend's son is married to your cousin. What is my sister to me?'

Ayesha said promptly, 'Your sister will remain a sister to you.'

By now Basheer had heard enough. Here was a really intelligent woman—his ideal bride. He met Ayesha's father, who agreed happily to have his daughter marry this sober young man. Soon the two got married and set off for Basheer's village.

When Ayesha reached the village and saw her new house, she realized Basheer was a very rich man. There were servants here to wait on her every wish, cooks to rustle up the most wonderful meals and gardeners to look after Basheer's vast gardens and orchards. There was no need for her to lift a finger! Ayesha decided she liked this new way of living and slowly she lost her earlier hard-working nature. There were enough people who wanted to be friends with her now that she was rich, and soon she gathered a group of good-for-nothing lazy friends around herself. They did nothing but eat and gossip the whole day.

A few years passed, and no one from Ayesha's own village would have been able to recognize her, so fat and lazy was she now. Then one day she fell sick. Doctors came, they examined her, asked all kinds of questions, scratched their heads, and prescribed medicines. But Ayesha still didn't get well.

Finally, word reached her father's village. And the person who was saddest to hear about Ayesha was the very old man who used to throw those riddles at her. He decided he would do something to bring back the clever, sweet Ayesha of old. He reached her house and announced he would stay there for a while. In return, he promised to cure her of her illness. Ayesha and Basheer agreed and the old man started staying with them.

The next day the treatment began. The man said, 'You will get well only if you eat the special food I cook for you. No one must come to the house and it should stay sparkling clean at all hours.' Ayesha agreed. So the man cooked a small meal for her and left it in a box a few yards away from the main house. Ayesha would have to walk up to it. It was a simple meal, but tasty. And Ayesha had to work so hard to keep the house clean without the help of servants that she was always hungry; whatever she ate tasted wonderful.

Many months passed like this. Ayesha got used to the work and the new food habits. She started learning how to help with her husband's business and in the fields. With no one to gossip with, she had to think through everything on her own, and slowly her old intelligence shone forth. Every day she went to bed tired out and slept soundly. The next morning she woke up at the crack of dawn, refreshed, and started her day's work. She realized she was happier now than she had ever been.

She went to the old man and said, 'I am cured at last, Great Uncle. What was the secret of your therapy? I will tell my friends about it too.'

The old man laughed and said, 'I did not do anything. Once upon a time, when you were poor, you were healthy and active. You used to do all the work yourself. Then you became rich and lazy. You had so many maids to do all the work for you. I only gave you healthy food and made you work like before. Your illness disappeared. Rich or poor, it is good to do our own work and be fit. You were always a bright girl, and now you use your energy for better things.'

Basheer was listening to all this silently. Now he smiled. He knew the Ayesha he had loved and married was back for good.

The Magic Drum

Ramachandra and Rama were an old couple. They had worked very hard and saved every paisa they possibly could, to make their dream come true. They wanted to visit Kashi and offer puja to Lord Vishwanath. They saved for many years, and one day were delighted to find they had enough money for their pilgrimage.

They set out on the long and dangerous journey. They had been warned that there would be many thieves on the way and hence were quite careful with their belongings, especially their small pouch. They had put all their money in it.

On the way to Kashi they passed Souveera, a small village. They had heard that it was a good place to stay the night. So the old couple decided to stop and spend the night in one of the dormitories there.

Kamesh, the owner of that dormitory, told the couple to leave their belongings with him and freshen up for dinner. But the two refused to do so. Rama sat holding the bag containing their money while Ramachandra went to take a bath. After he finished, he sat holding the bag and Rama went to wash up. Then they had dinner, chatted with Kamesh for some time and went into their room.

They decided to use the pouch as a pillow and Ramachandra slept with it under his head. The first thing they did when they woke up the next morning was check for their money bag. To their horror, they discovered it was missing! While they were sleeping, the lodge-owner, Kamesh, and his wife had entered the room and removed the bag from under the old man's head.

The two cried in despair; now they would not be able to complete their pilgrimage. Then they went to Kamesh to complain. But Kamesh coolly replied, 'I don't know anything about your bag. You are old, you must have dropped it somewhere. This is an honest person's lodge.'

After some more arguments, the elderly couple walked out clutching their small bag of clothes and some food. As they walked through the village, they told many people their story. A teacher, sitting and teaching his students under a tree, heard them and decided they should be given justice. He told them to go to the city, where Krishnakant, the king's counsellor, lived. He was famous for his sense of fairness.

Krishnakant heard their story and said, 'I have a drum in my house. If you tell the truth in front of the drum, it starts beating by itself. You come to my house tomorrow morning and carry the drum to the court. On your way, tell the drum your story. I will send word to Kamesh to come and carry the drum back in the afternoon. I will see how the drum behaves and be ready with the verdict in the evening.'

The next morning, Rama and Ramachandra started walking with the magic drum to the court. It was very heavy. The court was at a distance and the two were soon tired. They saw a big banyan tree and decided to rest in its shade. They put the drum down and sat under the tree.

Rama said, 'We will never get justice in this strange kingdom. Let us go back home.'

Ramachandra replied, 'I was so careful with the money, yet we lost it. Maybe the lord does not wish us to visit him.'

As soon as he said these words, the sound of beating came from the drum. The old couple was very happy. 'We may have no witness, but god knows we are speaking the truth.' Then they stood up and, after drinking some water from a nearby stream, they picked up the drum. To their surprise, they found it had become much lighter. 'God must have heard us,' they told each other happily. 'That is why he has made our load lighter.'

In the afternoon, it was the turn of Kamesh and his wife to carry the drum back from the court. They too found it very heavy and decided to sit under the big tree to rest. As soon as they sat down, the wife started blaming her husband. 'Why did you have to steal the money? Now see what a mess we are in.'

Kamesh replied angrily, 'You are a good one to blame me. Who unlocked the door and showed me where the pouch was kept? Anyway, do you really believe this is a magical drum? I think it is all a lie.'

Now Krishnakant himself opened the top of the drum and jumped out. 'I am the witness. I have heard every word you said, and also what Rama and Ramachandra said. You will return the stolen money and also pay three times more as penalty.'

Rama and Ramachandra were delighted when they heard the verdict. They went on to complete their pilgrimage in comfort, all the while blessing Krishankant and his magic drum!